D0174986

Recent Titles by Cynthia Harrod-Eagles from Severn House

The Bill Slider Mysteries

GAME OVER
FELL PURPOSE
BODY LINE
KILL MY DARLING
BLOOD NEVER DIES
HARD GOING
STAR FALL
ONE UNDER
OLD BONES
SHADOW PLAY

Novels

ON WINGS OF LOVE
EVEN CHANCE
LAST RUN
PLAY FOR LOVE
A CORNISH AFFAIR
NOBODY'S FOOL
DANGEROUS LOVE
REAL LIFE (*Short Stories*)
DIVIDED LOVE
KEEPING SECRETS
THE LONGEST DANCE
THE HORSEMASTERS
JULIA
THE COLONEL'S DAUGHTER
HARTE'S DESIRE
COUNTRY PLOT
KATE'S PROGRESS

SHADOW PLAY

SHADOW PLAY

A Bill Slider Mystery

Cynthia Harrod-Eagles

This first world edition published 2017
in Great Britain and the USA by
SEVERN HOUSE PUBLISHERS LTD of
19 Cedar Road, Sutton, Surrey, England, SM2 5DA.
Trade paperback edition first published
in Great Britain and the USA 2018 by
SEVERN HOUSE PUBLISHERS LTD

Copyright © 2017 by Cynthia Harrod-Eagles.

All rights reserved including the right of
reproduction in whole or in part in any form.
The moral right of the author has been asserted.

British Library Cataloguing in Publication Data
A CIP catalogue record for this title is available from the British Library.

ISBN-13: 978-0-7278-8751-1 (cased)
ISBN-13: 978-1-84751-865-1 (trade paper)
ISBN-13: 978-1-78010-928-2 (e-book)

This is a work of fiction. Names, characters, places and incidents
are either the product of the author's imagination or are used fictitiously.
Except where actual historical events and characters are being described
for the storyline of this novel, all situations in this publication are
fictitious and any resemblance to actual persons, living or dead,
business establishments, events or locales is purely coincidental.

All Severn House titles are printed on acid-free paper.

Severn House Publishers support the Forest Stewardship Council™ [FSC™],
the leading international forest certification organisation.
All our titles that are printed on FSC certified paper carry the FSC logo.

FSC
www.fsc.org
MIX
Paper from
responsible sources
FSC® C013056

Typeset by Palimpsest Book Production Ltd.,
Falkirk, Stirlingshire, Scotland.
Printed and bound in Great Britain by
TJ International, Padstow, Cornwall.

ONE
Foresight Saga

Where roads and railways cross old established ground, there are bound to be odd triangles left over, too small or too ill-favoured for development. This one was bounded in steel, concrete and noise, by the railway, Wood Lane and the A40 flyover.

Along one side of the plot was a motor repair workshop, occupying some old wooden buildings that seemed once to have been stables – three loose boxes, what had probably been the tack room, and a larger structure with big double doors, perhaps formerly a fodder store, now fitted out with a lube-pit and car lift. Beyond them were two crude concrete garages with up and over doors. Above the door of the tack room, now the office, was a board bearing a name painted in faded, peeling letters: E. Sampson.

On the side bounded by the high steel security fencing of the railway, two ancient, derelict car-body shells lurked under a vigorous overhang of buddleia. Rosebay willow herb and cow parsley, ghostly now at the season's end, sprouted through a muddle of metallic debris in the corner beyond them. It must have looked quite festive in midsummer.

Access to the yard was down a narrow track off Wood Lane, running between windowless rail depot buildings. The first few yards were tarmac'd, but beyond that it was bare earth. After several days of rain, track and yard alike were sodden and muddy.

The SOC unit had laid boards for safe passage, but multiple feet had muddied these too. Detective Sergeant Atherton picked his way delicately like a cat through broken glass, grumbling. He was wearing rather natty grey shoes. Detective Chief Inspector Slider, a country boy by birth, always had wellingtons in his car boot. He stepped more confidently, but he grumbled too.

'No CCTV cameras, no overlooking houses, no passing traffic or pedestrians. That means no witnesses.'

'Lots of tyre tracks,' Atherton offered.

Slider would not be comforted. 'Too many. Let's hope deceased is clutching a scrap of paper with the name of the murderer on it.'

Atherton nodded. 'It's always wise to write the name of your worst enemy on your cuff before going out. That's foresight.'

Slider smiled reluctantly. 'Cuff! You dear old-fashioned thing.'

The man who had found the body was squat and swart, probably in his fifties, though so weathered it was hard to tell. His expression was dour, his mouth a hard line, and he spoke tersely, in a roughened voice, never making eye contact, giving the impression that he did not often have call to communicate with other members of his species.

He was dressed in workman's dungarees, liberally streaked with oil and mud, over a chunky green sweater with a surprisingly cheery motif of red reindeer and white snowflakes. Slider suspected it had not originally been bought for him. The elbows were worn through, revealing some kind of grey undergarment. His hands, scarred and broken-nailed, were swollen and stiffened by hard work into the appearance of wooden clubs. Still, they were nimble enough while constructing a skinny roll-up, which he inserted into his prow and lit. It clung there, smoking sulkily, waggling as he spoke.

'Mr Sampson?' Atherton enquired. It didn't do to make assumptions.

Sampson scowled, nodding minimally. He poked his tongue out of the opposite side from the roll-up and removed a shred of tobacco from it.

'What does the "E" stand for?' Atherton wanted to know.

'Eli,' he acknowledged, with a look that said, *Go on, then, make something of it. Give me an excuse.*

With regard to the corpse in his yard, he was sullen. 'I don't know nothing about it,' he said. 'Ask me, someone's playing a joke on me.'

'A joke?' Slider said, pained.

'Trick, then. Having a go at me. Tryna get me into trouble.'

'Do you know who he is?'

'Never seen him before in me life.' He brooded a moment, then added, gratis, 'He's not from round here.'

'How do you know that, if you don't know him?' Atherton asked.

'Look at his close,' he said succinctly.

Slider admitted he had a point. The corpse was wearing a good-quality charcoal wool overcoat over a two-piece black suit and white shirt, tieless and open at the neck. His shoes were black leather, highly polished. His dark, grey-speckled hair, kinky like wire wool, was cut short. He was clean-shaven and gave off a faint aroma of expensive aftershave.

'Dressed up like he's going up the West End,' said Sampson.

'How long have you had this place?' Slider asked.

'Been here twenty year,' said Sampson. 'Ask my satisfied customers.'

It was his way of offering his credentials. Slider did not really suspect him of having put the body there. To call the police would be a bold double bluff, but it was rare even among professional criminals to find anyone willing to try it. On the whole they liked the more basic defence of being as far from the scene as possible. Being a good twenty miles away at the time was a lot simpler than arguing, 'If I was guilty, I wouldn't have called you, would I?'

That didn't mean he didn't know the deceased, or have anything to do with the death, of course.

He answered Slider's questions tersely, resentment bristling in every word. His business was servicing and repairing cars, his clients the unlucky souls who did not have the luxury of a warranty. The cars were mostly old bangers and rust-buckets, which he kept limping along for the owners, who relied on them for their own precarious livings. He was here most days, working, or tinkering about with his own motors – he bought old MGs and restored them as a sideline. He had been here until six last night, give or take, and had arrived at seven this morning to find the unwelcome visitor lying in the mud at the side of the yard.

'Took you long enough to call it in,' Atherton remarked. It was logged at seven twenty.

'Didn't know what to do. I knew you lot'd look at me suspicious. As if I'd plant a body in me own yard!'

'Did you touch him, or move him?' Slider asked.

'Never went near him,' Sampson said, 'only to see he was dead and not drunk or whatever. I could see he was dead all right, without touching him. So I went in me office and had a fag while I thought what to do. I was shook up. Then I rung you lot.'

He hadn't seen any strangers hanging around lately. And the only people who'd been in his yard in the last week had been his customers coming and going, all people known to him. 'Why'd anybody come down here, unless they was looking for me?' he said logically.

Another point, Slider allowed. The opening to the track was unobtrusive, and didn't look as if it led anywhere but behind the blank warehouses.

A tube train rattled past, down in the cutting beyond the security railings. Overhead, the sky was grey and messy, like wet dishrags, but too high for rain. The wet spell was passing over. 'You're pretty isolated here,' Atherton remarked, glancing about.

'That's the way I like it,' Sampson said. 'I like me own comp'ny.' He glowered at the police and the SOC crowd infesting his space. He jerked his thumb towards the corpse. 'What was he doing here, that's what I want to know.'

'That's what we all want to know,' Slider said.

'He never brought no motor in,' Sampson observed. 'That one's mine,' he pointed to a beat-up Ford Focus which he'd parked in one of the garages, 'and that one I'm working on.' He indicated a frail-looking Cortina, practically a museum piece, which was in the shop. 'So what'd he do, wander in here drunk?' he concluded irritably.

Slider beckoned LaSalle over and left him with Sampson, while he followed the boards across to where the forensic pathologist was kneeling beside the body. The SOC unit had laid tarpaulins around it, and Freddie Cameron had the protective suiting on, but he still looked less than happy. 'Mud,' he said by way of greeting as Slider reached him. 'I hate mud. Slipped off the damn board walking up here, now I've got wet knees. And I'm particularly fond of these trousers.' He looked penetratingly at Slider's wellies. 'Foresight is a lovely thing.'

Hear a new word and you'll hear it again within the day, Slider thought. 'I never leave home without them,' he said.

'Smug bugger!'

'How did he die? He looks peaceful enough.' The corpse was supine, arms to his sides, and his clothing was not torn or disordered.

'Broken neck,' Cameron said, pointing out the unnatural angle of the head. 'I don't know if there are any other injuries – that will have to wait until I've got him back and stripped.'

Slider studied the face. A man in, he guessed, his mid to late fifties; a firm face, naturally sallow, and weather-tanned; a strong fleshy nose and chin, large ears with big earlobes. A face of resolve, he thought: someone who knew what he was doing, a businessman, perhaps – a small trader. The clothes were nice but he didn't have the air of a mogul.

Cameron went on: 'There are no defence wounds.' He lifted a hand. 'Well-kept fingernails. Doesn't look as though we'll find a handy skin specimen of the assailant under them.'

The sleeve tipped back a little with the movement, revealing a handsome watch. Cameron caught Slider's glance. 'Patek Philippe,' he said. 'Very nice. The sort you don't own, you just look after it for the next generation. Still showing the right time.'

Atherton leaned closer to examine it. 'It's a Calatrava,' he concluded.

'Expensive?' Slider asked.

'They start about five thousand. Connoisseur's choice,' Atherton said. 'Not your usual swank-pot's show-off job. Interesting.'

'Doesn't seem as if robbery from the person was the motive, then,' said Slider.

'You say that,' Freddie Cameron answered, 'but all his pockets are empty.'

'How empty?' Slider asked.

'Completely. Not a sausage. No wallet, cash, keys – not even a handkerchief. And what gentleman goes out without a hanky?'

'We don't know that he was a gentleman,' Slider said, 'watch or no watch. But I take your point. In any case, we know he didn't walk in here. Look at his shoes.'

'Good quality. Leather soles,' Atherton observed.

'But no mud,' Cameron said.

'Quite,' said Slider.

Hart, coming up behind them, caught the exchange. 'Someone could a' driven him here, then whacked him.' She jerked a thumb backwards towards Sampson. 'Laughing Boy over there, maybe. He looks tasty. And his is the only motor here.'

Slider shook his head. 'There's no mud on the *soles* of the shoes,' he said. 'So he couldn't have stepped out of a car, even if he was driven here. He couldn't have moved anywhere in this yard under his own motive power without getting mud on the soles.'

'So he was dumped?' Atherton concluded.

'That would be my guess. Killed somewhere else, pockets emptied, driven here and bundled from the car.'

'But why dump him here?' Hart asked, staring around.

'Ah, now you're getting onto the expensive questions,' Slider said, shaking his head. 'The Christmas and birthday questions. I'm not sure you can afford 'em.' He turned to Freddie. 'Time of death?'

'Between twelve and twenty-four hours ago, give or take,' Freddie said. 'Rigor's well established. Sometime yesterday, in all probability.'

'If Sampson's telling the truth, he has to have been dumped here between six last night and seven this morning,' said Slider.

'That's OK, time-wise,' said Freddie.

'But of course, he could have been killed earlier than six, and stashed somewhere else first, then moved after dark.'

'That's about the size of it,' Cameron agreed. 'Right, I'm ready to roll. I take it you'll want fingerprints, since there's nothing else to identify him by? OK. I'll take a DNA sample and do the teeth as well. And I'll report again, as soon as I've done a full inspection.'

'So what now?' Atherton asked as they turned away.

'A quick word with Bob Bailey,' said Slider, 'and then we might as well get some breakfast.'

He talked to Bailey, the Scene of Crime chief, about tyre tracks. 'If you can work out which was the latest one, before Sampson drove back in, it might help.'

'Won't be able to tell you more than the make. But I'll take a cast if there's anything clear,' he said. 'Course, it won't help until you get something to compare it *to*, but . . .' And he shrugged.

Then Slider led the way back down to Wood Lane where all the official wheels were parked.

'Breakfast, where?' Atherton asked, when they reached the department car. 'There's nothing round here.'

'You'd be surprised,' said Slider. 'Chummy had the good taste to get himself dumped only yards from one of the best eateries in West London.'

'More foresight?' And then he stopped to look around disbelievingly. 'I find it hard to believe. What's the name of this gourmet establishment?'

'Sid's,' said Slider.

Sid's was in the centre of the flight of shops between the Westway and Du Cane Road.

'Been here donkey's years,' Slider said. 'It's an institution.'

'So is a mental hospital,' Atherton countered.

'Don't be sniffy until you've tried it.'

It was an unglamorous place, an old-fashioned transport caff, surviving through the nostalgia and dogged loyalty of the many commercial drivers who passed up and down Scrubs Lane. The original Sid was now in his eighties, and the heavy lifting was done by various children and grandchildren, but he was generally to be found stationed behind the griddle, flat cap on his head, cooking the endless relays of the famed all-day breakfast. His frying of an egg was poetry in motion.

But when Slider and Atherton went in, the griddle was manned by one of his sons, Young Barry, a tall, fleshy man in his fifties. 'Ullo,' he said pleasantly. 'Long time no see.'

The counter was being tended by Barry's daughter Tiffany,

while Mrs Sid, a mere spritely seventy-nine, did the rest of the cooking.

'Ooh, look who it is. I 'ope we're not in dutch,' Mrs Sid said jocularly.

Tiffany was lively, with platinum hair and a lot of teeth, and was very popular with the customers. 'I hear you got a bit o' trouble up at Jacket's Yard,' she said.

Slider filed the name gratefully – it didn't appear on any maps. 'Who told you that?' he asked.

'Some drivers who were in earlier,' she said.

'Our Tiff gets to hear everything,' Young Barry observed. 'She gives 'em a smile and they tell her all their secrets.'

'No Sid today?' Slider asked.

'Dad's stopping upstairs,' said Young Barry.

'Not ill, I hope?'

'Nah, just his bronichals,' said Mrs Sid.

'So what'll it be, gents?' Tiffany asked.

'Breakfast for me,' said Slider.

'Double soss, bacon, egg and beans? Fried slice with it?'

'Please.'

'Same for you, is it?' She examined Atherton, noted his faint shudder, and added, 'We ha'n't got any tofu, darlin'.'

Slider smiled. 'She's got *you* down all right.'

She took pity on him. 'How about a nice bowl of muesli?' she offered. 'Home made. I make it up meself. All organic.' Atherton accepted gratefully.

They went and sat down. Across the other side, two lorry drivers were lingering over their tea and newspapers, and in a corner an old man was slowly consuming an all-day, eating the baked beans one by one to make it last. The morning rush was well over.

Tiffany brought their food, and two cups of tea that went with it, and said in a low voice, 'Is that right then, a dead body's turned up in Jacket's Yard?'

How did these things get out? Slider wondered despairingly. But it would be in the papers soon, anyway. And if they didn't find out who the corpse was, they'd have to appeal to the public. 'That's right.'

'It's not Eli, is it?' she asked anxiously.

'No, he's all right,' Slider said. 'You know him, then?'

'Oh yes. He comes in here sometimes, for his breakfast, or just a cuppa.'

'What's he like?'

'He don't talk much, but he seems decent enough. I'm glad it's not him. You don't like it to be someone you know. He was in for his breakfast Sunday, Eli. I don't think his wife's very kind to him. But you ought to talk to Grandad. He knows all about Jacket's Yard and everybody round here. Why don't you go up when you've finished your breakfast?'

'He's not too ill to see us?'

'Nah, he's fine,' Tiffany said. 'He'd sooner be down here, truth be told, but Barry said his coughing wasn't nice for the customers. He'll be glad to see someone – it drives him mad, not working. You go on up when you've finished. You can take his tea up, save me a trip.'

The flat above the shop, which had once been home to Sid and his family, was now part pied-a-terre and part store room. No one lived there now, but there was a small kitchen and a bed, if anyone needed an overnight doss, and the sitting room was still furnished, acting as a rest area for whoever was on duty downstairs.

Sid was on the sofa watching the racing, and the air was blue with cigarette smoke. He started up in alarm when Slider and Atherton came in, then relaxed when he saw who it was. 'Thought you was Young Barry,' he said with a shamefaced grin. 'He's always on at me about smoking.'

'Brought your tea,' said Slider. 'Mind if I open the window a bit?'

'Help yourself,' said Sid. He turned down the television and sat down again. He was in grey flannel trousers, held up by braces over a collarless shirt, and carpet slippers, but his tweed cap was firmly in place. Slider had never seen him without it. He wondered if he slept in it.

Sid had a good cough, wiped his lips, and said, 'It ain't the fags, anyway, it's the brown kiters. Damp weather brings it on. Bit o' trouble down Jacket's Yard, so I heard. S'at what you've come about?'

'I thought you'd be good for a bit of background,' said Slider.

Sid looked pleased. 'Always glad to oblige. Sit down, sit down.' He waved his hand magnificently. 'They give you tea downstairs?'

'We had breakfast,' said Slider. 'Why's it called Jacket's Yard, anyway?'

'Well, that's what we always called it,' said Sid. 'Everyone round here. Used to be a rag-and-bone yard, see, back before the war, and right up into the Sixties. Old man Jacket, he was the big boss, used to have twenty carts and ponies, maybe more, went all over this area, Shepherd's Bush, White City, Ladbroke Grove. Everyone knew 'em. That's what Steptoe and Son was based on, didn't you know that?'

'Hard to believe there was ever horse-drawn traffic round here,' Atherton said, as lorries rumbled endlessly by, darkening the windows like a migration of mastodons.

Sid nodded, lighting another cigarette. 'Oh, it was big business, rag and bone – though it was more scrap metal towards the end,' he added fairly. 'Made a fortune, too, old man Jacket, with his ponies and carts. Blew it all on the racing, though. Funny, that – made it on the ponies and lost it on the ponies.' He laughed happily at his own wit, which brought on another coughing fit.

'Tell me about Eli,' Slider said, when the noise subsided.

'Oh, everybody knows Eli,' said Sid. 'He's always there, Sundays and Christmas included, fiddling about with his motors. I reckon he just goes to get away from his wife. Mother don't like it when I say that, but she's a right harridan, his missus. So is he dead, then, Eli?'

'No, he was the one who found the body.'

Sid looked vaguely glad. 'He's a gyppo, you know – Eli? Proper Romany – old Romany family, the Sampsons. There was quite a few of 'em round here before the war. Give up the road and settled down. His wife, she was a Lee before she married. Another Romany family. Eli took over Jacket's Yard, ooh, must be, what, twenty-five, twenty-six year ago. Before that, it was a bloke called Gerry Philips, he had a car repair shop there, and Eli used to work for him, on and off. Done other stuff, seasonal. Fruit picking. Flogging stuff round the streets. Worked at the fair, and the circus when they came to the Scrubs – there was Sampsons them days at Billy Smart's, relatives of his. Then when Gerry retired, he offered the place to Eli. Helped him out with the rent till he got going. Like a son to him, Eli was. Course, the business has gone downhill since then.'

'Why is that?' Slider asked. 'Is he not good at it?'

'Oh, he's good with cars, is Eli. None better. But cars've changed, it's all computers now, you can't mend *them* with a spanner. And he's no good at business. This place has changed, Wood Lane, with all this development round here, nobody knows he's there any more, and he won't shift himself to advertise, or get himself known, or put in new equipment. So all he gets is the old bangers, and word-of-mouth. Won't even put up a sign on the main road. Says he's happy as he is.' Sid shrugged, to signify that people were as people were, and there was nothing you could do about it.

'Does he make a living?' Slider asked.

'That I can't tell you. I can't see how he can do, the way he goes about it.'

'So – is there something else? Something on the side? A bit shady, maybe?'

Another shrug. 'I wouldn't say he's up to anything crooked. Not that I know of.'

'But it wouldn't surprise you?' Atherton put in.

'I wouldn't say he's *never* been a naughty boy,' said Sid, circumspectly, 'but it wouldn't be anything big. He's too lazy. If something fell in his lap, maybe. If it was just a case of no questions asked, maybe he'd just roll with it.'

'Knock-off watches, you mean? Duty free cigarettes?' Atherton suggested.

'I don't know anything about that. I'm just saying.' He blew smoke upwards, and looked at them with faded but steady blue eyes. 'But you're looking at a dead body. Eli'd never have nothing to do with a thing like that. That's big stuff. How'd this bloke die, anyway? Lorry driver come in here this morning, says they reckon it's a gangland boss, some turf war or something.'

Slider supposed someone had told someone else the victim was smartly dressed in toff style, and it had snowballed from there. 'We don't know anything about the victim,' he said, 'and that's the truth. So, Eli owns the property, does he?'

'Nah, he just rents it,' said Sid.

'Only it must be worth a bit.'

Sid chuckled. 'You'd think so, wouldn't you? Used to be owned by a property comp'ny, I'll think of the name in a minute. Begun with a T. They bought it off Gerry Philips, reckoned to develop it. Target, that was it. But they couldn't, see, on account of the access. That road that goes in there, the first bit of it's a bridge over the railway tunnel, and it's not strong enough to take heavy traffic. London Transport owns that bit, and they're not willing to rebuild it, given they never use it. So o'course you couldn't get lorries in. Site was a white elephant.' He chuckled again, pleased with the deserved misfortune of the naïve. 'So they was glad to rent it out for whatever they could get.'

'So Target still owns it?'

'Nah, they sold it about two year ago. To another developer. That big company, what's it called, that's been buying up plots all over the place to put up luxury flats. Another lot of idiots, never did their homework. So *they*'re stuck with it now. What's their name again? Some posh name, like a big house somewhere.'

'Grosvenor?' Slider suggested.

'No, not that one. Something like Buckingham Palace. I'll get it in a minute.' He screwed up his face. 'Blenheim, that's it. Blenheim Property Development. So they're renting it to old Eli on a short lease, hoping God'll come down and reinforce that bridge for 'em so's they can stick up a mansion block and make their fortune. Good luck to 'em!'

'So Eli is shady, but not *very* shady,' Atherton said as they emerged again into the day. There was a thin patch in the clouds through which the sun was trying to slide. It was blurred and whiteish behind the grey, like a half-sucked acid drop. 'That, by the way, was surprisingly good muesli.'

'Told you so,' said Slider.

'The muesli in our canteen looks like something a pigeon regurgitated to feed its young.' He went round to the driver's side of the car. 'I wonder if our Eli is just enough connected to the demi-monde for someone to know about his yard and fancy it for a dumping ground.'

'Possible. And if it implicates Eli and has us chasing about investigating him, so much the better?'

'I hadn't thought that far, but it's a good line.'

Slider got in at the passenger side. 'The bugger of it is, we'll have to look into Eli anyway, just as a matter of—'

'Routine,' Atherton supplied.

'Common sense,' Slider finished.

TWO
That'll Do, Pig

With the corpse taken off to the forensic suite at the Charing Cross, Sampson taken back to the station to 'help with enquiries' – in the delicately non-committal parlance of the early stages of an investigation – and the SOC team laboriously examining tyre prints and searching the yard for weapons, Slider decided they might as well call on Mrs Sampson before heading back. Sampson had given his address as a housing association flat in North Pole Road. 'That's only two minutes away.'

The flat occupied the upper floor of a two-storeyed edifice in the centre of a terrace. It had three bedrooms, kitchen, bathroom and sitting room, which sounded extensive, but it was in fact a miniature place, built before the war for a smaller race of natives with more modest ambitions. The largest room was only ten feet by twelve, and in the kitchen and bathroom two people couldn't have passed each other without risking intimate contact.

Someone had already rung Mrs Sampson with the news – how things got about! – so she was not surprised to see them.

Not pleased, either. The police, it was evident, were not at the very top of her list of welcome visitors, and only Slider's most gimlet stare kept the opprobrious epithets that were hovering on her lips from taking to the air.

But when he made it clear he was not prepared to talk on the doorstep, she reluctantly let them in and admitted them to her sitting room. Though it was tiny, it was crammed with furniture and ornaments, and everything was shiningly clean and obsessively neat. It put Slider in mind of the inside of an old-school caravan or narrowboat. There were lace doilies under everything, antimacassars everywhere, plastic flowers in every vase. Bits of china and brass occupied every surface, and every inch of wall was covered in framed photographs, some of them hand-edged with lace, and cheap prints of sentimental pictures: faithful dogs, kittens playing with wool, whimsical children, whitewashed cottages infested with rambling roses and monstrous hollyhocks.

Mrs Sampson was short and stocky with a face like toothache. Where her husband was sullen, she bristled with suppressed fury. Her body seemed to strain outwards against her clothes as though ready to burst with it. She was an entire womanful of anger – possibly two.

'That old fool! I'll give him what for when I get hold of him, the useless article!' she raged. 'What's he got himself into this time?'

'I don't know that he's done anything,' Slider said mildly. 'Perhaps *you* can tell *me*.'

'Are you trying to be funny?' she snapped.

'Not at all. You asked what he'd got into *this time*. What has he got into before?'

She was momentarily floored, but soon recovered. 'What you saying? What you tryna pin on him? He's a hard-working man, tryna make a living, no thanks to the likes of you – and young Skippy, here!' She had saved a glare for Atherton. 'Still wet behind the ears. Bumfluff still on his face. What you staring at, sonny? Try getting your hands dirty for a change, same as working people, if you pigs'd leave us alone for five minutes, coming round here accusing honest folk of I-don't-know-what . . .'

She'd been forgetting to breathe in and now as her face went from scarlet towards black she had to pause at last to gasp, which gave Slider a chance to get a word in. He was treasuring her assessment of Atherton – especially 'Skippy' and 'bumfluff' – to be enjoyed more fully later. For now he had to get her to calm down.

'At the moment, your husband is just helping us with our enquiries. But we are investigating a serious matter, so I recommend that you try to help us too. Tell me, do you know this man?' He passed over the deceased's image on his tablet.

She glanced, blenched a little, and tried to give it back. 'Is this the dead bloke?'

'Who is he?'

'*I* don't know. Never seen him before in my life.'

'Look again. You didn't look for long enough to be sure.'

'I looked long enough! You take me for a fool? Coming in here, making me look at dead people! I tell you I don't know him! What's he got to do with my Eli?'

Slider still hadn't taken the tablet back, and she couldn't resist taking another peep. He watched her face. He was sure there was something there. 'You *do* know him, don't you?'

'No, I don't!' she declared. Her eyes met his and slid away. 'He just looks a bit like somebody famous, that's all. Like some film actor or something. That Gene Hackman,' she said on an inspiration. 'That's who it was. I thought at first he looked a bit like him.'

She thrust the tablet at him determinedly, and he took it, and threw Atherton a glance to take over.

As Slider was now Bad Cop, Atherton tried buttering her up along the 'nice place you've got here' lines.

'I do my best,' she said rigidly, unwilling to bend far. 'Best I can do with a man forever messing things up, coming home all grease and dirt, fingermarks everywhere, everything in the wrong place, clothes hung up on the floor. Why the good Lord created men in the first place I'll never understand. I'm glad to see the back of him when he goes off to his daft old yard, I can tell you, so's I can get on with my work.'

Atherton slipped into the crack she'd opened. 'He must be doing all right, though, all those long hours he puts in.'

'Long hours? He's never home. Might as well be a widow, married to that object.'

'But I've heard he's very good with cars. They say he can fix anything.'

She snorted. 'Fat lot of good it does him! Or me! I'm not a fiver better off at the end of the week, for all his messing. All those so-called friends of his that never pay him – "Oh, I'll give it you next week".' She put on a whining voice. 'Only next week never comes, does it? He's an idiot when it comes to business. Only a fool would have signed that lease.' She stopped abruptly, and looked suspiciously from Atherton to Slider. 'What you taken him down the station for? You don't think *he* had anything to do with this? He couldn't kill anyone if he tried. Soft as muck, he is. He'd mess it up, anyway – probably shoot himself by mistake.'

'What makes you think this man was shot?' Slider asked.

She gave him a cunning look. 'Oh no you don't. You don't catch me like that. I don't know anything about it, and nor does Eli, and if I don't see him back here double-quick, I'm going to make a complaint. We're honest citizens. You can't go harassing us. I know my rights.' She folded her arms and her lips with a triumphant look.

'What was that about the lease?' Atherton asked smoothly, with an air of innocent interest. 'You mean the lease with Blenheim? I thought he had it on good terms.'

She mottled with fury. 'Good terms? *Good terms?*' It burst from her. 'One year rolling with a six month notice? I told him, I said what security you got now? They can have you out any time they like. If I'd been there – but no, he goes and signs it without asking me, the stupid lummox. Just because some slick-talking bastard comes round his yard – and what do they want it for, answer me that! Those big companies don't go buying up land if there's no profit in it – profit to them, not profit to someone who's worked on it for thirty year!' Again she stopped to breathe. 'I think you better go, now,' was her next effort. 'I got washing to take out, and dinner to get started.'

Ooh, that's cold, Slider thought. *Playing second fiddle to washing.*

'When's Eli going to be home?' she went on before he could speak. 'You got nothing on him, you can't keep him.'

'We're not keeping him now,' Slider said smoothly. 'He's voluntarily helping us with our enquiries.'

'Right! If it's voluntary, he can voluntary come home. He don't know nothing about this geezer, and neither do I. I've warned you. If I don't see him back here by dinner time, I'm putting in a complaint. So you're told!'

Outside, Atherton said, 'Phew! I feel like the victim of reverse police brutality. Was she feigning anger to distract our attention, or was it real?'

'There was nothing feigned about that. But I still think she knew deceased.'

'That stuff about Gene Hackman didn't work for you? I was convinced.'

'Ooh, irony? You could put someone's eye out with that. But all the same, I agree with her, I don't think he did the killing. She may think he's an idiot, but surely not idiot enough to leave the body there?'

'Elaborate double bluff?'

'Not that much of a Moriarty, either,' said Slider.

Sampson's statement had been short and sour. He'd said only what he said before, that he'd come in at seven and found deceased there, and that he'd never seen him before in his life. Hart had questioned him about his customers, on the off chance that one of them was involved, but he was sure they couldn't be. They were all good blokes, he said, though when it came to details about them, he was vague in the extreme. He had no surnames, knew them only as Dave, Mikey, Phil and so on, and had no addresses for any of them.

'He could tell me the make and model of their cars and what was wrong with them down to the last wing nut,' said Hart, 'but the owners were "just some bloke".'

'How did he know them, then?' Slider asked.

'Word of mouth,' Hart said. 'Tom, Dick and Harry recommend him, and Jim, Jack and Paddy just drive in, leave their motors, and he fixes 'em.'

'He must have phone numbers, or how does he tell them when the car's ready?' Atherton said, sitting on the cold radiator and contemplating his shoes. He'd had to wash them when he got back to get the mud off, and dry them with the hand dryer in the gents. He was hoping there wouldn't be a watermark.

'He jots the number down on a piece of paper when they leave the car,' said Hart, 'but he doesn't keep 'em. He's not what you'd call devoted to the office work. When I asked about receipts, he looked at me as if I'd started talking Swedish. I gather it's a cash business, in so far as it's a business at all.'

'He's got a land line at the yard,' LaSalle said helpfully. 'We could get the records.'

'Do we want to?' Hart said with a weary look. 'Trawling through his customers'd take ages, and do we really think he's got something to do with the corpse, boss? He dun't seem the type to me.'

'We have to account for the body somehow,' said Slider. 'Someone put it there – so why there?'

'It's got to be someone who knew the yard existed,' Atherton said. 'You can't tell from the road.'

'Well, that'd be a bugger, having a corpse dumped on you, just cos someone knows you've got a yard,' Hart said.

'What are friends for?' said Atherton.

'Normally if you've got a body to get rid of,' said Slider, 'you bury it in the woods or throw it down a remote quarry.'

'Shepherd's Bush is notably short of both,' Atherton observed.

'If they was in a car,' Hart pointed out, 'they could've driven off and found one.'

'So perhaps time was short,' said Slider. 'The good thing about Jacket's Yard is that it's not overlooked. If they knew that, maybe it was enough, just to get the body away from wherever the killing happened.'

'Or maybe they panicked,' Atherton said.

Slider shook his head. 'It doesn't look panicky, exactly. They took the trouble to empty his pockets. It looks more like time-saving. But until we know who deceased *is*, we can't tell if he's connected to Sampson or his customers in any way.'

'I don't think there's any point in sifting through his

contacts,' said Atherton. 'I don't believe he would have called
it in if he'd had anything to do with it. He'd have loaded the
body up and driven it away somewhere.'

'I've already said that,' said Slider.

'Well, I'm agreeing with you.'

'But in my case it was reasoned deduction. With you it's
just laziness,' said Slider.

Doc Cameron had sent over the fingerprints, and LaSalle went
off to run them. Slider was getting on with some other stuff
when Loessop, who had been running Sampson through
records, came in. He was swarthy and piratical, a look he
cultivated for street-cred purposes with the Captain Jack
Sparrow locks and plaited beard, earning him the nickname
of Funky. Slider noted he was also wearing a dangly earring,
a silver skull. His women detectives knew he did not allow
danglers, but it obviously hadn't filtered through to Funky. He
mentioned it mildly, and Loessop hastily removed it.

'Sorry, sir. It's just part of the image.'

'If some low life on the street grabs you by it, it'll be part
of a visit to A&E,' said Slider. 'What've you got on Sampson?'

'He's got no criminal record,' said Loessop.

'That's a surprise. I'd have thought there'd be a little something. Receiving stolen goods. Driving without insurance.
Looking iffy in a public place.'

'Well, he's either been virtuous, careful, or lucky,' Loessop
said. 'I'd bet lucky: he's been drawing long-term disability
benefit for nearly ten years.'

'He looked spry enough to me.'

'Yeah, guv. He doesn't look like a bloke with chronic back
pain and crippling sciatica, does he?'

'I suppose he's got a note from some doctor or other?'

'It's Dr Bajwa in St Mark's Road. He's come on the radar
before, for giving out medical certificates for cash.'

'There's a lot of it about,' said Slider.

'And another thing, guv – I checked with the Inland Revenue,
and Sampson's not troubled them since he went on the sicker.
No declared income. He's what you might call part of the cash
economy.'

'That explains why he doesn't have to hustle to make a living,' said Slider. 'A nice benefits cushion, and mends cars for cash as a sideline.'

'And no paperwork to catch him out. Doesn't get us any nearer the mystery corpse, though,' Loessop concluded, tugging fretfully at his beard plaits.

'What it does,' Slider comforted him, 'is give us a handle if we should need to put the bite on friend Sampson at some stage. Benefits fraud and tax evasion are enough to lock him up and lean on him.'

Loessop brightened. 'D'you want me to have a go, guv?'

'We've got nothing to ask him yet,' said Slider. 'You can let him go. I think his wife wants a word with him.'

LaSalle came back with the news that deceased's fingerprints had not found a match. With no one to canvass and no lines to follow up until they had an identity, there wasn't anything more they could do for now. 'We can't even ask Mispers without a name,' said LaSalle discontentedly.

'I'm sure you've got plenty of other work to get on with,' Slider said. 'As I have.'

LaSalle took the hint and went away, and Slider tried to clear his mind of annoyingly misplaced bodies and concentrate on police community relations initiatives. He was about to go home when Freddie Cameron telephoned.

'You sound tired,' Slider said.

'It's been a long day,' said Cameron. 'And the mud's gone right through my nice grey bags. Both knees.'

'You should know better than to wear nice clothes to work.'

'I spend my entire life at work, when else am I going to wear nice clothes? If I'm reduced to wearing tough corduroys and big boots every day like some urban James Herriot, I might as well retire, because life won't be worth living.'

'Dilettante!' Slider jeered. 'What about my corpse?'

'I've only done the visual so far,' Freddie said. 'The full necropsy will have to wait until tomorrow. But I can say that death was almost certainly caused by a massive blow to the cervical spine, with a heavy blunt instrument with a rounded profile. A blow of considerable force.'

'Ah, typical suicide,' said Slider. 'He accidentally brutally hit himself on the back of the neck with a baseball bat.'

'Ho ho,' said Cameron. 'It rather rules out accident as well as suicide. You couldn't fall on something with that much force without leaving other injuries. And there were no other visible injuries or bruising.'

'So it wasn't part of a beating?'

'No, just the one blow. I suspect he didn't see it coming, since there were no defence injuries. For the rest, deceased was probably in his mid-to-late fifties, but fit for his age – good musculature and a low body fat percentage. He was well-nourished, clean, circumcised, no evidence of homosexual activity or drug use. There was one old scar around the ribs that looked like a knife wound, but that must be going back twenty years or so. The hands were well-kept but there was some old scarring of the knuckles, together with some thickening, typical of someone who's used his fists for fighting. No wedding ring, though that doesn't mean he wasn't married, of course. No jewellery other than that nice watch.'

'So he was a naughty boy in his youth, come upon something more lucrative and less physical to do in later life. How long was he dead before they dumped him, can you tell?'

'It was probably quite soon after death. The hypostasis is consistent with the position in which the body was found,' said Cameron. 'It doesn't become fixed until around six hours, but there are usually some traces – earlobes and fingernails, for instance – if the body's moved after it sets in.'

'I suppose he didn't have his name and national insurance number tattooed on his arm?'

'Interesting you should say that,' Freddie began.

'You're kidding me!'

'Yes, of course I am. However, we did find one thing. We thought the pockets were completely empty, but in the inside breast pocket of the jacket we found a lottery ticket. I'll send it over. It was flat against the lining under the buttonhole, so you couldn't feel it just by putting your hand in. We missed it at the site. We only found it when we had the clothes off the body and turned every pocket out, which presumably the murderer didn't have the luxury of doing.'

'A lottery ticket,' Slider said. 'Recent?'

'Saturday's,' said Freddie. 'Something?'

'Could be. We still don't know who he is.'

'No one's rung in asking for him, then?'

'It's early days for that. And the fingerprints came up blank.'

'Interesting. I'd have thought the fighting might have got him into trouble. Well, I'll circulate the dental profile. And I'll send off a DNA sample. You can decide if you want it processed. We'll go over the clothing for any fibres or other deposits, but that'll have to wait until tomorrow as well. I'm going home now.'

'Good idea,' said Slider.

'Have you got plans for this evening?'

'No, I'm all alone tonight. Joanna didn't have any work for a couple of days, so she's gone to visit her parents, and taken George with her.'

'You're welcome to come and feed with us,' said Freddie – a generous offer given how tired he was.

'Thanks all the same,' said Slider, 'but I'm quite looking forward to pretending to be a bachelor again. I shall have a curry on my knees in front of the telly.'

'Sounds like heaven,' said Freddie politely.

Slider smiled to himself. He couldn't imagine Freddie ever eating other than at a table, and with a knife and fork. 'It is to me,' he said.

'And the whole bed to yourself,' Freddie added. 'Martha's miniature dachshund gets on the bed between us, and I wake up to find myself clinging to the very edge and Merry sprawled out in the middle. It's amazing how much room a small dog can take when he puts his mind to it.'

'Shut him out of the room,' Slider suggested.

'Then he howls outside the door,' Freddie sighed.

Slider chuckled. 'It's not like you to give in to emotional blackmail. If you'd brought your children up that way . . .'

'They didn't have such piercing voices,' said Cameron.

Slider didn't sleep well, despite having the whole bed to himself. Perhaps it was the curry, or the gloomy Australian film he'd watched, featuring dead teenage girls and corrupt policemen in a grim outback settlement. Perhaps it was having the whole bed to himself. He kept surfacing, about every half hour; jerking awake as though he'd heard something. Then he went through that tiresome process of calculating, 'if I can go to sleep now, I'll still get four hours'; then three, then two. At six he gave up and went downstairs, made some tea, and had bacon frying when the phone rang.

'Did I wake you?' Joanna asked.

'No, I was up. I had a bad night.'

'So did I. Kept waking up thinking it was morning, and finding I'd only been asleep half an hour.'

'Same here. Can it be that you miss having me beside you?' he asked.

'Always. Are you making yourself a proper breakfast?'

'Yes, Mama. Are you having a nice time? How is everyone?'

'They're all fine. Dad is spoiling George – bought him a chocolate ice cream as big as his head yesterday, so of course he was sick. George, not Dad. Mum keeps asking when he's going to have a little brother or sister. She says it isn't good for children to be "onlies".'

'She has met *me*, hasn't she?'

'You're the exception that proves the rule.' She paused. 'What does that even *mean*?'

'"Proves" as in "tests",' said Slider.

'Oh!' she said, with an air of discovery. 'You are a fount of knowledge.'

'We did it in school.'

In the background a person said something he couldn't make out, and she said, 'I have to go. Someone's just spilled a whole glass of water over someone.'

'I hope both someones are my son,' Slider said.

Slider's immediate boss, Detective Superintendent Porson, was back after a week off. It didn't seem to have sweetened him. He seemed to regard the body at Jacket's Yard as having been deliberately planted to annoy him. In fairness, they did have a lot on, and this sort of body boded a lot of work. Nobody liked boding first thing in the morning.

'What did they want to dump him there for?' he demanded,

fretfully leafing through the paperwork that had arrived on his desk in his absence. 'What's wrong with the countryside? Plenty of it around, isn't there? What did they have to come cluttering up our ground for?' Slider took those as rhetorical questions. 'And you've got no ID? Nothing at all?'

'Nothing from the fingerprints. We've had no enquiries after anyone matching his description, and it's too early for Mispers. We'll circulate his photograph to the other boroughs, and the usual places – hospitals, taxi firms. If nothing turns up, we may have to go to public appeal.'

'We're a long way off that,' Porson said hastily. 'He can stay in the cooler until someone misses him or you get a name. No use knocking yourself out.'

'We could process the DNA—' Slider began.

Porson scowled. 'We could not! There's enough wailing and gnashing of feet upstairs 'cause we're over our budget. I'm not lashing out for some low-life that nobody's missing.'

'No, sir,' Slider said. The nice clothes, watch and manicure suggested he was quite a high-living low-life, but the principle was the same.

'Don't go borrowing trouble,' Porson advised. 'It's not as if you're short of something to do. Murder's a priority, of course, but you'll have to do this one on the cheap, until there's a reason not to.'

Slider looked up as McLaren came into his room. 'You've got something on your mouth,' he said sharply. 'Is that chocolate?'

McLaren's hand stole guiltily to his upper lip, even as he said, 'No, guv. I'm growing a moustache.'

'Really?' said Slider.

McLaren smirked. 'It's a surprise for Natalie.'

Slider contemplated the statement. 'I don't think you're going to be able to keep it a secret,' he concluded.

'She's *had* the surprise,' McLaren explained. 'The surprise was me doing it. She says every man should have a moustache. She thinks they're macho.'

It was the reason, of course, that so many policemen sported facial hair.

McLaren seemed to have fallen into a reverie. His new

girlfriend had that effect on him. Slider broke his dream. 'Did you want something?'

'Oh – yes, guv! This come in the bag from Doc Cameron.'

It was the lottery ticket from the corpse's pocket. Slider followed McLaren to the door of the CID room, caught Swilley's eye, and when she came over, handed her the ticket and said, 'See if you can find out where this was sold. If it's a local shop, there's a possibility the vendor might recognise the mugshot.'

THREE
Arose By Some Other Name

The National Lotteries Board reported that the ticket in deceased's pocket had been purchased from a newsagents called Randal's in Hammersmith Road. Swilley punched up the details of the shop. There had been a Randal's on that spot for sixty years, but it was now owned and run by an A. Patel and a B. Patel.

'The chances of them knowing anything are slight to nil, Norm,' Hart complained. 'You'll have a wasted journey.'

'At least it gets me out of the house,' Swilley said, slinging on her coat.

'Bring us back a pasty,' McLaren called. Swilley glared at him. 'Go on, Norma. I'll give you the money when you come back.'

'Maurice, it's well past lunchtime,' Swilley objected, looking pointedly at her watch.

'That's why I'm hungry,' said McLaren.

'You're always hungry. It's pathological,' Swilley said. 'Obsessive eating's a displacement activity for sex.'

'Well, you won't have sex with us, so bring us a pasty,' McLaren said logically.

Swilley snorted and whirled out.

* * *

The shop was just like any other in the area: tiny and dimly lit, with the counter at the far end. The newspapers were stacked at floor level, and above them were racks of sweets on one side, crisps and snacks on the other, with a passage one-customer wide down the middle. Cigarettes were in a locked cupboard behind the counter, and the Cerberus in front of them was a chubby-faced Pakistani, who folded his arms defensively across his chest and narrowed his eyes at the sight of Swilley. *How did they know*? she wondered. She was rather offended – she went to some lengths *not* to look like a copper. They might as well have 'Metropolitan Police' tattooed across their foreheads and be done with it, she thought with an inward sigh.

He relaxed slightly as she explained her business and produced the photograph. She was fully expecting a blank stare and a what-did-you-expect denial, but A or B Patel took one look and said, 'Oh, yes, we know him. He's one of our regulars.'

Swilley's spirits lifted. 'Do you know his name?'

He rolled his eyes upward, contemplating the ceiling for inspiration. 'Wait one moment. I will think of it.'

Contemplation went on too long. This wasn't the Sistine Chapel. Swilley prodded him, 'How often does he come in?'

He lowered his gaze with apparent relief. 'Oh, many times. He comes in for cigarettes. Chocolate bars. Also a lottery ticket every Wednesday and Saturday.'

'Just one?'

'Always the same numbers,' he explained. 'He said he was afraid to change them in case that was the week they won. Many, many people say the same. He has never won. Nobody ever does. But they go on buying a ticket every week. It is very strange.'

'And what's his name?' Swilley said, hoping to trick it out of him.

He just looked bothered. 'Yes, yes, I will think of it in a minute. It's Mr something.'

No kidding, Swilley thought.

'Also we deliver his newspaper,' he went on. 'He lives just across the road, in Ruskin House.'

Swilley endured a brief struggle between excitement and impatience, both of which required her to scream. Then she said patiently, 'Perhaps you could look him up in your books.'

'Oh yes,' he said brightly. 'What a good idea.' He got down a large, battered-looking loose-leaf folder from the shelf behind him, and began laboriously thumbing through, with plenty of licking between pages. 'I am remembering now, his name I think is Mr King. I am almost certain is it Mr King.' And at last, 'Yes, here it is. Mr King. Flat 16, Ruskin House. One *Guardian* newspaper every day.' He looked up, pleased with himself, for her thanks.

'Have you got a phone number?'

'We don't have phone numbers. It is not necessary.'

'Is he married, do you know?'

'I do not know.' His face clouded. 'Has something happened to him?'

Swilley avoided that one. 'Thanks for your help, Mr Patel,' she said.

'I am Mr Wassan,' he told her gravely. 'Mr Patel is my uncle.'

'Well, thanks anyway,' she said, heading for the door.

'If something has happened to him, do you think I should cancel his order?' the voice followed her, rather wistfully.

Ruskin House was a handsome 1930s art-deco block in white stucco. It was five storeys high, and the corner flats on each floor had those curved windows so beloved of the period, which for some reason made the building look like an ocean liner. Number 16 was on the second floor. All the flats had three-panelled wooden doors, with a spy hole and a bell push. She pressed the bell, and knocked long and loud for good measure, but there was no answer.

A slight sound made her turn her head, to see the door of the next flat open a crack. An eye was peering through at little-old-lady level. As Swilley approached, the door was snapped shut. She knocked on it, more temperately, and said, in her most conciliatory voice, 'It's the police, ma'am. Can I have a word?'

'Go away!' was the muffled cry from inside, but from close

by the door. Swilley concluded there was curiosity there, as
well as apprehension.

'I'd just like to talk to you about your neighbour. Look, I'm
holding up my warrant card so you can see it. I am a plain-
clothes police officer. Would you just open the door, ma'am?'

There was some heavy, contemplative breathing behind the
door, then a fumbling rattle as the chain was applied, and the
door opened to its limit, revealing a shrivelled face surmounted
by a puff-ball of spun white hair, like a dandelion clock.
Swilley was tall, and the head appeared at around waist-level
for her. She crouched and offered the warrant card again,
smiling as unthreateningly as she knew how.

The suspicious eyes travelled up from the warrant card to
Swilley's face. 'You don't look like a police officer,' the old
lady objected.

'Thank you, ma'am. I take that as a compliment, Mrs . . .?'

'Greenwood.'

'I'm Detective Constable Swilley. It's about your next-door
neighbour—'

'Has something happened to Mr Kimmelman?' Mrs
Greenwood interrupted.

'Kimmelman?'

She jerked her head. 'Next door. Number sixteen. Leon
Kimmelman is his name. Has something happened, you should
come round asking about him? Such a nice man – always so
polite. He holds the lift if he sees me coming – I don't walk
so fast any more. I have one of those frames. A mixed blessing!
It slows me down, but he never gets impatient. "Good morning,
Mrs Greenwood," he says, so pleasant, all the time in the
world, and he holds the door open for me. A real *mensch*. Not
like *some* people.'

'Is he married?' Swilley asked.

A toss of the head. '*That* well I don't know him. He's just
a neighbour.'

'I mean,' Swilley hastened to repair, 'does he live there
alone? I was knocking but there was no reply.'

'Alone, as far as I know,' Mrs Greenwood allowed, placated.
'And usually, a quiet neighbour, you would never know he
was there, no parties or loud music.'

'When did you last see him?'

'I don't remember. Was it Saturday? I looked out and he was just letting himself in. Friday or Saturday, I don't remember. But Sunday night, I could hear him moving around, very late, banging doors and such, not like him. And now the police here, asking questions! Such goings-on we *don't* like in this house. A quiet, respectable house it has always been.'

'Mrs Greenwood, would you just take a look at this photograph, so I can be sure we're talking about the same person. Is this your neighbour Mr Kimmelman?'

A monkey-paw came through the gap and snaffled the photograph back through. The face disappeared for a moment, and then the photo was returned and the face was at the gap again, concerned and anxious. 'That's him,' she said. 'Leon Kimmelman. In that photo he doesn't look so well. Has something happened to him?'

'I'm afraid he's dead, Mrs Greenwood,' Swilley said as gently as she could. She was afraid the old bird might faint away, still on the wrong side of the door chain to be helped.

But she only closed her eyes and shook her head and said something under her breath that sounded like a prayer, or an imprecation. Then she opened them sharply and said, 'Was that what it was, on Sunday night, the noise?'

'We don't know,' Swilley admitted. 'What sort of noise was it?'

She contemplated her memory. 'Bumping against the wall. Things dropped on the floor. Furniture being moved. I thought maybe he was packing to move out.'

So that might be where he was whacked, Swilley thought. 'Voices?' she asked.

'I heard no voices. But these flats are well-built. You don't hear quiet noises. I had to put my ear to the wall to hear, after the bumps woke me up.' She scrutinised Swilley's face. 'Was he dying? Was that what I heard? I don't like to think he was dying in there all alone. I could have rung for an ambulance if I'd known. What happened to him?'

Swilley ignored the question and put one of her own. 'What time was it, do you remember?'

'Late,' said Mrs Greenwood. 'I couldn't say exactly. Maybe

after midnight. I was in bed. I'd been reading. I don't sleep so good any more. But I'd fallen asleep, and then the bump against the wall woke me up, right by my bed. Then I got up and put my ear to the wall.'

'Did it sound like a fight?'

'A fight? No! Who was fighting? Is that what you think? Like someone packing to leave, is what it sounded like to me. And I haven't heard him go out or come in since, not yesterday or this morning.' Her worried old eyes stared up as she thought about it. Sooner or later a penny would drop. Swilley sought to distract her.

'Do you have a spare key to his flat?' she asked.

'I do not,' Mrs Greenwood said, slightly offended. 'I'm a respectable widow. A key to a single gentleman's flat I would not have.' Swilley began to excuse herself, but Mrs Greenwood said, 'The managing agents have spare keys in case of emergency. Not to *my* flat,' she added, with a cunning look. 'Thirty-five years I've lived here, when we first came they were very nice people, a Mr Bergman took care of the house personally. Him, I didn't mind having a key. But nowadays, they come and go, flighty young things, you don't know who works there. I don't want any Tom, Dick and Harry having my key. So I changed the lock.' She gave a triumphant smile.

'What if there's an emergency?' Swilley couldn't help asking.

'What will be, will be,' said Mrs Greenwood, and snapped the door shut.

Now *that's* good theatre, Swilley thought.

Cameron rang with the result of the autopsy. 'Death was certainly due to the blow. It was very violent – fractured three vertebrae, shattering one of them. There's no head trauma, and the brain shows no sign of concussion, which suggests he must have crumpled, rather than being knocked over, so death was probably instantaneous. There's no pathological evidence of poisoning or sedation, though of course I will send off tox screens to be sure, but you know how long that takes.'

'I'm happy to take your word that he wasn't drugged.'

'Kind of you. His last meal had passed out of his stomach,

but there was alcohol in there. Whisky – but not enough for him to have been drunk at the time of death.'

'So he was having a drink with someone, and annoyed them enough for them to wallop him, leaving them with an embarrassing body to get rid of,' Slider mused.

'If you say so. You're the detective. I'm just a lowly scientist.'

'Lowly!' Slider scoffed.

'Also those knuckles showed signs of old fractures, there was a long-healed fracture to one of the ribs, and a dent in the forehead, consistent with a blow. And the nose had been fractured, again a long time ago. Our friend was something of a pugilist in his former life, it seems.'

'Thanks,' said Slider. 'I'm not sure any of that helps.'

'Have you found out who he is yet?'

'Unlike you, I had nothing to work with.'

'You need a visit from our old friend, Neil Desperandum,' Cameron advised.

The excitement of Swilley's return brought Slider out of his room. The relief of having a name was profound. A body without a name was as unsettling to a policeman as a raspberry pip stuck between the teeth.

Two names.

'I wonder why he gave a different one to the paper shop,' said Gascoyne, adding the new information to the whiteboard. He had taken over the role of office manager for major investigations, now Colin Hollis was dead. No one else ever wanted to do it, and though it might have been dumped on him, as the most recent recruit to the CID, he actually didn't mind doing it, having an orderly mind and endless patience.

'Probably couldn't be bothered spelling Kimmelman to the Patels,' Swilley said. 'Everyone can manage "King".'

'She said the noises next door were late at night?' Slider queried.

'She said after midnight, probably. Why?'

'Because if it was that late, it probably wasn't the murder she heard. Doc Cameron gave twelve hours plus for the time of death. It's never exact, but he's not likely to have been that far out.'

'The murder could have been earlier, and the murderer was still there,' Gascoyne suggested.

'Doing what?'

'Frozen in panic, maybe.'

'For several hours?' Hart said derisively. 'Nah, if it was panic, he'd have legged it.'

'I think it's more likely the murderer came to the flat after dumping the body,' said Atherton.

'How would he get in?' asked Fathom, a meaty lad, getting meatier since he joined the firm under McLaren's pie-and-pasty regime. He looked at Swilley. 'You said there was no sign of a break-in.'

'He'd have the keys, dumbo,' said Swilley. 'He went through deceased's pockets, remember?'

'Mightn't have been the murderer,' Fathom said, driven to defence. He didn't like being out-thought by a female. 'Could've been anyone with a key.'

'Anyone with a key who knew Kimmelman was dead,' said Swilley.

'Well, one way or another, we'll have to go and have a look,' said Slider.

'Let's hope all the evidence hasn't been removed,' said Atherton.

'Let's hope Kimmelman didn't change his lock, like Mrs Greenwood,' said Swilley.

The managing agents, Wiley's, provided a key, along with the information that they had him down as Leon Kimmelman, rather than King.

'So perhaps that was his real name,' said Slider.

'Perhaps?' Swilley queried his caution.

'People with two names generally have something to hide. If two, why not three or four? But it's a jumping-off place. You can start searching records for it.'

He took Atherton with him to Ruskin House, along with Hart and LaSalle to start canvassing neighbours. It was getting late enough now for people to start arriving home from work.

At the first glance, Kimmelman's flat looked as though a bomb had hit it.

'Trashed!' said Atherton, taking photos from the doorway.

'Someone didn't like him. I'm amazed the other residents didn't hear something,' said LaSalle.

'We don't know they didn't,' said Hart. 'People who live in flats learn to mind their own business.'

'But this must have made a hell of a noise,' said LaSalle.

'Not necessarily,' said Slider. 'If you put things down rather than throwing them. And if it was the murderer, he'd know he wasn't going to be disturbed, so he could take his time.'

'Uh-oh. Trouble,' Hart said. Doors to either side were opening. Neighbours were getting curious. Hart and LaSalle peeled off, while Atherton went on taking photos and Slider stared slowly around.

Finally he said, 'Stand back from it, mentally. Get the wider picture. This isn't just random destruction.'

'No, it's total destruction,' Atherton agreed.

The flat, as they knew from the floor plan, consisted of a large living room, with a kitchen area at one end, divided off by an island unit, and a bedroom and bathroom. From the viewpoint here at the door, the kitchen was at the near end, and the bedroom was through a door off to the left, backing onto Mrs Greenwood's flat – presumably, onto her bedroom. Straight ahead in the far wall was a window, and beside it a door opened into the bathroom, which was housed in a rear addition which jutted out from the back of the building.

Everything within view had been violated. Every drawer had been removed and upended, every cupboard and shelf emptied, the sofa and armchairs gaped, their upholstery ripped. The curtains were down, the pictures had been taken off the walls and their backs slashed.

'It's not mindless violence,' Slider said. 'This is a search. They've taken down the light shades. They haven't smashed them, as they would if it was destruction.' There had evidently been two wall sconces and a central light, and the art-deco glass covers were lying, intact, on the disembowelled sofa, while the metal plates at the back of the sconces had been unscrewed from the wall. 'Not just a search, but a professional one. See, they've even prised off the picture rail and skirting board.'

'And they've taken the carpet up,' Atherton noted. The flat had 1930's parquet floor all through, but there was a square Turkish carpet in the living-room area, which had been rolled up. 'Very thorough.'

'That's why it didn't make much noise,' said Slider. 'They didn't want to be disturbed. Even the neighbour who did hear something only thought he was packing. And another thing,' he went on, 'if the search had to be this professional, they must have thought Kimmelman would be equally professional at hiding whatever it was. Your average bod doesn't get much further than the inside of the lavatory cistern. They must have believed he'd be a lot more cunning than that. So what can you deduce from all this?'

'It must have been something important they were looking for. Something small, or they wouldn't have taken off the picture rail.'

'But not flat,' Slider suggested, 'like a piece of paper, or they'd have had the wallpaper off.'

'Can you hide things under the wallpaper?'

'Ease it off at the seam, and glue it back down afterwards,' said Slider. 'I would also deduce,' he added, 'that they probably didn't find whatever it was.'

'Now you've lost me,' Atherton said.

'As soon as they found it, they'd have stopped,' said Slider. 'The whole flat has been taken apart, which suggests that the search was unsuccessful.' He reached up a hand and eased his finger along the top of the architrave above the door out in the passage. It came down dusty. 'That's good,' he said.

'It is?'

'If you're hiding something from a professional searcher, the best thing is to hide it *outside* the room, not inside. But the searchers didn't look up here. Which suggests they're not quite as professional as they think they are. There's a chance that Kimmelman was smarter than them, which means . . .?'

'There's a chance it might still be here. Whatever it is,' Atherton concluded. 'But where do we look?' And, after a beat, 'And what are we looking for?'

'We'll know if we find it,' said Slider.

* * *

They had to get SOC in, which was frustrating; but the flat had to be properly gone over, in case the murder had been carried out there, and in case the murderer/searcher had left traces. Slider propounded his theory to Bob Bailey, but Bailey was sceptical. 'Sounds like ordinary vandalism, to me,' he said. 'Someone with a grudge just took the place apart. But I'll keep an eye out. What am I looking for?'

Slider was forced to say, 'I really don't know,' which did nothing to convince Bailey. He gave Slider a long stare, which stopped short of pity by the amount he respected Slider's previous record, though as a civilian expert he was not under Slider's command so didn't have to take orders from him. Or agree with him.

'Right,' said Bailey at length, and went away.

Meanwhile, they could at least get on with the canvassing, and with a name they could search records and put out enquiries. But not tonight. SOC would take as long as they took, but Slider could not authorise overtime for non-urgent activities, not when Mr Porson had instructed them to be frugal. He told Hart and LaSalle to knock off at six thirty, unless they had a hot lead, in which case they could phone him. And he went home himself. Joanna would be back from Sussex. He couldn't wait to see her.

FOUR

Ubi Caritas

By Wednesday morning the weather had returned to its previous unseasonal warmth. The sky was a hazy blue, the sun shone, and the leaves were hanging on to the trees, a little bedraggled from the rain but determined not to let go. The fact that it was as warm as early summer was vaguely unsettling, as when you see a slim blonde walking ahead of you in the street, and when you pass her she turns out to be in her sixties.

Kimmelman had no criminal record, did not even appear as a 'person of interest'. Under that name, at least, he had left no trace in police intelligence. Reports so far from the canvass of neighbours were that no one knew him other than to say hello as they passed. It was thought he lived alone, and the neighbour on the other side from Mrs Greenwood believed that he was not often at the flat at all, though this judgement proved to rest on his quietness rather than any firmer information. The same neighbour confirmed Kimmelman never had parties. He did not think he even had visitors – but again, how would he know?

The neighbours underneath had not noticed any noise on Sunday night, but acknowledged they were heavy sleepers. A tenant on the ground floor thought she had heard someone going out through the street door in the early hours of Monday morning, but could not say at what time, and had not looked out to see anything.

Everyone was excited and intrigued, and in some cases disturbed, that Mr Kimmelman had been murdered, either glad or disappointed that it had probably not happened on the premises, and quite sure that they could not help any further. It was, as far as the investigation was concerned, the usual Three Wise Monkeys.

'But if he *had* had any sort of friendly relationship with anyone in the building, it would have emerged,' Slider concluded, 'so I think we can assume he kept himself to himself.'

'Doesn't help with the next of kin,' Gascoyne complained.

'Maybe there'll be something at the flat,' said Atherton.

But when Bob Bailey reported halfway through the morning, it was to say that there was little in the way of personal possessions amongst the ruins.

'Clothes, some toiletries, that's about it. It's almost like a hotel room. Nothing in the way of personal papers – if there was anything, chummy's taken 'em with him. Some books and a coupla newspapers and magazines. There's not even a TV – dunno what he did for pleasure.'

'Read books,' Slider suggested.

Bailey snorted as though that could never be regarded as a pleasure. 'And no mobile phone.'

'He probably had that in his pocket,' Slider said. 'No computer?'

'No, but there's a mouse, keyboard and speakers on a table, and from the space left it looks as though he had a laptop set up there. Suppose chummy took that as well. But like I said, it's like a hotel room. Not much in the way of food, either – tea, coffee, sugar. Milk in the fridge, half a loaf of bread. Some frozen ready meals – not frozen any more, obviously, since they've been taken out of the freezer and slashed open. So, it looks like he had toast for breakfast and ate out most of the time. *Or*, possibility, he never actually lived here, just dossed down now and then.'

Thank you, we'll do the deductions, Slider thought. 'Any sign of the murder?'

'No blood anywhere or anything that looks like the weapon. But with the flat turned over the way it is, if he was whacked here, we can't tell. Fingerprints are all deceased's. There's quite a few glove smears, so they knew what they were doing.'

'And have you found what I'm looking for?'

'If I knew what it was I could tell you. Haven't found anything anyone might be looking for, but what do I know?'

'When can I get in?'

'We should be finished about lunchtime. Lucky the place was minimal furnished, or the mess would have really slowed us up.'

Canvassing with only negative results was pretty boring, and Hart had stepped outside to get a breath of air, and chat to the uniform on the door, which happened to be big, blonde, handsome Eric Renker, whom she quite fancied. It was warmer outside the flats than inside, and she undid some buttons. 'Ridic'lous weather,' she said to him.

'Tell me about it,' he said, looking down at her. 'At least you don't have to wear this lot.' He was in shirtsleeves, but the vest, necessary to carry all the kit, including the Airwave, cancelled much of the benefit. That and the helmet.

'Yeah, we have to wear a jacket, though,' said Hart. 'Mr Slider's hot on that when we're in public.'

'Well, boo hoo, poor you,' said Renker.

'Up yours, Eric. I'm just tryna be friendly.'

'Gawd, I'm dying for a fag,' Renker said, shifting his weight. 'Ullo, here comes another of 'em,' he added as someone came up the path from the road. 'I bet there's been more people visiting their friends in this block today than the rest of the year put together.' He made it clear that 'visiting' had inverted commas round it. He put on his official, quelling voice as the woman drew near. 'Yes, madam, can I help you?'

The nervous eyes flitted from his helmet to Hart's face, and seemed to find the latter more agreeable. 'Are you, um, the police – like, a detective or something?' The doubt in the voice, Hart thought, came more from nervousness than distrust of Hart's status. It was a thin young woman in a very short black skirt, a tight, white, low-cut top that left everything to be desired, a boxy denim jacket, and ankle boots with tassels. She had very foxy make-up on, under which she seemed to be in her mid-twenties, and rather plain. Her hair was a long straggle of mid brown, but clean and shiny. Surprisingly, it seemed a natural colour.

'I'm Detective Sergeant Hart,' said Hart. 'Did you want something?'

She cast a nervous glance at Renker, and moved away a step. 'Um, can I talk to you?' she said in a low voice.

Some members of the public were intimidated by the uniform, and Renker was in himself an imposing figure. Hart rolled an eye at him, stepped away two paces, and said pleasantly, 'Yes, love, what can I do for you?'

The woman writhed a bit, chewing her lip, and then said almost in a whisper, 'They're saying – I heard someone say – it's Mr King? That something's happened to him?'

'And what's your name?' Hart asked.

'Shanice,' she replied. Hart waited pointedly, and at length she got it and said, 'Shanice Harper. I – I live just round the corner. In Sulgrave Road.'

'And what's Mr King to you?'

Shanice cast her eyes down, twisting her fingers together. 'He's – we're – friends,' she managed at last.

Hart smiled. 'Oh, right! We're very anxious to talk to any

of his friends. Would you like to come and sit in my car and have a chat?'

'Yeah, all right,' she said. 'But – can you tell me – is he in trouble?'

'Let's get private, and we'll have a chat,' Hart said.

Shanice seemed reassured by the privacy of the car, but she was still anxious about Mr King, and the first thing she said when Hart got in was, 'They're saying in Randal's that he's dead? That he's been . . . murdered?'

'I'm afraid so,' said Hart.

Shanice's eyes widened, and she drew a sharp breath, but she kept it together admirably. 'That's what they said. I didn't believe it. Who would do such a thing? He was such a nice man.'

'Tell me about him,' Hart invited, knowing it was the one thing Miss Harper wanted to do right then.

She was, by trade, a freelance masseuse – 'I've got me own portable table and everything,' she said proudly – but her relationship with Leo King, as she knew him, was of a more intimate nature.

'I'm not a pro,' she said sharply, 'so don't you think it. I don't do that stuff with anyone. Leo's special. He comes to my flat – I don't see anybody else there. And sometimes I give him a massage, if he's really tense, but mostly we . . .' She hesitated.

'You're lovers?' Hart suggested kindly.

Harper seemed to appreciate the upgrade. She almost smiled. 'Yeah.'

'But he gives you little presents, does he?' Hart suggested delicately.

She proved not so delicate as that. 'He pays me,' she said bluntly, 'but that's not why I do it. I really like him. I wouldn't take the money now, but he insists. He says he's got plenty and he wants me to be comfortable. He's a lovely man. He gives me presents as well,' she added. 'He bought me this watch.' She extended her arm to show a very nice Citizen, probably costing around £100. She wore it with the face on the inside of her wrist, perhaps to conceal its value to the natives in case of theft.

'How did you meet him?' Hart asked.

'In Randal's. I was putting a postcard in their window. I go in there for ciggies, anyway, and he was in there, buying 'em as well, and we sort of . . . got talking. When I said I was a masseuse, he asked if I would come up his flat and do him. Well . . .' She blushed at some memory. 'A lot of people get the wrong idea, especially men, when you say you're a masseuse, and I said to him pretty sharp that I wasn't, you know, on the game. And he said, ever so gentle, that he never thought I was, and he really just wanted a massage, 'cos he had neck tension. I was mortified.'

'So you went to his flat – the one across the road?'

She nodded. 'Just that once. After that, he said he'd prefer to come to my place. Ever so nice it was, his flat – all wood floors and that low furniture. Like IKEA, but posh. But he said the neighbours were ever so nosy and he didn't want them seeing him bringing a young lady in, so we'd have to meet at my place after that. I didn't mind, except his place was nicer.'

'And when did you become lovers?'

'Oh, that first time. I give him a full body massage, and then it – sort of happened.' She grew frank. 'Men often get a hard-on with a massage, and sometimes I'll give 'em a hand job, if I like 'em, but that's all. But it was different with him. We were just sort of attracted to each other, right from the start. He never asked,' she added, 'but when I'd finished, it just sort of happened naturally. He's ever so nice,' she added dreamily. Then she gave Hart a minatory look, as if she'd spoken. 'Nothing kinky – never! Straight and normal every time. Ever so energetic, he is, but gentle. And afterwards we have a smoke and talk. I love that bit. It's . . .'

Just like real life, Hart supplied for herself. Like having a proper boyfriend. She felt terribly sorry for Shanice, who had evidently never managed to bag a man in the normal way, and was making her living as best she could, given what seemed to be her handicap of general haplessness.

'So you talked a lot,' Hart said. 'What about?'

'Oh – stuff. I dunno. Just talk.'

'Did he tell you what he did for a living?'

She frowned in thought. 'Not exactly. He said he was a right-hand man to somebody. That's what he called it. I didn't really understand properly what he did. He said when things needed fixing, he fixed them. Not like a plumber or anything, but, like, with business things.'

'You think maybe he was an enforcer?' Hart suggested.

Her eyes widened. 'You mean like beating people up and shooting them and stuff? No! Leo's not like that. He's too nice. I can't believe he'd ever hit anyone, not unless it was self-defence.'

Which didn't fully accord with the old broken knuckles, Hart thought. Of course, if he was an enforcer, he probably wouldn't tell his dippy date anyway. But perhaps that was in his past and he didn't need violence any more. Depended a bit on who he was right-hand man to.

'Did he tell you who he was working for?'

'No,' she said. 'We didn't really talk about his job much. But it must've been a good one, because he had plenty of money. Always wore nice clothes, and had cash in his wallet.'

'Was he married?'

'No. He said he'd never had time to find someone. I think that's why I was important to him. I think he was a lonely man.'

'How often did you see him?'

'Coupla times a week. Not regular days, but he'd phone me when he wanted to see me.'

'And when did you last see him?'

'Thursday night. He rung me really late, apologised for waking me up. Always had lovely manners. I said I wasn't asleep anyway, which was true. And I was always glad to see him. Well, he come round. He was quite keyed up. I give him a shoulder massage because he was so tight with it, and then we . . . you know. Like usual. He said he had a big job on, on Friday, and that he'd have big money coming because of it.'

'How big?'

'He didn't say, but I think it must have been really big,

because he'd been saving up to retire, and he reckoned this money would be enough to do it. I was a bit, well, put out – I mean, if he retired, I wouldn't see him again. I didn't want to lose him. But I had to be happy for him. It was what he always wanted.'

'To retire?'

She nodded. 'That's why he did the lottery, 'cause if he'd won big, that's what he was going to do. He was going to buy a big house on the Isle of Wight.'

It was so unexpected, Hart needed all her professionalism to control her features. The Isle of Wight? How the hell did that fit in with a scarred-knuckle enforcer who ended up dead in a yard with his neck broken? The *Isle* of *Wight*?

'He said he'd been there as a kid, and always wanted to go back. It was like his dream.' Shanice's eyes filled now, and her lower lip trembled. 'So I guess he'll never go there now,' she said pathetically. 'What happened to him? Who killed him?'

'We don't know,' said Hart. 'That's what we're trying to find out.'

'Was it this big job he had on Friday? Did something go wrong?'

'Did he give you any idea what the job was? Or where?'

Shake of head. 'He never told me anything about it. Just that he had big money coming because of it.'

'You've got to *think*, Shanice. You owe it to him. We need to know who he worked for, what he did. Anything you remember, any little detail of what he told you could be important. Doesn't matter if you think it's silly, it could be the one thing we need to know.' Hart laid it on thick, to penetrate the foggy brain.

'I will, I will think,' she vowed tearfully, 'but he never really told me anything about himself. I'd tell you, honest, if I knew. I want to *help*. I loved him. He was so nice to me.' A sob broke from her, but she choked it back.

Hart was impressed. Usually they were only too eager to let go, having seen Extreme Emoting practised so often on TV. She patted her hand. 'You're doing great, girl.'

'You'll find out who did this to him?'

'We will,' Hart said.

Shanice looked at her a long time with swimming eyes, and Hart waited, hoping some useful snippet was about to emerge. But what she said in the end was, 'What's it like, the Isle of Wight? I've never been there.'

Hart thought for a moment. How to describe it? What could she say about that blessed isle, Kimmelman's Eldorado, that would make sense to his grieving doxy?

'It's nice,' she said at last.

When Bob Bailey gave the all clear to go back to the flat, Slider took Atherton and LaSalle with him, and realised as they drove over that he had chosen two tall, thin people on the subconscious basis that they wouldn't take up so much room, or disturb anything. Daft!

There were small changes in the chaos, caused by the SOC's activities, but they hadn't moved anything they didn't have to move. There was no need for gloves, since everything had been cleared, but they put them on anyway, out of good habit. But in any case, Slider told them, their searching should be done mainly with the eyes. 'Anything you can touch, the murderer will have touched before you. It's something that *hasn't* been disturbed we're looking for.'

There wasn't much of that. 'I wish I knew what we're looking for,' LaSalle complained.

Slider didn't comment. After a long, fruitless period, he was wishing he was still sure there was anything to find. Perhaps he had been wrong, and it *had* been mere mindless vandalism, a furious retaliation by whoever had killed Kimmelman. Or, if it had been a search, perhaps they had found whatever it was. There was no reason they could not have found it last rather than first. He was beginning to feel foolish, and only his stubborn devotion to thoroughness was keeping him going.

Eventually they all gathered in the middle of the flat to straighten their backs.

'Well, I don't know about you,' said Atherton, 'but I've enjoyed the experience. It's been a slice. I feel I know the victim so much better now.'

'Don't reckon his taste in books much,' said LaSalle. The paperbacks scattered among the debris, some with their covers ripped off, were crime novels, mostly American – John Grisham, Michael Connelly and so on – and cowboy stories.

'I think we *have* learned something from the magazines,' Slider said. '*New Electronics. Electronics World. EPE. Tech Briefs.*'

'Yes, he was fond of gardening,' Atherton said. 'How does that help?'

'You said we were to look for something that hadn't been disturbed,' LaSalle put in. 'About the only thing I can see that hasn't been moved is the bathroom window. It doesn't open.'

Slider gave him an arrested look. 'You may have said something important.'

'Have I? I didn't mean to, guv,' LaSalle apologised.

Slider went in and stared at it. Its immobility was due to many coats of paint which had stuck it closed. The bathroom had an extractor fan for ventilation, so presumably Kimmelman hadn't needed to open it. It was glazed with heavily frosted glass, presumably because it was right angles to the living-room window, meaning that anyone standing there could have seen in. Slider became very still, absorbed in a train of thought.

'It obviously *hasn't* been opened,' Atherton said, trying to fathom what was going on in his boss's mind.

'Outside, not inside,' Slider said at last.

'Eh?'

'The best place to hide something. I wonder . . .'

'Can you wonder a bit louder, so we can all share?' Atherton said, following him back into the living room.

At the window, Slider examined the locks. 'They're all engaged. If they'd opened the window, would they have bothered to re-lock? I don't think so.'

It was a typical Crittall double casement. He unlocked, opened one side and leaned out. The window sill both on this and the bathroom window was a narrow metal strip about three inches deep, curved at the edge, hardly more than a drip sill.

'I've seen this done before,' he said.

He felt carefully along underneath the living-room sill, and found nothing. To reach the bathroom sill he had to lean out so far that Atherton was afraid he'd take a header, and grabbed a handful of his jacket. At full stretch, he was putting weight on Atherton's grip; then he grunted and said, 'Pull me in, will you?'

Back on terra firma, Slider said, 'It's there. On the underside of the window sill. This boy knew his stuff. I could feel something, but I didn't want to pull at it in case I dropped it. It calls for a taller person. LaSalle, you're up. But photograph it in situ first.'

LaSalle being much taller and with such long arms his nickname was Rang – short for Rangatang – was able to angle the tablet so as to get a shot of the underside of the sill where the package was taped.

'I hope he held a fishing-net underneath while he was doing it,' Atherton said. 'It's a long way down to go and fetch it if he'd dropped it.'

'All right, let's have it,' said Slider. 'Careful, now!'

LaSalle gave Slider the tablet to hold and leaned balletic-ally out of the window, with Atherton acting anchor again, to retrieve the package. He handed it to Slider, who found he had been holding his breath until it was safe, and photographed it again to record the state of the packaging.

'What is it? Open it! Open it!' Atherton did the Homer Simpson hop-and-finger-waggle.

'Can't you wait for Christmas?' Slider said sternly. 'I'll need a knife, or scissors. There's a lot of this tape.'

LaSalle produced a penknife.

And as in a game of pass the parcel, the contents proved to be much smaller than the original package. The outside was completely covered in tape, presumably to keep out moisture. Under that was brown paper, and then bubble wrap. Denuded of its protection, it was about the size of Slider's little finger.

It was a memory stick.

'Oh-ho,' said Slider.

'I was hoping for diamonds,' Atherton complained.

FIVE
Sausage Roll

They received Hart's report while McLaren was setting up the memory stick.

'So now we're supposed to believe he was a nice ordinary bloke with a regular girlfriend and a craving for a retirement bungalow?' Atherton said.

'She wasn't his girlfriend,' Swilley objected. 'He paid her for sex. And he obviously wasn't intending to take her to the Isle of Wight.'

'And she didn't say bungalow. She said big house,' Hart corrected.

'Doesn't matter. It's just a bungaloid sort of place.'

'When were you last there?' Swilley demanded.

'I've never been there,' Atherton said. 'Don't need to. It's a totally justified irrational prejudice based on subliminal impressions gained over a lifetime.'

'I wish you came with subtitles,' Loessop complained.

'Anyway, why shouldn't he be a nice ordinary bloke?' Swilley said. 'We're basing the idea he was a villain on . . . what?'

'He was murdered and dumped with his pockets emptied, and his gaff was turned over,' Atherton said kindly, 'which suggests some kind of criminal connection.'

'Shanice said he talked about a big job,' Hart added doubtfully. 'That sounds criminal.'

'Not necessarily,' said Swilley stubbornly. 'If you were an electrician, rewiring an entire block of flats would be a big job. Or a carpenter fitting out an exhibition centre.'

'Is anybody interested in this?' McLaren called from his desk. 'It's video footage.'

'Coming, Mother!' Atherton trilled.

They all gathered round to watch his monitor.

What appeared had the hallmarks of surveillance film: the fixed camera angle, the muffled sound, the people moving in and out of shot, voices mingling with thuddy background music and speaking across each other.

There were three people, male, and all of them were naked. McLaren jumped up and jokily tried to block the view from Swilley. 'Don't look, Norm! You'll go blind!'

She pushed him aside with easy strength – she was as tall as him and much fitter. 'Get off! I've probably seen more willies than you in my life.'

'I'm looking at a prick right now,' Hart said. 'Sit *down*, Maurice. I can't see.'

They settled down, and there was silence as they watched. Two of the men were young, slim and white, and the fact that their pubic area had been waxed suggested they were prostitutes. The head-hair of one was spiky and straw-blonde on top and short and black round the sides and back. He had the high cheekbones and flattened nose of a Rudolf Nureyev, and a Slavic accent to go with them. He had snake tattoos up both forearms.

The other had longish dark hair and was very slender, almost girlish. He had a bit of a look of Keira Knightley about him. His accent was mid-European, and he had a small gold ring through his foreskin and a butterfly tattooed on his shoulder.

At first they couldn't see much of the third man. He was doing something across the other side of the room, and the two young men, dancing together, obscured the view. Then they parted, one to pick up a glass and drink, the other to light a fat roll-up that was probably a reefer. Now, between them, could be seen the third man, who had been bending over a coffee table and now stood up, grinned, and said cheerily, 'OK, boys, come and get it!'

He was shorter than them, and a little chubby – not obese, but with a sneaky padding of fat around the waist and chin, and a little telltale roll slumped into a fold above his wedding-tackle. He was white, freckly, with short-cut reddish hair and ginger pubes, and his accent was Scottish. 'This is good stuff,' he promised. 'Come and get it 'fore it gets cold.'

'Oh my God,' Swilley said. 'You know who that is?'

'Yeah, and I wish I didn't,' Hart answered. 'That's more of him than I ever wanted to see.'

'I'm never going to eat a hot dog again,' Swilley agreed.

'Isn't he an MP?' McLaren said. 'I recognise him, anyway. His face,' he added hastily.

'He *was*,' Atherton said. 'Then he lost his seat and got elected to the London Assembly instead. He's Director of Diversity, or some title like that. One of the big players, anyway.'

'It's Kevin Rathkeale,' Slider said, in case anyone hadn't got it yet.

On the screen, the three men gathered round the coffee table, which had a glass top. They knelt, and the way the two rent boys positioned themselves suggested they knew the camera was there. On the table Rathkeale had chopped out six lines of white powder, and now he rolled up a twenty-pound note, bent and snorted up one line, then another, and passed the note to the boys, who followed suit.

'And there's your money-shot,' said Slider. 'I'm betting that's not cornflour or talcum powder.'

Rathkeale was rubbing his nostrils and grinning. For the furtherance of absolute clarity, the Nureyev-looker said, 'Man, that is good cocaine!'

'Nothing but the best for ma friends,' said Rathkeale. 'Coupla grams of this and you can go all night. Rock on, boys!'

'Where ever you get such good stuff?' asked Rudi-looker, enunciating clearly.

'Oh, I got my contacts,' Rathkeale said airily, boastfully. 'I can get you as much as you like. Any time. You just say the word.'

'Come dance with me,' said Keira-looker, getting up and holding out a hand to Rathkeale.

They began slow-dancing, arms around each other. Soon they were smooching, and the boy was grinding his pelvis into Rathkeale's. Rudi came and joined in, and after a bit, action was moved to the sofa and became more graphic. Fortunately, there wasn't much more of it. The film stopped abruptly, suggesting that this was an edited section of a longer tape.

'Just the highlights, then,' Slider said, straightening up.

'Lowlights,' Swilley corrected. 'Oh, so low!'

McLaren had restarted it and frozen the first frame, and was examining it closely. It was a sitting room of some kind, with a sofa, chairs, lamps. A couple of vodka bottles and several lager cans were standing about on various surfaces along with dirty glasses and ashtrays.

'Where *is* that place?' Atherton mused. 'It looks like a tastelessly expensive and yet curiously small hotel room.'

'The room may be bigger than it looks,' Swilley said. 'You can't see all of it.'

'But the ceiling is so low,' Atherton complained.

'I like the chandelier,' Loessop said.

'That's what I mean by tasteless,' said Atherton. 'And a Regency-stripe sofa? Shoot me now!'

'The point is,' Swilley said impatiently, 'it's obviously an attempt to frame Rathkeale.'

'Frame?' Atherton queried.

'Well, roll him, then.'

'Lot of people get up to worse naughties than that,' said Loessop.

'He's married,' said Hart, who had gone to her own desk and looked up Rathkeale on her computer. 'Second wife, no kids, but he's got two by his first wife, young teenagers. That's four people to be shocked.'

'And he's a public figure,' said Gascoyne. 'The papers would have a field day.'

'Yeah,' said Hart, still reading, 'especially when he's in Youth Services.'

'Really?' said Swilley.

'Diversity and Urban Renewal Director,' Hart said. 'And chair of the Youth Equalities Taskforce. Very right-on. Very newsworthy.'

'Ripe for blackmail, then,' said Swilley.

'He's always been a bit holier-than-thou, as I recall,' said Atherton, who kept up with politics more than the rest of them. 'Always banging on about inner city deprivation and youth opportunities.'

'Maybe he was sincere,' said Swilley, who often took the opposite view to anything Atherton said, on the principle that

someone had to rein him in. 'Don't be so cynical. Somebody's
got to stand up for the deprived inner-city youth. And oppressed
minorities. You can't pretend there isn't a problem. At least
he was *doing* something about it.'

'Yeah, fondling rent boys and snorting white,' said Hart.
'Come on, Norm, he might be Mother Teresa as far as his job's
concerned, the point here is if this got out, he'd be ruined.'

'Quite,' said Atherton. 'The thing above all else that the
press likes to attack is hypocrisy. Sincere or not, this behaviour
lays him right open to blackmail. And you've got to admit it's
pretty unsavoury.'

'Depends on your point of view,' McLaren said.

'I always did wonder about you,' Atherton said politely.

McLaren was unfazed. 'Nobody's forcing them boys,' he
pointed out.

'You don't know that,' said Atherton.

'Well, they look like they're having a good time.'

Slider intervened. 'We're not here to discuss the morality
or otherwise of prostitution. This footage was recorded,
presumably without Rathkeale's knowledge, and presumably
with the purpose of blackmailing him. We need to know why
Kimmelman had this film.'

'It's obvious, isn't it?' said Loessop. 'This was his big
job, the one that was going to make him the big money. So
he *was* a villain.'

'I should have thought what we need to know more immediately is who was trying to get it back,' Atherton said.

'Rathkeale's heavies,' Hart said. 'Who else would care?'

'Why did Kimmelman care?' Gascoyne said. 'Who on earth
was he?'

'Just a crook who needed enough for a bungalow in Worthing,'
Atherton said.

Mr Porson was not pleased. 'Bloody hell-fire, not another MP!
I think you do it on purpose.'

'He's not an MP now, sir. He's a member of the GLA.'

'And that makes it better how?' Slider didn't answer that.
'Well, we'll have to put on the gas now. It's moved into high
profile. And for Gawd's sake don't let that video get out.'

'I'll guard it with my life, sir,' said Slider stolidly.

Porson gave him a suspicious look. 'You've got a funny sense of humour. Do you realise how unpopular you are with our lords and masters?' Again, Slider kept schtumm, and Porson jerked restlessly into motion, pacing up and down the strip of carpet between his window and the desk. Slider fully expected him to go through to the floor below one of these days. 'Right. Top priority now. Get your firm in gear. Who *is* this geezer Kimmelman?'

'We know nothing about him. No record, and whoever searched his flat did a good job – no diary, letter, bill or bank statement. Nothing to give us a handle on him.'

Porson threw him a moody glance. 'Don't forget, that female – Sharon?'

'Shanice.'

'She said he was someone's right-hand man. So he may not be the primary blackmailer. Find out who he was and who he worked for. But don't forget it's the murder we're interested in. And Rathkeale's the most obvious suspect, God dammit. You'll have to look into him.'

'He'll have friends in high places,' Slider observed.

'They won't want to be seen protecting him over something like this,' said Porson. 'And nobody likes a blackmailer. They'll think, if him, maybe me next. They've all got their little secrets, people in the public eye. Nobody gets that high without standing on someone else's head.' Slider was impressed, as he so often was, with Porson's insight. 'Has Rathkeale got the akkers? How much was Kimmelman after?'

'Enough to buy a bungalow,' Slider said, without thinking.

Porson scowled. 'What?'

'If Kimmelman was his real name.'

The scowl cleared. 'Nobody'd make up a name like that. Don't get paranoid. He was a crook, not a secret agent.'

Back in the office, Slider gave out jobs: trying to find out more about Kimmelman, tracing his movements. And getting background on Kevin Rathkeale.

'Anything about his recent movements, too. I want a full work-up before I go and see him tomorrow.'

'You're going to ask *him* about the blackmail?' Hart queried.
'Who would know more about it?' Slider said.

On record, at first sight Kevin Rathkeale looked white as the
driven. Born in Glasgow, he'd studied law in London, and
practised it for a while in Leeds. He'd become active in politics, served for a while as a councillor, then stood for Parliament
in Leeds but failed to be elected. He'd evidently caught the
eye of the party, however, for at the next election he'd been
parachuted into a safe seat in North London, which he'd kept
for two terms before losing it by a narrow margin. Then he'd
got himself elected to the Greater London Assembly and had
quickly been given important jobs. During his time as an MP
he'd been prominently involved with KidZone, a high-profile
charity organisation that aimed to help black and ethnic
minority young people in deprived areas. So far so good.

Digging deeper, however, Hart discovered there had been
one or two little glitches along the way. In Leeds, there had
been some questions about the large postal vote in his favour:
suspicions of fraud and vote rigging, though as he'd lost the
election anyway it had not been pursued. In London, he had
been disciplined by the party and narrowly avoided prosecu-
tion for having accepted campaign funds from a foreign
national.

He had been one of the MPs named during the Expenses
Scandal campaign for 'flipping' – changing the designation
of his main residence so as to avoid capital gains tax – though
he had produced a semi-plausible excuse and had avoided
discipline for it.

And on a separate occasion he had been exposed by a newspaper for employing an illegal immigrant as his cleaner, and
for improperly using his influence to try to get her and several
of her family members passports. However, a House of
Commons enquiry had concluded he had done nothing wrong
in the latter case; and in the former case deserved nothing
more than a mild reprimand. The newspaper had tried hard to
keep the story going, but they had not managed to get much
traction against him. Few people enquired into the residency
status of their cleaners; and when he had discovered she was

illegal, it appeared he had tried to remedy the situation in his own way. Public opinion seemed to conclude that he had tried to do a good thing, though cutting a few corners in the process. Verdict: not guilty-ish.

Then there was the matter of KidZone, which had always been high profile because of the large number of celebrities associated with it, thanks to its charismatic CEO, Myra Silverman. It had come to unwelcome prominence when an investigative journalist brought into question how much good it was actually doing, and where all the money was going. Eventually there had been a Commons committee hearing, at which Rathkeale had been called, and had defended the organ-isation and his former colleague. The conclusion was reached that no wrongdoing had been intended, and that naivety and poor accounting practices had led to the problems. Rathkeale had escaped that one as he had not been involved with the charity for several years, and the accounts were too erratic to tell exactly when anything had gone awry.

The conclusion one might draw, Slider thought, was that here was a generally good man, although, like most politicians, he had developed a sense of entitlement that led him to bend the rules in his own favour from time to time. He tried to keep that in mind when he and Atherton were shown into Rathkeale's office, mainly in order to distract it – his mind – from the knowledge that he knew what this man looked like naked.

Rathkeale stood up to greet them, and offered his hand across the desk, which Slider feigned not to see. He didn't like shaking hands with members of the public anyway, and there was something about the pale, pudgy hand with gingery hairs on the back that convinced him it would be damp. Rathkeale was wearing a better-than-average dark blue suit over a pale blue shirt and an expensively colourful tie – jazzy but tasteful – that would have got him a good table at most restaurants. He smiled a politician's smile: wide and white and automatic, a smile that was picked dew-fresh and quick-frozen for instant use anywhere. Overall, his face was not unattractive, but there was in his eyes that blank watchfulness you saw in most citizens receiving an unexpected visit from the Bill.

'I'm afraid I can't give you long,' he said. 'I'm due in a committee in a few minutes.' His Scottish accent was much milder than it had been in the video – the merest trace. He evidently had more than one persona, which interested, though it didn't surprise, Slider.

'I think you may want to give us a lot more than a few minutes,' Slider said. 'This is a matter of importance, and of great delicacy.'

'Oh Lord, what now!' Rathkeale said with a jokey, rueful smile. 'Have I been caught speeding?'

Slider produced the memory stick. 'I have here a video sequence that you will want to see. Is your computer secure? You won't want anyone else to watch it.'

A little spark of alarm showed in Rathkeale's eyes, but he still seemed determined to carry it off lightly. 'All right, I suppose I'd better see what you've got,' he said, as if the idea bored him. 'I hope it isn't long.'

He sat down and plugged in the stick. Atherton moved round the desk so that he would see what Rathkeale was seeing, but Slider remained where he was, the better to judge Rathkeale's reaction.

From the first frame it was shock and alarm. 'How the hell did you get this?' he cried. 'Oh my God! Oh my God, I—' His face crimsoned. 'I don't want to see any more.' He kept watching, though, and belatedly, anger came to help him out. 'Those little tramps! They were filming me! I didn't— Oh my God!'

The last 'Oh my God' was different from the others. It sprang from realisation of the trouble he was in as opposed to embarrassment and shock. Now he went from crimson to a pallor that was almost yellow. From Atherton's tiny nod, Slider knew the coke-snorting sequence had been reached. It was an 'oh my God' of deep apprehension.

The recording stopped and he looked up, his faint blue eyes shiny with shock. 'Who did this?' he asked. And, 'Where did you get this?'

'We'll go into that later,' Slider said. 'For the moment, I want to know who is blackmailing you.'

'I don't know,' said Rathkeale.

Slider kept his patience. 'Blackmailers always tell you not to go to the police, but it's too late for that. We're here, so there's no point in trying to keep it secret any longer. Blackmail is a disgusting crime, and right now, we are on the same side as you. We want these people caught and prosecuted, and we will do what we can to mitigate the damage to you. But you must help us. Who is blackmailing you, and what do they want?'

Rathkeale looked up, rather pathetic, now, in his bewilderment. 'I don't know. I mean, I *really* don't know. Nobody's asked me for anything. I've never seen this film before. Where did you *get* it?'

Before Slider could answer, there was a tap at the door, which opened to reveal a PA looking enquiring. 'Kevin? You aren't forgetting that committee, are you?'

Rathkeale looked confused, as though coming back from a long way off, and then straightened his face, and said in a businesslike manner, 'Something's come up, Val. It's rather important. I'm going to have to miss it. Can you ring everyone who needs to know? And see if you can reschedule the URT meeting.' She looked as though she was going to argue, and his voice sharpened. 'Just do it, please. And I don't want to be disturbed again.'

When they were alone, he put his head in his hands, and moaned softly.

Slider said, 'Let's get this straight. Are you telling me that no one has approached you over this incident?'

'No! I mean, yes, I am saying that.' He looked up. 'I've never seen this film before. I didn't know it was being recorded. No one's said a word about it to me, except you. Now you're telling me someone's blackmailing me? But why haven't they come to me? How did you get it? What the *fuck* is going on?'

'I'd really like to know that myself,' Slider said mildly. 'I can't think of any reason for anyone to make this recording *unless* they were intending to blackmail you. Do you have any enemies?'

'Of course I've got enemies,' he said, as if exasperated. 'You can't be in politics without making enemies. But no one in particular. No one I can think of who'd go that far. And what could they want, anyway? I'm not a rich man.'

'You're sure?'

He bristled. 'What d'you mean by that? You think I've got hidden hoards, ill-gotten gains? I've been a public servant all my life. I'm decently paid, but that's all. I own a property, I've got a mortgage on another, I have a couple of consultancies, but I've got two kids at private school, so I'm just about breaking even. A blackmailer'd have a thin time of it getting money out of me.'

'What are your relations like with your wife?' Atherton asked.

'Fine, fine. We're good. I mean, she doesn't know about . . .' He gestured towards the screen. 'I've always been discreet.' His eyes widened. 'Oh my God, you don't think she hired a private detective?'

'The thought occurred,' Atherton said.

He shook his head slowly. 'But – if she suspected anything she'd say something to me. We've always agreed not to let things fester. That's why our marriage is so solid. We talk about everything.'

'Well, not everything,' Atherton pointed out.

He looked pathetic. 'You're not going to tell her, are you?' Receiving no answer, he looked from one to the other, still thinking it out. 'Look, she's happy. I'd know if she wasn't. I can't believe she'd put a detective on me – that's not her style. If she wanted a divorce she'd have talked to me about it. And the house and most of the good stuff is in her name anyway, so what would she have to gain from a contentious divorce? Besides,' he added with a frown, 'why are you here asking about it? If it was just a private detective on a divorce case, that wouldn't merit using up police time and facilities.'

'You're quite right,' Slider said. 'I think it's much more serious than that. This recording was found in the home of someone who had been murdered, and his home had been ransacked – very professionally searched. We are proceeding on the assumption that it was this recording they were looking for.'

There was a silence, and then Rathkeale said voicelessly, 'Murdered?' He looked pale now, his freckles standing out by contrast, his eyes still, and seeming almost to have gone farther back in his head. 'You said – someone's been—?'

'So you see,' Slider went on inexorably, 'that this matter has become extremely important.'

Rathkeale was staring at nothing, his dry lips moving as if rehearsing phrases he could not speak. He looked like a guilty man who had been found out – but whether guilty of boying and coke-snorting, or of having paid a hitman who had not quite completed his task, it was impossible to say. Best, Slider thought, to let him think they hadn't thought about the second option, lull him, see what he said or did. The seriously guilty were often arrogant enough to think they could fool the police, and to delight in it, and that sort of over-confidence was the copper's friend.

'It's possible,' he went on, 'that a blackmail was being set up, and that we have intercepted it before it could be completed. If you definitely haven't been approached?'

Rathkeale became eager. 'I haven't! I swear to you!'

'But even though we have this recording, there may be others, and we can't be confident that they won't still try to get to you.'

'Get to me? You mean – try to blackmail me?'

'If what they want is money, yes. If it's revenge they want, they could go from blackmail to more direct harm. You could be in danger.' He let that sink in. 'So I am asking you to think very carefully: who is your enemy, and what do they want?'

'I don't know. I don't *know*! If I did, I'd tell you – my God, I don't want this coming out. It would ruin me! Think what the papers would make of it! I wish to God I'd never—'

'I'm sure you do,' said Atherton smoothly.

Rathkeale found a little spurt of self-righteousness. 'It's not illegal! It was all consensual. Those boys were over age, and they were well paid.'

'Cocaine is an illegal substance,' Atherton reminded him.

'But everyone takes that,' Rathkeale asserted. 'It's – it's no different from vodka. You can't go to a party without finding it these days. My God, the entire House of Commons is at it. Nobody thinks of it as being illegal any more.'

'I'm afraid we have to,' Slider said. 'But if you really don't know who is out to blackmail you, we had better start working from the other end. Do you know this man?'

Rathkeale took the photograph and studied it. Slider watched him closely, but he only looked puzzled. But, of course, he was a politician; and he knew he was being watched. 'No, I don't recognise him. What's his name?'

'Leon Kimmelman.'

'I don't know the name, either. Is this the man who—?'

'Was murdered? Yes. It was in his flat that we found the tape. You're sure you don't know him?'

'I've never seen him before in my life.'

Rathkeale's phone rang. He reached for it automatically, then remembered and drew back his hand, and after a moment the ringing stopped.

Slider said, 'The two men in the recording with you – who are they?'

'I don't know.'

'Mr Rathkeale,' Slider said sternly, 'you are in a great deal of trouble. Whatever you think of it, cocaine is an illegal substance and I could arrest you for that. At the moment, I'm trying to help you, but don't try my patience.'

Rathkeale blushed again. 'I mean, I really don't know. I picked them up at a club. They said their names were Rudy and Stefan – of course, they're probably just their working names. I paid them cash. That's all I know about them.'

'You say you picked them up?' Slider said. 'Did you approach them, or did they approach you?'

'I—' He stopped, an arrested look in his eyes. 'Oh. They approached me. I suppose that's it. It was a sting.'

'It looks that way. When was this?'

'Last Friday. At this club I go to. They came up to me at the bar. We got talking. They suggested going back to their place. I mean, it's not unusual. I didn't think anything of it. I thought they just—'

'Fancied you?' Atherton suggested.

He looked annoyed. 'Well, *obviously* they were looking for customers. I knew that. In their case. But I've had my share of ordinary pick-ups. People *like* me, you know. How d'you think I got elected? I'm a nice bloke.'

Slider cut across this. 'The club where you picked them up

– are you a regular there?' He didn't seem to want to say it. He nodded. 'How often do you go?'

'Most weeks,' he said reluctantly. 'Friday. Friday's my night.'

Slider rolled inward eyes. For someone in his position to lay himself open like that, by going to the same place on a regular basis – well, it showed the arrogance that believed it could never be found out. And perhaps the same arrogance that believed it could have someone put out of the way and not be called to account. 'Had you seen them in there before?' he pursued.

'I'm not sure. I may have. Boys come and go all the time. I think maybe I'd seen Rudy before, but with different hair. It's quite dark in there, you know. I don't think I'd seen Stefan before, but I couldn't be sure.'

'What's its name, this club? Where is it?'

'It's called Ivanka's. It's in Soho.'

'All right,' said Slider. 'We'll start from there, see if we can pick up these men. Meanwhile, I recommend you to be discreet. Don't tell anyone about this.'

'As if I would!'

'And try not to change your behaviour or routines in any way. If we have intercepted a blackmail attempt, it's important the blackmailers don't know that we know. We need to flush them out.' Rathkeale looked uncomfortable at that. 'And of course,' Slider said, laying down his card, 'you'll let us know at once if anyone *does* contact you. As I said, we don't know that this is the only copy – it's very likely not.'

Rathkeale nodded, looked at the card as though it might bite him, then put it into his inside jacket pocket.

Slider and Atherton headed for the door, when Slider remembered one more question. 'You said the men took you back to their place. Where was it?'

'Chelsea. Well, just past Battersea Bridge. One of those houseboats moored alongside the embankment – a big one. I don't remember the name.'

Outside, Atherton looked at Slider, enlightened. 'A houseboat! I said it was a funny sort of hotel room.'

'We'll have to keep an eye on him. If he ordered the hit, he may lead us to the murderer. I'd like to get his phone and email records.'

'You don't think he did it himself?' Atherton queried. 'He's a bit of a chubster, but if he took Kimmelman by surprise, and with a heavy enough weapon . . . But he seems a bit too woolly for desperate deeds.'

'I don't know,' said Slider. 'Desperate is the key word. Fear, plus a sense of entitlement, can do wonders for resolve. And he's a politician – hiding things is in their nature. It's the old problem – when you're dealing with an actor, how do you know when they stop acting?'

'Well, he's still the obvious suspect,' Atherton said as they walked back out into the thin sunshine of the Embankment. There was a grey-green smell of water on the air, and the light was reflecting prettily off the Thames. It was running fast, the outgoing tide combining with the normal flow towards the sea. 'Actually, the only suspect,' he added.

'How you do comfort me,' said Slider.

SIX

Never Say Leather Again

Rathkeale had seen the necessity of coming in to make a statement. Though he didn't like it, he agreed to follow them as soon as he'd battened down his office. He point-blank refused, however, to allow his phone records or emails to be searched.

Porson agreed with Slider that there were no reasonable grounds, of the sort that would persuade a magistrate to issue a warrant. 'No point in even trying, until we get something more to go on. But there's no reason you can't go round asking his nearest and dearest what he's been up to lately.'

'He won't like that,' Slider said, not without satisfaction.

'He can do the other thing, then. I suppose he thinks he's

being smart, denying he's been blackmailed. Just bright enough to realise that would put him smack in the frame. You'll have to come at it from the other end.' He moved restlessly. 'Damn, this is an awkward business. Well, see what you can winkle out of him. Meanwhile . . .'

'Yes, sir,' said Slider. You didn't have to draw him a picture. Although he liked it.

In the office, everyone was busy: checking Rathkeale's recent movements, seeking out who his contacts were, beginning the exhaustive business of searching for CCTV cameras and checking their records. And looking for information on Kimmelman.

'So are we dropping Sampson, guv?' Gascoyne asked, hovering by the whiteboard.

'Putting him on hold,' Slider said. 'I don't think he's our man, but I still think he must be connected with Kimmelman in some way. There must be *some* reason the body was left there.'

'Meanwhile, who's going to Ivanka's?' Atherton asked, following him back to his office.

'Well, definitely not you,' said Slider. 'With your boyish good looks, we'd never get you back.'

'I'm trying to think of a way to take that as a compliment.'

'On the other hand, we can't send anyone who looks too much like a policeman, or it'll scare them off. I think Loessop's the obvious choice. And LaSalle can go with him.'

'Funky, I grant you, but Rang?'

'He'll get the pity vote. Besides, he's got a moustache.'

'So has McLaren – almost.'

'What did I just say about not frightening them?'

The afternoon was absorbed by the interview with Rathkeale. He gave an account of his recent movements without much fuss, though it was not much help. On the critical day, Sunday, he said he'd been at home alone all day, his wife having gone away for the weekend to see her parents in north Norfolk. On earlier days, he was vague about some timings and muddled, even contradictory about some activities. 'For God's sake, I can't remember every little detail,' he cried at one point, when

Slider's stoical patience pushed him over the top. 'I mean, nobody can remember like that, at the drop of a hat.'

'No, sir,' Slider agreed in a provoking monotone.

'Anyway,' Rathkeale said, adding the fatal second justification, 'I'm upset about this business – wouldn't you be? You try thinking straight when someone's just landed all this in your lap.'

'Just take your time, sir. We've got all day.'

But by the time he went tottering off into the dusk, they had learned little more. He still insisted he had never seen or heard of Kimmelman, had not seen the film footage before, and had not been blackmailed.

'I'd almost be ready to believe him, if he wasn't such a repulsive little squit,' Atherton said as they climbed the stairs.

'I object to the word "little". That's sizeist,' Slider said, looking down at him from the advantage of two stairs up, the only way he ever could overtop his tall lieutenant.

At the door to the office, he was met by Gascoyne. 'Your wife rang,' he said. 'She wants you to call her back.'

Slider parted from Atherton and went to his desk. Joanna answered straight away, in a voice that assured him nothing was wrong.

'I've got Emily here,' she said. 'We've had a nice domestic afternoon, and she's staying for supper. She says can you bring Jim home with you, because there's nothing at their house.'

'Yes, if I can catch him.' He looked through into the CID room, where Atherton was putting on his coat, and caught his attention. 'OK, got him. Do you need us to bring anything?'

'No, it's all under control. I'm just doing a big pot of bolognese, and Emily's making garlic bread. Your dad and Lydia are going to a dinner dance at the Red Lion, so it'll just be the four of us. Oh,' she said as he was about to ring off, 'I don't know whether you ought to warn him, but she's getting very broody over George. She's giving him his bath as we speak. Gales of merriment are pouring down the stairs. I think she may be wanting one of her own.'

'On the whole,' said Slider, 'I don't think I'll tell him.'

'Tell me what?' Atherton asked, catching the glance.

'No,' said Slider, 'you should have all the fun of discovering it for yourself.'

The house was warm and lit, glowing through a thin fog like the paradigm of a traveller's rest. Joanna opened the door and a smell of garlic and herbs engulfed him. Home!

'You just missed your dad,' Joanna said, when coats had been shed and Atherton and Emily were catching up. 'They came up to say goodbye.' Slider's father and his new wife Lydia lived in the sub-basement granny flat, a wonderful arrangement for childminding. Fortunately, they thought it was wonderful too. 'He looked *gorgeous* in black tie. I practically fancied him.'

'Hey!' Slider protested.

'Now I know what you'll look like in black tie when you're his age. Gorgeous, and slightly shame-faced. Why are men so reluctant to put on a dinner suit?'

'We don't like to be made monkeys of,' said Slider.

'*Au contraire*, it's the far other end of evolution.'

Slider knew when to leave an argument. 'I'll just pop up and see my boy.'

'Don't wake him up,' said Joanna, heading for the kitchen.

But George was awake when he went in, though heavy-eyed and fighting it. 'I betted I could stay awake till you came,' he said.

Slider went to kiss him and tuck him in. 'Did you have a nice time with Aunty Emily?' he said.

'We played submarines in the barf,' George said. 'I like it when she plays with me. She makes funny noises. Daddy, can she come and live with us all the time?'

'I don't know if there's room. Where would she sleep?'

'In my bed.'

'And where would you sleep?'

'In my bed too,' George said, as if it was a silly question.

'I think she might want to go home to her own house,' Slider said, seeing his son's eyelids drooping. The effort of staying awake was taking its toll.

'But will you ask her?' George murmured, eyes closed now. 'Pease. I like it when we do fings . . .' He was gone.

On the way downstairs, Slider planned to say to Emily,
'You've made a hit,' but thought better of it. He knew Atherton
had always had difficulty with committing himself to one
woman, and he and Emily had already had some ups and
downs. If she *had* started thinking about marriage and reproduction – and she was in the right age-bracket for it to become
a priority – it wasn't for him to stir things up. Let Atherton
find his own way through that particular minefield, and at his
own pace.

'Kevin Rathkeale,' said Emily in tones of surprise and interest.

'This goes no further,' Atherton warned her.

'Of course,' she said impatiently. 'You know you can
trust me.'

Atherton had told, with some relish, what happened on the
secret film. Slider drifted a little, thinking about mankind's
propensity to turn any invention to harmful purposes. It started
off with someone making shadows with their hands on the
wall, as he'd done for his children – the rabbit, the goose,
the old man chewing. Innocent shadow-play; then bigger and
better shadows from a magic lantern; then the fuzzy, jerking
moving pictures in black and white – Queen Victoria on the
terrace at Osborne, King George V on horseback inspecting
troops; and on, all the way up to fabulous modern movies
with CGI and special effects that baffled the brain and dazzled
the senses. And then back again, to grainy images of a chubby
public servant, two rent boys and a packet of white. Oh
Mankind! Would you *ever* get your act together?

'Rathkeale, though!' Emily was saying. 'I didn't know he
liked boys. I know a bit about him, because a friend of mine
from the *Mail*, Jenna Cargill, was one of the team that invest-
igated KidZone, and we talked about it quite a lot. He must
have been *very* discreet to keep that to himself.'

'What's your impression of him?' Slider asked.

'I don't do impressions. Journalism's my field,' she said,
straight-faced.

'You've been a rotten influence on that girl,' Joanna told
Atherton with a sad shake of the head.

Emily grinned, chomped some bread, and said, 'I always

thought he was really more of a klutz than a crook. He was like one of those big, clumsy dogs, always dashing about barking and knocking things over. He'd latch on to something with big dumb enthusiasm without realising the implications or looking into the background. The dog that tries to bite a hedgehog. In my view, Myra Silverman was the one to watch over KidZone. Now, *she's* one smart cookie. She paid herself a huge salary, you know, and she had directorships with some of the companies that were getting money from the charity. She's a big one for directorships.'

'So how come she got away with it?' Joanna asked, filling glasses.

'No one ever established that there was any actual wrong-doing, though of course we all suspected it like mad. We journos, that is. But anyway, she's the kind that always will get away with stuff. She's the Queen of Schmooze – contacts all over the place, hence all the celebrity endorsements. Hence Kevin Rathkeale going to bat for her in front of the select committee.'

'So you think he was innocent?' Slider asked.

'I wouldn't go that far,' Emily said thoughtfully. She pondered a moment. 'I think when it comes to wrongdoing, he's like a man with no sense of smell. He knows what wrong is, but can't detect it on himself. The man that chucks on so much aftershave it makes your eyes burn, and can't smell the dead rat under the sink.'

'Interesting. Do you think him capable of having someone bumped off?' Slider asked.

'My personal opinion – I could see him doing it, if he had reason enough. But I tell you what,' she added with a smile. 'He'd probably leave a big old obvious clue just lying around for you to trip over. Mister Smooth he ain't.'

'You don't think it was Rathkeale himself that killed this man and turned over his flat, then? With his own hands, I mean,' Joanna asked.

Slider shook his head. 'It was a professional search. Maybe Rathkeale has those skills. It seems unlikely, but I don't know.'

'Well, I suppose he'll have an alibi,' Joanna said.

'Probably Sunday evening, and in the early hours of

Monday for the search,' Slider said. 'He says he was at home and in bed.'

'His wife . . .?'

'They have separate rooms. And she was away, anyway. So no alibi there. But sadly, at that time of night most of the nation is likewise in bed, so it's a universal alibi which is difficult to prove one way or the other.'

'Oh dear. So what can you do?'

'Keep looking.' Slider shrugged. 'Somebody somewhere knows something.'

'Rathkeale will crack,' Emily predicted comfortingly. 'He's no Moriarty. And there must have been a big movement of money – either what he was assembling to pay the blackmail, or what he used to pay the assassins – probably the same money.'

'Unfortunately, we haven't enough reasonable grounds for suspicion to look into his bank account.'

Joanna got up to clear the plates, and Emily rose too, to help. When she came back from the kitchen carrying the plates for the cheese and fruit that was to follow, she said casually, not looking at Slider, 'I could have a bit of a dig around, if you like. It's amazing what you can find out if you know where to look.'

'You know I can't possibly authorise that,' Slider said sternly.

'Oh, I know,' she said. 'Actually, of course, you can't stop me. I'm an investigative journalist, it's my job.'

'You could compromise the case if—' Slider began.

'Relax, I'll be discreet. I know the rules. And anything I do find out must be in the public domain, so your own people could find it equally well. I'm only going to look into Rathkeale's background – and see if I can find out anything about this chap King, or Kimmelman.'

'Well, just don't tell me you're doing it,' Slider said.

'Or me,' Atherton added. 'And we never had this conversation.'

'Of course we didn't. What conversation?' said Emily.

Atherton took up his glass and leaned back with an air of relaxation. 'I wonder how Funky and Rang are doing. Sooner them than me.'

*   *   *

Loessop had tied a bandeau round his head and smudged a bit of eyeliner on his lower lids to enhance his resemblance to Captain Jack Sparrow. LaSalle did his best with a pair of tight, low-slung trousers and some gold neck chains borrowed from Hart. He was never going to be love's young dream, but then, how many true Adonises looked for love in a Soho cellar?

In the entrance foyer was a very large bald bouncer. His shoulders and chest were big enough to warrant their own postcode, and made the rest of his body appear unnaturally tapered. He looked like what you'd get if you shaved a buffalo. He blocked their way politely, while managing to convey that impoliteness was being retained as an option, and told them it was members only. But membership only involved handing over a sum of money at a booth at the back of the foyer and receiving a card, and they had drawn a fair sum of contingency expenses.

Once certificated members of Ivanka's Gentlemen's Club, they decided to go in separately, not only to double the search power, but so that Rang could come to Funky's rescue if he attracted too many suitors. The place was as such places are, moodily-lit, loud, crowded, and over-represented in the leather and facial hair departments. LaSalle found a table where he could watch the door, and fiddled with his mobile to avoid catching anyone's eye, while Loessop went and sat at the bar. There was no sign of either of the young men from the tape.

Loessop ordered a vodka tonic, and since the barman, a young Australian, seemed friendly, he asked if Rudy had been in. He'd decided to ask about Rudy as he thought he'd stand out more than Stefan, be more likely to be remembered.

The barman looked blank, and Loessop added, 'Tall guy, blonde on top, snake tatts up his arms? Looks a bit like Rudolf Nureyev?'

'Oh, I know who you mean,' said the barman. 'He was here, but he went off with someone. If it's Russians you're after, Ivan's in the back room. He's very butch,' he added cautiously, eyeing Loessop as if wondering whether butch was what he was after. It was hard to tell these days.

'No, I really wanted to see Rudy,' Loessop said, managing a bit of a pout. 'Thanks all the same.'

The barman moved away, and the man on the next stool swung round and said, 'Rudy know you're coming?'

'D'you know him?' Loessop countered.

The man shrugged. 'Seen him around.' He eyed Loessop with interest. 'He's probably coming back later. Guy he left with, I don't think he'll be long.'

'I might as well wait, then,' said Loessop.

After a pause, the man said, 'I'm Peter. Petey.' He was pale and goggle-eyed, like something that lived deep under the sea where sunlight never penetrated. He had sparse, fuzzy hair – his head looked like a moulting coconut. He held out his hand.

Loessop didn't touch it. 'Dick,' he said after a measurable pause, to let Petey know he wasn't interested in anything more than civility.

Petey didn't take the hint. 'My favourite name,' he said. 'I love Dicks.' He cocked an eye to see if Loessop would rise to it, then said, 'If you're waiting for Rudy, you could buy me a drink while you're waiting. I could tell you lots of things about him.'

'I'm cool, thanks,' Loessop said.

'Oh, come on, don't be so tight,' Petey whined. 'Just a drink. Be a bit friendly.'

Loessop caught LaSalle's eye across the room, and he got up and came gangling across.

'Hi!' said Loessop eagerly. 'I didn't know you'd be here.'

'I saw you, but I thought you were busy,' LaSalle said, and inserted himself into the space between Loessop and his tormentor.

'Very funny,' said Loessop, sotto voce.

'Oh, *excuse* me!' said Petey, offended. 'I'm just part of the furniture. Who d'you think you are, then?'

Loessop craned his head round LaSalle to say curtly, 'Sorry. Old friend.'

'Old friend, is it? Does he know you're waiting for Rudy?' Petey said, arch and spiteful.

'I can leave you two alone if you like,' LaSalle murmured so only Loessop could hear him. 'You make such a pretty couple.'

'Shut up, you dork. He says Rudy's probably coming back, so it might be worth waiting – for a bit, anyway.'

LaSalle glanced around the room. 'We've got to keep it authentic. You might have to dance with me.'

'But then I might have to kill you,' said Loessop. 'Let's go back to your table. More private.' Petey was muttering a litany of complaint. 'And I've got to get away from Horace here.'

At the table they kept their heads together, pretending to talk, taking turns to watch the door. LaSalle went to get more drinks and was propositioned both on the way to the bar and on the way back. He didn't know whether to be surprised or gratified.

'So you better not say anything about me and Petey,' Loessop warned.

'You're supposed to fit in – that's what plain clothes are for,' LaSalle reasoned. 'But I draw the line at kissing.' The other couples sitting at the tables were getting a lot more friendly with each other.

'You could toy with my hair,' Loessop suggested, dicing with death.

Fortunately, at that moment LaSalle, who was watching the door, nudged him hard and said, 'There's one of our boys. Rudy.'

'Alone?'

'Yeah.'

'Let's go get him.'

Rudy was perfectly agreeable to going somewhere quiet with the two of them. There were booths in the back room, where the lighting was even lower, and LaSalle bought a bottle of vodka which they took in with them. The three of them squeezed in together, with Rudy in the middle, and having filled his glass, Loessop asked where his friend Stefan was.

'Stefan? Which one is he?'

'Long dark hair. Butterfly on his shoulder,' Loessop suggested.

'Oh, his name Stefan? I thought he Karel. Not seen him around. People come, people go. Maybe gone home to Czecho. Why you want him, anyway? Lots of nice guys here.'

'You and him went off with a bloke to a houseboat last week,' said LaSalle.

Rudy made a face. 'You cops?' he asked. He seemed remarkably relaxed about the idea.

'Yeah, but not vice cops. Detectives. We just want some information. We're not making trouble for you.'

'I know good well you not make trouble for Rudy,' he laughed. 'Rudy got lot of *bi-i-g* friends. You bust my chops, they break your legs, OK?'

Loessop couldn't help liking him. 'OK,' he said. 'No trouble, just tell us about that night.'

'Five hundred euro,' he said calmly. 'Pounds, I mean.'

'Dream on,' said Loessop.

'This working night. No talk for nothing. What you think?'

LaSalle laid a hand on his arm. 'See, we have to think of how it would look. If we give you money, people might say we'd paid for the information, so the information is tainted, won't stand up in court.'

'Two hundred,' Rudy said. He folded his arms. 'Rudy's memory not so good these days.'

'Two hundred,' LaSalle agreed after a nod from his colleague. 'And you come with us to the station and make a proper statement.'

'OK,' Rudy said easily. Too easily? 'Money first.' They slipped the cash to him under the table, and he wedged it somehow inside his tight jeans. Then he said, 'OK, we go, but not right now. People watching. I don't want get reputation for snitch. You—' he pointed at LaSalle – 'wait outside. You and me—' he pointed at Loessop – 'dance a bit. You don't look so much like cop. Then we leave, meet outside.'

LaSalle and Loessop exchanged a look, then LaSalle nodded and got up. 'OK. But no funny business.'

Rudy grinned wider. 'My business very funny business, no? Mama think her Rudy in very funny business if she know what I do.'

The capitulation wasn't all it seemed, for as soon as Rudy emerged onto the street, he took off like a greyhound. Fortunately, it's fundamental in a copper's DNA to chase someone who runs, so there was no lag for reaction and Rudy's lead was not long. He was younger and lighter than either of them; on the other hand they had the incentive of knowing they'd have to face Mr Slider *and* Mr Porson if he got away.

It was a glorious, adrenalin-fuelled chase, through the narrow streets of Soho, dodging the evening revellers and the crawling traffic; down Wardour Street, left into Noel, left again into Poland, across Broadwick Street, into Lexington. Onlookers stepped helpfully out of the way, even when LaSalle shouted, 'Police!' In the old days someone would have stuck out a foot. Loessop began to fall behind, but LaSalle had long legs. Where were the two men carrying the sheet of glass, the tottering stack of cardboard boxes, the young mother pushing a pram, when you needed them? Across Brewer Street and into Windmill, and if he got to Piccadilly Circus they'd lose him in the throng, or down the tube. LaSalle put on a spurt. As Rudy hit Shaftesbury Avenue he glanced quickly back, and ran into a clot of young people coming the other way out of Denman Street. The whole lot went down in a muddle of arms, legs, and swear words.

Loessop arrived panting as LaSalle reached into the tangle for the arm he wanted, and was in time to hear that sweetest refrain: 'All right sunshine, you're nicked.'

SEVEN
Feeling the Force

The chase seemed to have done Rudy good. He seemed quite invigorated on the drive back to Shepherd's Bush, and sang Russian pop songs in a melodious tenor. In the interview room, perhaps encouraged by the two hundred knicker down his trousers, and the promise that he would be released without charge if he co-operated, he was quite relaxed. They brought him tea, and a sandwich, which he inspected carefully before biting, with the air of a widow from the Bronx facing her first plate of snails in Paris.

Then he sat back, crossed his legs, and said, 'OK, what you want to know?'

Rudy had not really known Stefan before that evening. He'd seen him around the club, that was all. Mr King had recruited them separately. He didn't know why they had been chosen out of all the guys who were regulars.

For their looks, Loessop thought. Rudy was very striking-looking, and Stefan almost girlishly pretty. They'd look good on tape, and make an impression on the viewer. Two plainer or unremarkable figures wouldn't make nearly such good blackmail material.

Rudy didn't know Mr King, hadn't seen him before, to his knowledge, though he claimed to be a friend of the management. He'd asked Rudy if he'd like to do a special job for good pay, and took him outside to a big car with tinted windows. Stefan was already in there. Mr King gave them drinks and smokes and explained the job. They were to pick up a particular man, take him to a particular place, and have a good time with him. There would be a camera filming the whole thing. It would take a couple of hours, and they'd get five hundred apiece.

Stefan was worried that there would be trouble for them afterwards. Mr King said absolutely not, no trouble, and raised the money to seven fifty. Rudy wasn't worried about trouble, but he knew what the market price for such co-operation ought to be. He said a thousand each for the evening, and they were on.

That was last Thursday. Mr King took them to see the houseboat, the *Anna Rosita*. She was very big, very luxurious. He showed them where the camera would be, and warned them not to block the line of sight. There would be lots of drink, there would be cocaine, and they could go as far sexually with the customer as he and they wished – no pressure either way. As long as the customer got naked and there was some dancing and touching, the rest was up to them. They should just have a good time. It was money for jam.

Mr King showed them a photograph of the man they were to pick up. Rudy recognised him – he had been to the club before, one of the regulars. Stefan didn't recollect seeing him, but he didn't come in so often. Mr King said the man's night was a Friday. They should try to pick him up next evening. If he didn't come in, they must hold themselves ready for the following Friday. As it happened, he had come in – Friday last week, as it was now.

When they had picked him up, they must say they are ringing for a cab – except that they would ring a number Mr King gave them, and he would pick them up and take them to the boat, which they would claim belonged to a friend of theirs. They would say the friend was letting them live there until they got a place of their own.

'So what did you think was going on?' Loessop asked. 'Didn't it sound fishy to you?'

'Fishy? What fishy?'

'Like there was something dodgy going on? Something illegal?'

'No. Why think that? Lots of times, business guys, they want to make good time for client. Make him happy, do good business.'

'Pretending to pick him up? Pretending the houseboat was yours?'

Rudy shrugged. 'Make little play for him. What you say, role play? No harm.'

'And everything being filmed?'

Another shrug. 'Customer want movie afterwards, remember what good time he had. All part of play.'

The customer would not stay all night, they were told. He would have to get back to his wife and family, so it would be just a few hours' work for them. They must be sure he left first. Afterwards, the same car would pick them up. Mr King would drive them wherever they wanted to go, and give them their money. And that would be the end of it. They'd never hear any more about it.

'So, on the night, did it all go as planned?' LaSalle asked.

'Smo-o-oth as milk,' Rudy said, with a slow, sideways sweep of the hand. 'Mr King one smooth operator. No troubles. Go like clockwork. Customer have nice time, Stefan and me get nice money, say bye-bye, see you.' He gave a child's wave.

'Only didn't expect to see *you* guys,' he added. He examined their faces sternly. 'But you got nothing on me. I don't do nothing illegal.'

'I told you, we're not here to make trouble for you,' LaSalle said.

'So, who this Mr King? He private detective?'

'Is that how he seemed to you?'

He thought a moment. 'No, he not like 'tective. He was like fixer. He knew all about the cameras, lights and stuff, like the techno man, you know? But he tough cookie – see plenty of them back home. You want something done, you go to tough cookie fixer guy. Got no—' he searched for a word – 'emotion. No feeling with job, just job, you know?'

'So who was he working for?' Loessop asked.

'Mr King? He never say.'

'Did you know who the man was – the man you had to pick up?'

'Mr King show us photograph. I seen him before, round the club, but I don't know his name.'

'He must have introduced himself when you picked him up.'

'Given you some name to call him by,' LaSalle translated when the question elicited a blank.

'He say to call him Jimmy,' Rudy said, with a shrug that said, 'What do names matter?'

LaSalle gave Loessop a glance, and he produced the mugshot of Kimmelman. 'Just for the record. Is this Mr King?'

Rudy looked, said, 'Yeah,' then looked more closely and said with alarm, 'Hey, he dead?' He jumped up. 'No trouble, you say no trouble!' For the first time he was not smiling.

'No trouble for you,' LaSalle said, standing too. 'We're not trying to trap you. Sit down.'

'No more questions,' Rudy said. 'I go now.'

'*Sit down*! You're not finished yet.' Rudy sat, scowling. 'We've got to get out a statement for you to sign.'

'No sign nothing! I got nothing to do with *this*,' he said, shoving the photograph back at them. 'Give his customer good time, that's all. You got nothing on me.'

'We've got you on film taking cocaine. That's an illegal substance,' said Loessop, showing some steel. 'You sit down, be quiet, and sign the statement, and that goes away. All right? We're not interested in you. We're after the person who killed Mr King.'

He fidgeted, crossing and uncrossing his legs. 'You said no trouble for me,' he said again, sulkily.

'No trouble for you. Just the statement, then you can go.'

He seemed reluctantly reassured, and relaxed a little. '*Okay*,' he said slowly. He sighed. 'O-*o-kay*.' Then, 'What happen to Mr King?'

'He met with an accident,' said Loessop.

Swilley did not like loose ends.

Detective Constable Kathleen 'Norma' Swilley had many attributes that made her a good policeman. She was extremely fit, and an expert at hand-to-hand fighting: she knew several useful grips that would reduce an over-excited testicle-owner to meek, not to say watery-eyed, compliance. She was a crack shot; she had not applied to become a firearms officer – that was not her scene – but she belonged to a shooting club and enjoyed it as a hobby; and her unerring aim did mean she could project a screwed-up ball of paper from any distance into any waste bin in the CID room.

She was patient and painstaking, and above all she was methodical, which was why she had transferred to the Department in the first place. She had joined the Job from a desire to impose order on a disorderly world, but as a uniformed copper you were always being forced into last-minute reaction against the chaos created by the messiest section of society. As a detective, you could work at a more reasonable pace, and follow logic and deduction. Some craved the adrenalin rush of the fracas, but she found excitement in more cerebral challenges.

She had carried her desire for method into her private life. She had chosen her mate for the qualities which would make him a good husband, and more particularly a good husband for a copper. She had chosen the time to get married, when both their careers were at a suitable juncture, and her time to have a child, when she could safely take the time off, and when Tony's increased working from home would allow him to co-ordinate childcare with her. Her life was tranquil and satisfying; but her success in achieving balance outside of work made it all the harder for her to tolerate inconsistencies within work.

Fortunately, the job of a detective was specifically aimed towards tying up loose ends, which meant she was perfectly within her rights on Friday morning to indulge herself. The office of the property development company Blenheim was in a large new tower block at Hammersmith Broadway, on the Talgarth Road, which she passed on her way from dropping Ashley off at pre-school. The boss, James Hadleigh, was in – the receptionist rolled her eyes slightly as she mentioned that he was always in early, indicating he was a workaholic – and had no objection to seeing her for a few minutes.

He was already in his shirtsleeves, a tall, well-built man with thick, springing dark brown hair, which sprang at least partly, as was soon obvious, from his habit of running his hand backwards through it, a displacement activity when his brain was operating too fast for his tongue. His energy and bursting good health gave him an animal attractiveness that Swilley felt the moment she entered his sanctum, and he greeted her with a broad smile and a cheerful, 'What can I help you with?'

She recognised a busy man who would welcome points being got straight to. 'Jacket's Yard,' she said. 'I'm interested in why you bought it from Target. It seems odd that *two* development companies should get themselves landed with a white elephant, one after the other.'

'Ha!' He laughed. He had very good teeth. 'Jacket's Yard. Yes, I can see how it might seem to an outsider. We've got a tenant in there – virtually a peppercorn but it keeps the place warm.'

'Eli Sampson. Junk car repairs,' Swilley offered.

'That's right. D'you want to sit down?'

'If you do.'

He grinned. 'I'm game,' he said, and sat behind his desk; but he glanced at his watch. She took the chair in front of it and, after a moment's thought, crossed her legs. A police-woman, especially if she is good-looking, early learns not to radiate those pheromones that men take as an invitation. You must not be thought to be 'putting out', or you could quickly land in trouble. But as a detective, it could be a useful weapon in your armoury, judiciously used, for getting interviewees to let down their guard a little and tell you more than they meant to. So she crossed her legs, and put out just a little, and she saw his eyes gleam in response.

'So, what is it about Jacket's Yard? The weak bridge means it can't be developed,' she said, with the air of a serious journalist. He was smiling without answering, and she saw he wanted it to be a game. *Figure it out – you're a smart lady.* He looked the sort that'd say 'lady' and not 'woman'. Certainly not 'girl'.

'Unless you can get TfL to rebuild it,' she concluded.

He laughed again. 'Got it in one! You should be in the business. You see, Transport for London has an enormous estate of wasted land – old sidings and yards, unused warehouses, superseded engineering works, leftover bits alongside railway lines and so on. A lot of empty spaces. And a few years ago, the mayor – who's in charge of TfL, as you know – decided that they should start making use of it for revenue purposes, either sell it to developers or develop it themselves, and plough the money back into services. There's a shitload of modernisation work needed to the infrastructure, and the government doesn't want to raise the public subsidy any further.'

'I see. And Jacket's Yard is in a prime position,' Swilley suggested. 'Shepherd's Bush is up and coming, property prices are on the rise.'

'Right. The two biggest buildings flanking the yard haven't been used in years. Add them in, and you've got a prime developable footprint. I didn't pay much for Jacket's Yard, and sooner or later the pressure's going to be on for TfL to do something about the site, which means either they'll buy Jacket's from me – and believe me, they'll have to pay me a premium – or they'll sell me the empty buildings, and I'll make sure the price includes strengthening the bridge. Then I'll develop, and make the profit. Either way, I win.'

Swilley frowned. 'You can't be sure they'll fix the bridge for you, can you?'

'Oh certainly,' he said with ease. 'Otherwise it's no sale, and the mayor knows that. I've taken the precaution of slipping that thought into his consciousness ahead of the game.'

'You know the mayor?'

'It would be silly to be a developer in London without making sure of your contacts,' he said. 'I know the mayor, and the Minister for Transport, *and* the Housing Minister. Get on very well with all of them. I've got the bases covered.' She nodded, and left an alert, interested and inviting silence for him, into which to insert anything else useful he might have to say. His eyes drifted to her legs – she was glad she'd worn a skirt suit that day – and politely away again, and in payment for such inadvertent gaucherie, he gave her what she wanted. 'Of course, Target must have known all that as well. That's the only reason for buying the yard. No mystery about that. The puzzle is why, having held on as long as they did, they pulled out when the game was almost won. The current Housing Minister is also in charge of local communities, and the buzz word is development for the benefit of local residents.'

That's seven buzz words, Swilley's logical mind protested.

'So they're going to want that site turned into housing asap.' He shrugged. 'Target's loss is my gain.'

'Why do *you* think they sold?' she asked, implying by her look that his opinion would be gold.

'Money troubles,' he said bluntly. 'Between you, me and the grapevine, they've been divesting themselves for a couple of years now. It can only be because they need to cash out. Of course, I'd heard the rumours, so I gave them a hard time over Jacket's and got it for the bargain basement price.' He shrugged. 'Not my problem, but I think if you look into it, you'll find out someone's in trouble somewhere. That's the devil in this business – you've got to be able to hold out until the development's finished and the units are sold. Many a company's fallen down that crack, between buying the land and getting the return. That's why big is better in this game. You need long pockets.'

'And you're big,' Swilley said. For an instant she thought she might have gone too far, but he took her literally.

'We're big enough. And if Jacket's gets off the ground in the next six months, we'll be bigger still. That's why I've got the tenant on a six-month lease. You've got to stay nimble. No room for hairy mammoths in the development business.'

'Hairy mammoths?'

'Dinosaurs,' he clarified. 'They died out because they got too big and couldn't move fast enough.'

And there, she'd thought it was a comet hitting the earth. Not that it mattered. She had what she wanted. She stood up. 'Thank you very much,' she said. 'You've been most helpful.'

He grew serious. 'This is about that body found in the yard?'

'You heard about that?'

'Wiley's let us know – the managing agent. I hope it's nothing to do with our tenant?'

'He's not currently under suspicion,' Swilley said circumspectly.

'It's bloody odd,' he said, frowning for the first time. 'Why should anyone kill somebody there? Who was it, anyway?'

Swilley thought it worth a punt. She was pretty sure Hadleigh had nothing to do with it – even if he had a body to dump, he'd hardly jeopardise his upcoming TfL deal by dumping it *there*. 'His name's Kimmelman. Leon Kimmelman.' He shook his head. She pulled up the picture on her tablet and showed it to him.

He looked carefully, but handed it back saying, 'I don't know the name, and I don't recognise him. Sorry. What's he got to do with Jacket's Yard?'

'We're looking in to that,' said Swilley.

'I'd really like to know, when you find out,' he said, his eyes suggesting it would be a way for them to see each other again.

'I'll see what I can do,' she said.

Always leave them wanting more, she thought, as she headed out to the car.

The elation from Funky and Rang's successful operation had cooled somewhat by the time Swilley arrived back at the factory. The euphoria of finding stuff out faded when that information proved not to help you get any further.

'*Did* Kimmelman have a car?' Swilley enquired.

'Shanice didn't know,' said Hart. 'She never saw him in one – he just turned up at her door. And he was only round the corner from her anyway, so he could well have walked. Don't mean he didn't have one, but how'd we know?'

'There's got to be security cameras somewhere along the embankment there,' said LaSalle. 'If we can spot Rudy and Stefan getting out of a car, get the index—'

'Yes, but what then?' Swilley asked. 'Does that get us any further forward?'

'With that, we may be able to trace Kimmelman's other movements, find out who he met and where he went. Don't forget it's his murder we're supposed to be working on,' Slider said.

'Oh yeah. I keep forgetting,' said Fathom. 'All this blackmail stuff . . .'

'You can start looking for cameras along that bit of the embankment,' Slider said. It was slow, tiring and largely boring work, and Fathom usually got stuck with it because he was slow, tiring and largely boring. 'Once you've got the index, you might be able to fix him meeting with Rathkeale,' he added as a slight incentive.

'Oh yeah,' said Fathom, slightly incented.

'The problem, as I see it,' said Atherton, 'is timing. If the sting took place on Friday night, and Kimmelman was killed on Sunday night, that only gives two days for him to approach Rathkeale, for Rathkeale to sink to such despair that he believes the only way is to kill Kimmelman, for him to arrange the hit, and for the killers to get the job done. I'm finding it hard to see that timetable working.'

'Maybe he's got goons on standby all the time,' said McLaren. 'We don't know what stuff he gets up to. If he's getting drugs for his mates, he might need protection.'

'Hmm,' said Slider. 'That sounds a bit over the top. He's not some Mr Big at the centre of a criminal network.'

'He might be,' McLaren insisted. '*We* don't know.'

'Sir,' said Gascoyne cautiously. He'd not long transferred in from uniform and hadn't got the habit of 'guv' yet. 'Is it possible that Kimmelman had already *been* blackmailing Rathkeale for some time? He obviously knew about him being a regular at that club. He could have been putting the bite on him for weeks, and the tape was the icing on the cake, the last straw that Rathkeale couldn't let go past.'

Atherton nodded approval. 'That's good policeman thinking. The force is strong in this one.'

'It still only gives him a day and a half at most to arrange the hit,' Swilley objected. 'I can't see it.'

'Like I said, he's got his own squad already lined up,' said McLaren.

'I know you *said* it, Maurice. I was trying to *ignore* it,' said Swilley witheringly.

'We need to see his bank account,' said Hart. 'See if there was any big biccies flying out.'

'Most of all we need his phone and email records,' said Slider, 'but that's not going to happen, either.'

'Well, what about Kimmelman's bank account?' Swilley said. 'If Rathkeale has been paying him, it'll show up. And if *he* hasn't – well, blackmailers don't usually stop at one victim.'

'Yeah, but there was no bank statement in the flat,' LaSalle said, 'and none of the banks have come back yet to say he was their customer.'

'All right,' Swilley acknowledged, 'but he must have been paying his rent – or at least ground rent if he owned the flat – to Wiley's. They ought to be able to give us the bank and account number the money comes from.'

'Brilliant, Norm,' said Hart. 'And I been finking – if he owned that boat, he must have had money. They don't come cheap.'

'True,' said Atherton. 'You're talking £750,000 upwards, depending on the size.'

'If he owned it, why wouldn't he sell it to buy his dream house in the Isle of Wight?' McLaren objected. 'More likely he broke in.'

'No, he had a key,' Loessop said. 'Rudy told us – they wouldn't have wanted to get involved if there was breaking-and-entering. His mantra was, "I done nothing illegal".'

'Barring the coke,' said Atherton.

'Fighting a losing battle over that one, Jim,' said Hart. 'None o' the buggers think there's anything wrong with snorting white. Till their face caves in,' she added as an afterthought.

Hart came back later, after a long conversation with the moorings company, to say that the *Anna Rosita* was owned by a company called Farraday. 'A lot of 'em *are* company-owned nowadays, apparently. It used to be a little arty-hippy enclave, down there on Cheyne Walk, blokes with beards and dirty feet and women in corduroys paintin' the sunset and drinkin' gin. Everybody knew everybody else, according to this girl I spoke to. But given all the ritzy property around – I mean, it *is* Chelsea – prices were bound to've gone up, and now only rich people and corporate can afford to own a boat there – bar one or two nobby old ducks who've been there fifty years and won't budge. Bit like Wimbledon,' she added reflectively. 'The boxes used to be all serious fans, now only corporate hospitality can afford 'em, and they're full o' people eating smoked salmon and not watching the tennis.'

'So the world progresses,' said Atherton, who was sitting on Slider's dead radiator. It had never worked since Slider had been using that office. In really cold weather, he had to leave the door to the CID room open to let in some warmth. But it made him look like an approachable boss.

'What do you know about this Farraday?' Slider asked.

'Not much, guv,' said Hart. 'Directors are a Charles Holdsworth and a Mrs A. Holdsworth, and the address is Farraday House, Luxemburg Place.' She grinned. 'Sounds right posh, dun't it?'

'Positively multinational,' Slider conceded. 'That's Brook Green, isn't it?'

'S'right. Off Luxemburg Gardens. But it looks like a small outfit to me – could be one o' those mailbox companies. Maybe they just set it up for the houseboat – so's they can offset the mooring expenses against the rental.'

'Well, if they rented it out to Kimmelman, we may find out something about him from them. His bank details, at least. And his phone number.'

'Shall I give 'em a ring?'

Slider considered. 'No, it could be important. Could be a

way to get a handle on Kimmelman. If he rented from them, maybe they knew him. I think a visit is in order. Atherton, you can go. The weekend's coming up, so we're not going to get any more answers from banks and solicitors and that sort of cattle. It'd be nice if we could have *something* to put in the bag for Monday morning.'

EIGHT

Moor Often Knot Used

Atherton missed Luxemburg Place at the first pass and had to go round again. Some householder or house-holders in Luxemburg Gardens had sold off part of their back gardens for in-fill development, and Luxemburg Place was the little bit of road that gave access to the new house erected there. The road led nowhere else, between the blind side-walls of the existing houses, ending in a turning space before what had evidently been an expensive build, but owing to having been designed in the 1980s could have won Best In Show in a not-blending-in contest. While the surrounding houses were all typical Victorian/Edwardian, it was basically a giant brick box, but to justify his fee the architect had tacked on stuff – Hertfordshire-style hanging tiles, imitation Tudor beams across the gable, a cutesy cottage-style dormer, oversize windows from the 1970s, a gigantic integral double garage from the Florida collection. There was a large gravelled forecourt instead of a front garden, with tall iron gates, which were standing open and, to judge from the grass growing through them at the bottom, were never closed. At the end of what was effectively a private drive, perhaps there was no need.

Parked on the gravel were a rather dusty black Range Rover and a silver Skoda Octavia – his and hers cars, he thought. The gravel needed raking – there were heavy tyre tracks after the recent rainy spell that spoiled the look.

He followed one set, like railway lines, and slid himself in alongside the Skoda.

The door (glazed, of course) was opened by a small woman who seemed to be in her sixties, with carefully quoiffed and coloured hair. She was wearing an expensive skirt and jumper, polished court shoes and a preoccupied expression. She looked up at Atherton in a way that suggested she wasn't really seeing him, but was concentrating on whatever internal trouble was making her look worn under her practised make-up. Beyond her was the sort of interior he would have expected, with wood block floors, minimal architraves, track lighting, open spaces – he caught a glimpse straight through the house of the back garden seen through big sliding French doors – and the obligatory off-white conference-chic paint job.

'Mrs Holdsworth?' he asked. 'I'm Detective Sergeant Atherton from Shepherd's Bush police station.'

She was only just beginning to register his words, with a look of concern replacing that of internal discomfort, when a man stepped out into the hall behind her and said quickly and firmly, 'It's all right, Avril. I'll deal with this.'

He moved her, not roughly but definitely, aside and stepped between her and Atherton. 'I'm Charles Holdsworth, officer. What is it you want?'

'I'd like a word, if you don't mind, sir,' Atherton replied. Behind him, the little woman was hovering, and he heard her mumble something that seemed to include the word 'Charlie'. Without looking at her, the man said, 'Go inside, Avril.' Ditheringly, she moved away.

The man didn't look like a 'Charlie', which had a loose, bonhomous sound to it. Carefully styled grey hair, a firm-set face, conservative tie, an old but good charcoal suit, polished shoes – here was a Charles if ever Atherton saw one. He was tall, though not as tall as Atherton, probably in his sixties but well preserved, with a business-traveller's tan and an air of being in charge – or at least of wanting to be in charge.

'What's this about?' he asked, and then instantly cancelled the question and said, 'You'd better come into my office.'

He led the way into the room directly to the left off the

hall, whose window, onto the front gravel, was obscured by
a venetian blind. Inside was the paraphernalia of an office –
modern L-desk with screen and keyboard, executive swivel
chair in black leather, filing cabinets, side table with printer,
shelves stacked with ring and box files and one or two reference books. There were a couple of wire baskets filled with
papers, and a smell of furniture polish. The light was slightly
dim because of the blinds and it seemed very quiet. Of course,
it *was* quiet down this cul-de-sac, and Mrs Holdsworth wasn't
one to be creating riot in the background, if Atherton was
any judge. But he got the impression that nothing much had
happened in this office for a while. The deep and thorough
tracks of a professional cleaner's hoovering had not yet been
worn smooth.

Holdsworth did not invite Atherton to sit, nor did he sit
himself. He faced him in the middle of the room, seemed
about to speak, then turned his head towards the door. Mrs H
was hovering in the hall, looking anxious. 'It's all *right*, Avril,'
he said, with an underlay of impatience. 'Go and watch your
programme.' She turned without speaking and walked away,
like a dog hearing the command 'basket!' He waited until she
had disappeared, then subjected Atherton to a good, long
inspection, like an officer calculating what a rather unpromising-
looking recruit might be good for. 'Shepherd's Bush, eh?' he
said. 'How come?'

'Sir?' Atherton queried.

'If it's about Charlie, he doesn't have any connections with
Shepherd's Bush.'

'It's not about Charlie,' Atherton said. On top of one of the
filing cabinets was a framed photograph of a very handsome
youth who bore some resemblance to the man standing in
front of him. A rapid course of deduction suggested that the
handsome boy had been in trouble before, probably more than
once. In the photograph he looked in his early twenties, but
if the Holdsworths were in their sixties he was probably older
than that now – at least in his thirties – so if he was still
troubling them he must be a hardened case. And if Mrs H was
wearing that look of internal trepidation, he had probably given
them cause for grief fairly recently. Interesting.

However, he was not here to give them more pain. 'It's about your boat, the *Anna Rosita*,' he said.

There was a moment's silence, during which Holdsworth surveyed his face rather blankly while internal recalibration went on. 'What about it?' he asked at last.

It, Atherton noticed, not *her*. Whatever the boat was, she was not the treasured companion of the Holdsworth leisure hours. 'I believe you rent it out?'

'Sometimes,' he said. 'It's really more of a company asset – entertainment and so on. Visiting businessmen like a weekend on the water – very historical, merry old England and so forth. But I do let friends borrow it when it's not needed, and I occasionally let it. I let it out for the whole of the Olympics to some very nice people from California. They loved travelling to the Olympic Park by water taxi. Very different. Quite a thrill for them.'

Atherton had not expected him to be chatty. He put that together with the undisturbed carpet and made himself a retired businessman who missed the business.

'Have you rented it recently?'

'Not for a while. Some family members had it in the summer.'

'When did you last go there?'

'Not for a long time. I'm not really a houseboat person. I like my comfort.'

'Would you be surprised to learn, then, that someone was using the boat last Friday?'

He seemed to lean back a little, as though to get a better view of Atherton's proposition. 'Yes, very.'

'You didn't give anyone permission?'

'Indeed I did not. If someone was there, they must have broken in.' He sighed. 'It's not unusual, I'm afraid. You can't secure a houseboat in the same way you can a house. There have been break-ins before.'

'This person used a key,' Atherton said.

'Ah,' he said. 'Well, I'm afraid that's happened before, too. They keep duplicate keys at the office down there, and it's not difficult for someone to lift one while the girl's attention is distracted. Or when she pops out to – you know. Powder her nose.' He made a *tchk tchk* noise. 'What a nuisance! Now I shall have all the trouble of changing the locks. Did they do much damage?'

'Apparently not,' Atherton said. He was taking it very calmly – obviously the *Anna Rosita* was just a business asset to him. 'It seems they just used it to hold a party.'

'Oh dear,' he said. 'That will mean getting a cleaning firm in, I suppose. What a *dreadful* nuisance! Well, thank you for letting me know, officer. I ought to sell it really. I don't use it enough to justify keeping it. But you know how it is – one gets fond of a boat, somehow. A sentimental attachment.'

The one thing Atherton knew about boat owners was that it was always the last thing they sold, even though most of them went on board about once a year, and then with sighs of reluctance and grumbles about the amount of time it took at either end to wake it up and put it back to bed. The total asset value locked up in all the boats in all the marinas in all the world that never left the dockside must run into trillions. Of course, he was thinking of motor cruisers, but it was probably the same thing.

'Just one more thing, sir,' he said, and brought out the photograph. 'Do you know this man?'

He took the picture and looked at it for a long time, so long that Atherton was sure he was going to say, in the end, 'he looks familiar'. But finally he handed it back and said, 'No. No, I don't know him.'

'His name's Leon Kimmelman.'

'Doesn't ring a bell. Is that the man who broke in?'

Atherton assented.

'How odd,' said Holdsworth. 'Well, I mustn't keep you, officer. I know you chaps are very busy, keeping the world safe for the like of us. Ahaha.'

Atherton allowed himself to be ushered out, thinking that if the Holdsworths were thirty years younger he would assume that he had called just as they were about to dash upstairs for some headboard-banging, lampshade-swinging hot sex. Mr H was eager to be rid of him, though trying not to show it. A lot of people felt that way about the police, as though a copper's contact with crime might be catching. Atherton felt Holdsworth hadn't asked nearly enough questions about the break-in; but apart from the not-liking-coppers thing, he was obviously not emotionally attached to the boat; and besides, was probably so relieved that the visit had not been connected with the errant son that nothing else mattered for the moment.

He drove away, wondering why Kimmelman had chosen the houseboat for the sting. It was actually quite a clever choice – a hotel was more traditional, but much riskier, with other people around, staff to bribe, and the possibility of more hidden surveillance cameras than one's own.

Porson was using his office to change into a dinner suit, but called, 'Come in,' anyway, so that Slider was treated to a vision of his pale hairy legs as he pranced into his trousers. Very, very hairy, in contrast to his shiningly bald pate.

He blinked at Slider in a way that dared him to comment on anything he might be seeing.

'I just thought you might like a progress report, sir,' Slider said, stoically not averting his eyes. He was impressed to see a proper black tie hanging over the back of a chair. He would have put Porson down as a twangy man – too impatient to tie the real thing and caring nothing that the upper echelons would despise the ready-made elastic band version. There was more to the old man than met the eye.

Porson gave him a blank look. 'Carry on, then. I might not be a multi-tasking woman but I can listen and get dressed at the same time.'

So he said, but as Slider unfolded the story so far, his fingers slowed and forgot what they were doing. They proceeded to putting on the tie, having done up the button on his dress trousers but not the zip. Slider wondered at what point he should intervene.

Finally he stopped moving altogether, and when Slider finished he was silent, pregnant with thought. 'On the whole, that's good,' he said at last. 'You're right, the timing's pretty tight for Rathkeale. Could rule him out – thank God. I want him fully cleared, and dropped – that's your priority.'

'I thought the murder was our priority,' Slider couldn't help suggesting.

Porson barked. 'Don't come the high and meaty with me! We don't work in a vacuum. We've got to get on with our political masters and that's all about it! Rathkeale's in the public eye – Kimmelman isn't. No one's been asking about him, there's no next of kin, nobody's interested, you can take your time sorting that one out, do it slow but do it right. But this Rathkeale thing is a hot potato. If it gets out what he's been up to, the papers may crucify him but there'll be some nails saved for us. He's popular, you know. And if the press gets a sniff that we liked him for Kimmelman with no bloody evidence, we'll be sued back to the Stone Age. You've got nothing on him, have you?'

'No, sir. Only the motive.'

'Then get him cleared and get rid of him.' He glanced at the clock. 'Bloody hell, I've got to get a move on.' His fingers rapidly finished the tie-tying. Without looking, too. 'Dinner at the Mansion House,' he complained, chin poking up as he settled the collar. 'Thank your lucky stars you've got me to do this sort of thing for you.'

'I do, sir, every day,' Slider said with sincerity.

'Glad handing, rubber chicken, boring speeches. Waste of bloody time, when I could be . . . Well? What are you hanging about for?'

When I could be – *what*? Slider knew nothing about Porson's private life. Playing canasta? Sticking stamps in my album? Doinking my teenage mistress? What a fascinating, frustrating caesura!

'Um,' said Slider. 'You haven't done your zip up.'

Joanna greeted him at the door. 'I'm suddenly hot!'

He slid his hands up inside her sweater. 'I can do something about that,' he offered. He kissed her. She responded. 'Like George, my breath was coming in short pants,' he murmured.

She laughed, but removed his hands and stepped back. Pity!

'I've got supper cooking. I'm hot as in suddenly in demand. You remember Martin Hazlett?'

Slider resigned himself, and took off his overcoat. 'Not personally. I think I've heard you mention him. Trumpet player?'

'Yes. Used to play with the RLP when they needed extras. Well, he's now first trumpet with the London Mozart Consortium, and also, by a pleasant coincidence, their fixer. And he rang me today with a whole lot of dates for January and February. Their number four is going off to have a baby, and he remembered me with kindness.'

'That's great,' Slider said, hauling his mind back from the day towards uxorious enthusiasm.

'It's better than great,' she said sternly. 'January and February, when dates are thin on the ground? And a promise to be on his list from now on? When the world is full of younger fiddlers? It's terrific. How about a little awe from you, feller?'

'Aww!' he said obediently.

She cuffed him gently upside the head. 'But that's not all.'

'There's more? I need a drink,' he protested feebly.

'Gin's all poured, waiting for the tonic.' She took his hand and towed him towards the kitchen door. He could feel her elation thrumming up his arm. He felt just a tiny pang of left-outness. In the early days of their relationship, *he* had been what made her this excited. In fairness, he got a buzz from his work, when he was hot on some trail, but still . . . A man's sexual ego was a delicate flower.

She unscrewed the tonic, splashed some in, positively *ran* to the freezer for ice cubes, shoved the glass into his hand, and said, '*Now* will you listen? You've heard of Sid Saxon?'

He raised his eyebrows and gave an intelligently neutral, 'Hmm?' The cold gin slid down his throat and a couple of bubbles made their escape from the glass up his nose. *Go go go! Good luck, guys! See you in hell, lemon slice.*

'I shall smack you!' she warned. 'The famous fixer, Sid Saxon. The famousest, fixinest fixer of them all!'

'*He* rang you today?' Actually, now he made the effort, he had heard of him.

'No,' she admitted, 'but Geraldine did – his assistant and widely supposed to be his mistress, though if you've seen Sid . . . However, she rang, and asked me if I was free for – wait for it – the Children in Need concert at the Albert Hall!'

'Hey!' he said. 'That's good, isn't it? Big star line-up—'

'Bugger the stars,' she stopped him. 'It's televised, you jug.

Concert fee *plus* television fee *plus* residuals. Two rehearsals and the filming. And the chance of being on Sid's books. He gets *lots* of recording work. Of course, the actual concert is going to be a long hack and the music will be terrible, but what do we care?'

'I remember you said, you just want to play the dots,' he said. 'How did she get on to you?'

'I didn't ask her and she didn't say, but there's plenty of suspects. Other fixers, people I've depped for. Once you're out there and people know you're out there . . .' She took the glass from his hand and took a drink.

'So the world is beating a path to your door,' he said.

'The world only beats a path to your door when you're in the bathroom,' she said. 'Still . . . I thought when I quit the orchestra that life on the outside would be cold and lonely, but it's turning out to be pretty damn good.'

'It's good *now*,' he said, his innate caution not wanting her to fall on her head.

She smiled and squeezed his arm. 'Darling, I'm a freelance. I know all about the ups and downs of fortune. You take the ups and try to put a bit aside to cover the downs. That's what you do. Are you ready for supper?'

She'd done her boasting and was back in hausfrau mode. She was like that – Miss Quicksilver. A dull old Plod like himself had to learn to be nimble to keep up.

'I'll just go up and kiss George and wash my hands,' he said. He sniffed. 'Lamb?' he queried.

'A good hearty stew for a damp grey evening.'

'I'm there!' he said – although actually he was heading for the stairs.

Over supper, it was his turn. She was always his sounding board.

'I agree, I don't think Rathkeale could have organised the murder, not that quickly anyway. Probably not at all,' she added. 'Ordinary people don't have hitmen on speed dial.'

'Politicians aren't ordinary men,' Slider pointed out. 'And they have minions.'

'Minions who know how to access a bloke in a mask who does murders for cash?'

'It's possible. But on the whole, I don't think Rathkeale is the killer, either in person or remotely.'

'Yet he must have *something* to do with it all,' Joanna said. 'I mean, Kimmelman was obviously *intending* to blackmail him, even if he hadn't got round to it yet. But then, what was he blackmailing him *for*? And who stepped in and stopped it?'

'Swilley put forward the thought that serious black-mailers don't stop at one victim. It becomes a bad habit. So maybe he was doing someone else, who decided he was a wart and eradicated him.'

'Or maybe,' Joanna said thoughtfully, 'the blackmail had nothing to do with it. Maybe it was just coincidental to the timing.'

'I thought you said Rathkeale had to be something to do with it.'

'I'm entitled to change my mind. I'm not the one whose job's on the line.'

'Oh, thank you. You think my hold is that precarious, do you?'

'Well, I didn't mean it like that, exactly. Anyway, it's early days yet,' she comforted him. 'What about that case that was on the telly the other day, that woman's body that was found in the woods, where they've just brought in the murderer after six years?'

'Hmm,' he said. 'I'd rather get this one out of the way before George goes to secondary school.'

'Do you have to work tomorrow?'

'Nope. There's only a couple of them going in, and they've got their orders. Bar anything important breaking, I'm all yours.'

'Ah,' she said regretfully. 'Would t'were that it were.'

'You're working,' he said flatly.

'As you'd know if you looked at the diary. Rehearsal and concert in Croydon on Sunday, and—'

'You were free tomorrow. I *did* look.'

'First rehearsal for Children in Need, all afternoon. I'm glad you're going to be here, because your dad's got something on. Some Scrabble tournament.'

'He'd cancel that in a good cause.'

'Yes, but I don't like to ask him. He does so much for us. But,' she added to comfort him, 'we can have a lie in. That'll be nice.'

'If George doesn't have other ideas.'

She grinned. 'I'll get up, dump him on your dad, and come back to bed. I'm not that altruistic! And you do owe me a remedy for my hotness,' she added in a purr.

'She remembered,' he told the casserole dish, gratefully.

NINE

I'm Always True to You, Darling, In My Fashion

The bulbous shape of London's City Hall, home of the London Assembly, squatted beside the Thames like a deformed headlamp, or an eyeball that had been popped out and then slightly trodden on. Less polite commentators called it the Glass Testicle. Hart did not have an architectural raw nerve, like Slider, but she didn't see the point of curved walls, because you couldn't put furniture, which was notoriously straight-sided, against it. Her common sense suggested a conventional oblong building would have given more useful internal space for the same money. But common sense generally took a duvet day when there was an architectural award to be won.

Rathkeale's PA, Valerie Case, had assured her that the Greater London Authority never slept, and that of course she would be in on Saturday; before adding prosaically, 'Saturday *morning*, anyway.' Hart found her in her office, an adjunct to Rathkeale's, and had to admit that the big window that formed part of the testicle's curved glass façade gave a stunning view up and down the Thames. It was a lovely day for it, too – soft, hazy sunshine, again more like spring than late autumn, and the trees along the Embankment were still green, only touched with gold.

'I dunno how you get any work done,' she said chummily to Call-Me-Val.

'Our work is tremendously important,' was the reply. 'Running the biggest and most diverse city in the world is a twenty-four-seven business.' Hart could practically smell the glossy brochure that came from.

'Yeah,' she said, 'it must be exciting, all the different sorts you get coming in here. Top people, celebrities – I bet you get some rough ones as well. Everybody wants something, dun't they? I bet you get some pretty dodgy underworld types tipping up now and then.'

Val looked at her coldly. 'Certainly not. We've got very good security downstairs.'

'But your Mr Rathkeale – Kevin – he's never been afraid to get his hands dirty, has he? I've always admired that about him. He didn't live in no ivory tower – he was always down on the street where the action was, getting real wiv the kids.'

She thawed. 'You're right. Kevin doesn't stand on his dignity. He's the least stuffy person I know. He's always made a point of talking to the real people.'

'Yeah, wiv the real problems. Kids in trouble wiv the police, that sort of thing.'

'Well, I suppose so,' Val said, seeming mildly puzzled. 'What is it you want to know?'

'What's on his mind. What he's been up to lately. Who he's been meeting. I'd like a squint at his diary.'

'I can't allow that,' she said. 'There's such a thing as confidentiality.'

'He won't mind. Ring him up, ask him,' said Hart, as if it was no biggie. Val hesitated. 'Go on, give him a bell.' While Val went to her phone, she went on, still casually, cosily, 'How's he been, lately? Had a lot on his plate, I bet.'

'He's always busy,' she said. 'He has a lot of high profile positions.'

Yeah, I've seen some of 'em, Hart thought.

'Has he been more worried than usual? Preoccupied? A bit short now and then? Like, I always know when my boss is up against it. He dun't know he's doing it, but you can see he's under the hammer.'

'I can't say Kevin's been any different recently,' she said, dialling a number. 'Just the same as usual. Except for . . . It's ringing. He might not be at home, you know,' she added.

'You got his mobile number, though. Except for what?'

Val held up her hand as the phone was answered. After a brief and deeply apologetic, not to say fawning, conversation, she hung up, and said, 'That was his wife. He's out walking the dog on Primrose Hill. She said not to disturb him. It's his down time.'

Ooh, down time on Primrose Hill! Hart thought sarcastically. She bet the dog was a Lab, as well. 'Give him a ring,' she said, making it just not a request.

'What's all this about?' Val asked doubtfully.

'He knows what it's about. Tell him his co-operation will be appreciated. Or I'll talk to him, if you like.'

She did like. Once having called him, she handed over responsibility and the phone, and Rathkeale, sounding irritable, supposed there was no harm in Hart seeing his diary, but for God's sake couldn't they leave him alone for five minutes. Yes, yes, anything she liked if it would get her off his back. Oh – and, not a word to Val about – you know – *anything*. She was not in the picture, and she wasn't to be put in it. There would be consequences if anything got out, he concluded, managing to threaten and beg at the same time, not a naturally sustainable posture. You could rick your back, Hart thought as she rang off and handed the phone back.

With Val hovering protectively at her elbow she went through the last few weeks and the one ahead, but every appointment seemed dull, normal and verifiable. Val knew all about them. She was sure there had been no extra visits slotted in that weren't in the book – apart from Slider's. That had thrown a lot of things out, she said sternly, necessitating some serious juggling, which accounted for the crossings out and writings in. *Bad* policeman! And there were no times unaccounted for. Apart from the Sunday, when he was at home, and that was not her business. Anyone was entitled to a day of rest, weren't they? What did she want, blood?

'You said, "he wasn't any different recently, except for . . ."'

and then you broke off. Except for what?' Hart asked, flipping the pages to look further back.

'I don't know what you mean,' Val said, puzzled.

'I was asking if he'd been upset about anything lately, or worried.'

'Oh! Yes, I remember. I was just going to say, except for Myra Silverman bothering him, but that's nothing really. Actually, I think she's given up on it, because she hasn't rung him the last week or so. So, no, there's nothing upsetting him.'

'Myra Silverman. She's that KidZone woman, isn't she?'

'Yes, and she caused Kevin a *lot* of heartache,' Val said severely. 'He was *completely* innocent of any wrongdoing, but because he stood up for her, purely out of a sense of chivalry, he got tarred with the same brush. It was wicked, what the press did to him. He's a *good* man. And then she's got the cheek to try and get him involved in some new scheme.'

'What scheme's that?'

'I don't know. He's not interested, anyway, and he told her so – in *no* uncertain terms. But she kept bugging him about it. But she seems to have got the message, anyway. She's stopped ringing him now, thank God.'

'Did he tell you anything about what she wanted?'

'No, he just said "some scheme".' She snorted. 'Something that'll line her pockets, if I know anything about it. The trouble that woman's caused him – and she's no spring chicken!'

The last words seem to leap out of their own accord, and given that they were as fine a non-sequitur as you'd hear in a long day, Hart concluded that Miss Case was a little bit in love with her boss.

She examined the well-controlled figure, the over-youthful outfit with the eye-poppingly short skirt, the careful make-up, the expensive haircut, and wondered whether naughty Kevin had been dipping his wick there as well. It was far from unheard-of for a man to use his secretary as a spare wife, and it would explain the intense loyalty, and the no-spring-chicken outburst – from someone the wrong side of thirty-five – plus the awkward deference to the official wife. Poor cow, Hart thought, not without compassion. She half wished she could tell Valerie Case what Rathkeale had been up to on the *Anna Rosita*, just to put her right, but it was not her secret to spill. Call-Me-Val would have to plough her own furrow.

At least they'd eliminated Rathkeale as far as they could without access to his bank account and phone records. And if he *was* so unimaginative as to doink his PA, he probably wasn't in the master criminal league. They'd had a look at his Facebook, Instagram and Twitter and found nothing there to suggest any leads. And she'd got the registration number of his car, which the devoted Miss Case just happened to know, so they could do an ANPR search on it and see if it went anywhere on Sunday, and in particular anywhere near Shepherd's Bush.

Rathkeale lived in Regent's Park Road, opposite the end of Albert Terrace. Hart looked the house up on Street View and marvelled at its size and opulence. He must be making a good bit of money somewhere. However, the tiny front garden had been sacrificed to make a concrete pad onto which it was just possible to cram a car, the only way to escape the anti-parking jihad of Camden Council – proving the adage that you couldn't have everything. There were no ANPR cameras in the immediate vicinity, though there were plenty between there and Shepherd's Bush. She put in a request for any pings on the Sunday, and while she was waiting, noted that Albert Terrace was a bus route, and that there was a TfL camera at the nearest bus stop which ought to be able to catch that section of Regent's Park Road in its range. She padded over to where Fathom was patiently trawling through security camera footage.

'Jezza mate, j'wanna do me a favour?' she said wheedlingly.

'Sorry to bother you, guv,' Hart said, not sounding a bit sorry.

Slider, with the phone clutched between shoulder and chin, stopped trying to get the car lift on the plastic toy garage to unstick, got up off the floor and said, 'What are you still doing there?'

'Something came up.' She explained about the bus-stop camera which, facing straight down Albert Terrace, had the front of Rathkeale's house as its ultimate back-drop. 'He said he didn't go out anywhere on Sunday, but his car backs out

of his parking space just after two o'clock in the afternoon
and doesn't come back until five Monday morning.'

Slider looked at the information from all sides. 'Can you
see who's driving?'

'No, guv, but he's said his wife was away for the weekend
– and he wouldn't lie about that because she'd be his alibi if
she was around – so it can't be her, and there's no one else
living there. Looks like he's been telling porkies. Can I go
and spoil his day?'

'Do you know where he is?'

'Yeah, I had a goosey at his diary, didn't I? He's at a council
meeting in Lambeth this afternoon and a benefit concert at
the Festival Hall this evening. Either one, he won't like the
filth turning up and asking questions.'

'You don't like him, do you?' Slider said mildly. 'It's not
part of our job to upset public figures for the sake of it.'

'Yeah,' she agreed, 'but just look at him! *And* he lied to us.'

'All right, you can go and talk to him. Someone has to.'

'Thanks, boss. You having a nice day off?'

'I *was*,' Slider said, and rang off. George was watching
him patiently, several toy cars at the ready. Two had not come
from that particular garage kit and were incompatible in
size with the lift – what had led to the problem in the first
place – but try explaining that to a three year-old.

Hart had rather fancied upsetting Rathkeale at the Festival Hall
in front of big donors in black tie and sequined evening
dresses, but she couldn't wait that long, and caught him instead
at Lambeth Town Hall. The meeting was just finishing, and
he greeted her with impatience, something of an eye-roll,
and the information that he had to get changed for the
evening and didn't have time for all this nonsense.

Hart gave him a cheerful grin. 'No trouble at all, sir. If you
don't want to talk to me here, I can escort you to the police
station and we can do it officially in a nice, comfortable
recording room.'

He paled a little, but managed to keep hold of his righteous
indignation. 'Are you arresting me, madam? Because if you're
not—'

'I can arrest you if you like,' she said with an air of trying to accommodate him. 'Obstruction's a nice open charge, covers a lot o' sins.'

'Obstruction?' Two people passing along the corridor observed him with interest, their ears evidently on stalks. He grabbed Hart's forearm and steered her aside. 'Look,' he hissed, 'can we not do this right now, with all these people around?'

'Here, or at the station. S'up to you.'

'But I haven't *done* anything,' he said, with as much passion as his sotto voce allowed.

'You *lied* to us,' Hart said, suddenly stern.

Two more people were approaching. A man with an armful of files came out of the room Rathkeale had just vacated, and said, 'Everything all right, Kevin?'

'Oh – yes – yes, thanks, Bob. Um – can I use this room for a few minutes? Private business to discuss.'

'Be my guest,' said Bob, subjecting Hart to a good old-fashioned up-and-downer. She grinned back at him, and as Rathkeale turned away, dropped him a wink that made his eyebrows shoot into his hair.

Rathkeale had hurried into the empty room, and Hart strolled after him. There was a scuffed and battered table, surrounded by cheap moulded chairs, and bearing a scattering of carafes and used glasses. As soon as she was inside, he snapped the door shut behind her and said, red now instead of white, 'What are you playing at? He probably thinks there's something going on between us.'

'What – you are the father of my baby, sort o' style? Oh Kevin, does that sort o' thing happen often? I *heard* you was the king of naughtiness, but—'

'Look, stop that,' Rathkeale said, a touch wearily. 'Tell me what you want, and be done with it. I'm a busy man.'

'What you been busy at, that's what we want to know. Where were you on Sunday?'

'Last Sunday? I told you, I was at home. Having a rare day off.' He said it with superb nonchalance, but his eyes flitted. He knew he was busted.

'Then why didn't you report your car was stolen?' she asked genially.

'It wasn't stolen.'

'Yeah, I know. Because someone come out of your house after lunch, drove your car away, and that someone was you, wun't it, mate? We got you on camera. There's cameras everywhere these days, ain't there? The most watched population on the planet, that's what they say. So where'd you go?'

'Go. Oh. Yes . . . er, I . . . er, I went out to get a newspaper. Just popped down to the shops. A newspaper and . . . er . . . a pint of milk,' he added on a fine burst of inspiration.

She looked at him sadly. 'Cameras, Kev, remember? The great invention of the dead hand of the state. Now, d'you want to limber up with a few more lies, or are you ready to get to the truth?'

'I've told you – I went to get a newspaper.'

'And then got lost? Because you didn't come back until five in the morning. And in case you think I'm just a stalker and mad for your bod, let me remind you that two in the afternoon to five in the morning nicely covers the period during which Leon Kimmelman was murdered and his gaff turned over.'

Rathkeale was pale again, his dry lips moving.

Hart oozed false sympathy. 'Come on, Kev, you know the game's up. Why not get it off your chest, eh? Confess and you'll feel better.'

He rallied. 'I don't have to tell you where I was. I've done nothing wrong. I'm a law-abiding citizen and I have a right to my privacy.'

'Then I shall have to ask you to come with me to the police station.'

'I can't go anywhere with you. I have a concert to go to,' he snapped.

'Tell me where you were, then,' Hart invited. He was silent. 'The man who was blackmailing you was murdered, at a time when you've got no alibi, and you lied to us about your whereabouts. You in trouble, mate.'

'He wasn't blackmailing me!' he wailed. 'I've never seen him before in my life.'

'Who's going to believe that? You weren't at home. Where were you?'

'I don't have to tell you!'

'Then I shall have to arrest you for giving false information to the police during the course of an existing investigation, under section five brackets two of the Criminal Law Act 1967—'

'*Don't arrest me!*' he cried desperately. 'Look, I'll come to the station, if that's what it takes to get you off my back, but I want to talk to a senior officer – and I can tell you, I shall be making an official complaint about your attitude.'

'Oooh, I'm scared,' said Hart. 'Come on, then. You can complain and explain at the same time.'

Porson clapped a hand to his head, hard enough to make his teeth rattle. 'You *arrested him*?'

'Not actually arrested—' Slider began.

'Threatened with arrest then. What part of "I want him cleared and dropped" didn't you understand?'

'My officer saw no alternative, when he refused to say where he was at the critical time,' Slider said sturdily.

Porson saw the point of that, and lowered the gas. 'I'm trying to keep this thing low profile,' he grumbled, 'and you go and clap the bloody darbies on him and drag him kicking and screaming—'

'He's our best suspect. With no alibi,' Slider said. He'd saved the best news until last. 'He wants to talk to you. Before he sends for a solicitor.'

Porson's eyebrows shot up in relief. 'He's not got a lawyer yet?'

'I think he wants to avoid publicity as much as you do,' Slider said. 'I tried to talk to him but I'm not senior enough for him.'

'I don't want to go in there naked as the day I was bald. Do we have *anything* on where he went?'

'We've put the index through the ANPR, but we've got no pings for that period. However, he could have got from Regent's Park Road to Jacket's Yard by the back streets. The problem would be, where did he meet Kimmelman and kill him?'

'Hmm,' said Porson, thinking hard. 'If they met some-where, and he transferred to Kimmelman's car, all the back

and forth could be done in that. But where would they meet?'
He thought a moment. 'You could draw a straight line between
Primrose Hill and Wormwood Scrubs, for instance. None
of it using main roads. Well, no use speculating with no
facts. I'd better go and see him. Meanwhile, you'd better start
looking for that car.'

'Yes, sir. But where?'

'Bloody Nora, I'm not doing your job for you!' Porson
exploded again, though Slider knew the frustration was not
directed at him. The words 'needle' and 'haystack' didn't
begin to describe the problem. 'You know he drove down
Albert Terrace. Work from there.' He stalked to the door, and
turned back to say, more quietly, 'I shall have to bail him,
you know. Once his lawyer gets here.'

'I know,' said Slider. 'But if we can make him agree to let
us see his bank and phone records . . .'

'I'll see what I can do,' Porson said.

Rathkeale had started to unravel. His was not the figure easily
to keep its cool. He was pudgy, pallid and moist, his hair
needed careful gardening to keep it smooth, and his shirts
had a tendency to lose contact with his waistband, for which
his vanity in clinging to a size just too small in each was
mostly to blame.

He still looked surprised at the sight of Porson. Porson
took a bit of getting used to: the knobbly bald pate, the
enormous bushy eyebrows, the considerable nose – and that
was before you got to his habitual mangling of vocabulary.
But though largely bony, Porson was tall and had been
powerful, and when he drew himself up he still looked impressive; and he had a natural authority, nurtured over the years,
that was more than equal to a slightly bent former MP.

'Yes, I'm Detective Superintendent Porson,' he said. 'I
understand you want to talk to me.'

'Have I been arrested?' Rathkeale demanded, attacking first.

'Not yet,' Porson said, with smooth menace.

'Then you have to let me go,' Rathkeale said triumphantly.

'Nobody's keeping you, sir,' Porson said, making the 'sir'
an insult, as only a policeman can. 'You are helping us with

our enquiries. Or, I hope you are. Because we don't take kindly to being lied to.'

'It's none of your business where I was on Sunday,' Rathkeale tried.

'I'm afraid it is, now. Why don't you get it over with? We'll find out sooner or later – nobody can move around a city like this without being traced – and sooner is better than later, as far as you're concerned. Less messy. Puts us in a better mood, too – makes us more sympathetic, like.'

'Are you threatening me?' Rathkeale blustered. 'Because I warn you—'

Porson made a show of turning away. 'We're just wasting time here. If you're not prepared to co-operate, I shall have to call in my officer and arrest you, then we can see what your solicitor says when he arrives.'

'No, wait!'

Porson turned back, and raised his eyebrows receptively.

Rathkeale bit his lip. 'Look, I didn't kill this man, whatever his name is. I didn't *know* him. I couldn't kill anyone, anyway – I'm not like that. Ask anyone. They'll tell you. I'm a *nice* bloke.'

'Then where were you on Sunday?' No answer. Porson turned away again with a large sigh that was meant to be heard.

'Look,' Rathkeale said. Porson paused, looked back indifferently. 'If I tell you – I don't want it to get out, you see. That's why I didn't say . . . Well, it's complicated.'

'It always is, sir,' Porson said pityingly. But he turned round fully. 'Well?'

'I went to . . . On Sunday . . . Well, my wife was away, and . . .'

Porson had a feeling he knew where this was going. He wasn't sure whether to be glad or sorry. 'Your wife was away,' he said patiently, 'and . . .?'

'Well, there's this friend of mine. Lives in Acacia Avenue – not far from where I live.'

'And what's his name, sir?' No answer. Rathkeale was still chewing the lip – in danger of going right through, as far as Porson could see. 'It's not an alibi without a name,' he advised Rathkeale. 'Your friend will have to corroborate.'

'It's not a him,' Rathkeale admitted, avoiding his eyes.

'Ah,' said Porson.

'And I don't want my wife finding out. Or anyone. If it got into the papers . . . I don't want policemen in big boots going round there and shouting my business to the rooftops. And I don't want my friend upset. She wouldn't like . . . That's why I wanted to talk to you before my solicitor gets here,' he added pathetically. 'She's a friend of my wife, you see. I know they're not supposed to . . . but I don't see how . . . That's why you've got to let me go. I can't have any fuss – any publicity. I've got my reputation to think of. My job.'

'I understand,' Porson interrupted, before the man got too far onto his knees. 'If you *are* telling the truth now, and you have an alibi for the time in question, I see no reason why anything should get out. But you must see that it has to be followed up.'

'Can't you just take my word?' he asked desperately.

'We did that once already,' Porson said unkindly.

Rathkeale blushed. 'There's no need to talk like that. I swear I'm telling the truth now.'

'Name and address, sir. If she confirms what you're telling me, there'll be no need to take it any further.'

'But she might not be in,' he wailed.

'That's all right, sir,' said Porson. 'We don't need to keep you here while we check up. We know where you live. Name and address, and then you're free to go.' He glanced at his watch. 'Might catch the end of the show if you hurry.'

'A mistress in St John's Wood,' Slider said. 'How traditional.'

'I just hope she's willing to back him up,' said Porson. 'Get him out of the way. Although I half hoped it *was* him did it. Would have been an explosion of shit, all right, but at least it'd be case solved. And it'd be nice to put him away for *something*.'

'There's still the cocaine,' Slider said.

Porson glared. 'When I want you to be funny, I'll send you a memo. Well, I suppose I can leave this to you now? Get off home?'

'I'm sorry to have spoiled your evening, sir.'

'I was only watching telly. Some crime film, Leonardo D. Capricorn, something about Boston. This trip to the pantomime's better entertainment. By the way, Hart did the right thing. Tell her well done.'

TEN

Press for Service

S lider was in early on Monday, feeling refreshed, and put in an hour clearing up some non-Kimmelman-related matters that had been piling up. Through his open door he saw McLaren creep in looking very much the worse for wear.

'You look hungover,' Atherton said cheerily.

McLaren put his hands to his head. 'Don't shout! Party last night. Some of Nat's friends. They can't half drink. Anybody got an aspirin?'

'You've been practising licence without a medicine again,' Atherton said sternly.

'Here,' said Swilley, throwing a pack over. 'Never mind, Maurice, your moustache is coming along nicely.'

'I can't believe how much it's grown in a week,' Hart said. 'What're you putting on it?'

'Nothing,' McLaren said, stroking it. 'It just does it on its own.'

'And Esau was an hairy man,' Atherton quoted. 'It suits you.'

McLaren took the praise cautiously. 'You reckon? I was sort of going for Burt Reynolds, but I think maybe I'm just coming off annoying.'

'Anything that covers up any part of your face is an improvement,' Atherton told him sincerely.

'Don't be mean. It's lovely, Maurice,' said Hart. 'Anyway, at least it proves you can grow one.'

'Here's something that's always troubled me,' said Atherton. 'Why doesn't Tarzan have a beard?'

Slider came out and broke it up. 'Report,' he said.

'Rathkeale's lady-love turns out to be a Labour MP,' Hart said. 'Married. Acacia Avenue's her London pad for when she's got to be in Parliament, and she's got a family home in Birmingham – that's where her seat is. And that's where she was yesterday, worst luck. But I give her a bell – discreetly.' She added hastily as Slider's eyebrow went up. 'When she knew what I wanted she got very antsy, said she'd have to call me back. I suppose hubby was around, listening. Anyway, she rung me later on her mobile and said she'd be in London today, so I said I'd go up to the House later and take her statement. But basically, she says old Gingernuts was with her all right. If you can call that an alibi.'

'Why would she lie? He's not very appetising,' said Atherton.

'D'you want me to try and check it any further?' Hart asked.

'You're getting his phone records?'

'Yes, guv.'

'Then you may be able to corroborate his story – there must have been communication between them over that weekend.'

'That's what I thought, guv,' said Hart. 'And if there's any funny-looking contacts, I can follow them up. Because if he *did* hire somebody to wallop Kimmelman, he'd take care to set himself up an alibi, wouldn't he?'

'True,' said Slider. 'OK, anybody got anything else?'

'I'm after a traffic camera, guv,' said McLaren. 'It's down Hammersmith Road. It's a bit of a distance from Ruskin House, but it's a straight bit of road and a clear view, and if there *is* anything there, we can follow it to other cameras in the area. Find out where Kimmelman went the last coupla days.'

'I've got Kimmelman's bank account details from Wiley's this morning,' Swilley said. 'Local branch of NatWest. I'm going to ask for the records, but you know what they can be like.'

'OK,' Slider said. 'Any thoughts as to further lines of investigation?'

'I was thinking about those fractures,' Gascoyne said, 'whether he was a boxer once. Is it worth making enquiries along those lines?'

'Can't hurt,' said Slider. 'We know so little about him.'

'And I was wondering whether he was in one of the services,' LaSalle said.

'Why d'you think that?' Gascoyne asked.

LaSalle looked puzzled. 'I dunno, really. He'd just got that sort of look about him. You can generally tell ex-army types. There's something about 'em. Maybe the way he'd polished his shoes, I dunno.'

The phone had rung and Hart, being nearest, had gone to answer it. Now she said, 'Boss, someone downstairs to see you. Penny Duckham. Says its about Kimmelman.'

She was the editor of one of the local newspapers, the wittily named *Bush Telegraph*. Most local papers lived almost entirely off their advertisements, so their interest in hard news was minimal, but Penny Duckham was new to the job, was young and enthusiastic, and had dreams of building up the *Telegraph* until it got noticed by the big press beasts, and she was elevated to stardom to one of the national dailies. *Manchester Guardian* syndrome, Slider called it. So she made a point of following any crime that could be classified as local, and any local government stories, particularly if there was an element of scandal to be wrung out of them. She had early made Slider her personal contact, and though the traffic had been pretty one way so far, he was never averse to having another pair of eyes looking out for him. So he encouraged her to contact him, on the basis that one day it would pay off.

She was waiting for him out in the shop, and he was encouraged to see that she had a file under her arm. 'Come on through,' he said, and led her into an empty room on the other side. She was a tall young woman, just a little chubby, with a very pale face which contrasted startlingly with her spiky dyed black hair. She wore glasses with heavy black frames, and scarlet lipstick, and a scarlet skirt-suit over a black top. Slider wondered vaguely if she was subconsciously motivated by the old riddle, 'what's black and white and red all over?'

She gave him a cheery, toothy grin, and said, 'I think I've got something for you this time.' She put the file on the table and opened it. 'You sent round that picture of the man at Jacket's Yard, and I've kept it on my desk, just in case I came across anything.'

'Very kind of you,' Slider said encouragingly.

'Got to help our boys in blue, haven't we?' she said whimsically. '*Well*,' she pulled something out and passed it across to him. 'I was trawling through the archives looking for something else, and I found this. It is the same man, isn't it?'

It was a copy of a newspaper cutting, a black and white photograph of a man coming out of a building into the street. He was tall and lean, very dark – almost swarthy; in his fifties, probably, wearing a dark overcoat over a good-looking suit. He had a look of prosperity about him. He was looking at the camera and his mouth was partly open, giving the impression that he was not happy about being photographed and was saying something like, 'Not *you* again!'

He was not, however, the subject of Penny Duckham's eager anticipation of praise. Coming out behind him, and clearly visible over his right shoulder, was a slightly shorter, chunkier man, also in a dark overcoat, whose eyes seemed to be flitting sideways in the manner of a bodyguard looking for trouble.

'That *is* him, isn't it?' she urged again.

'It certainly looks like it,' Slider agreed. The headline was DAVY LANE HOPES CRUSHED, and she had written the date over the top – a date about nine years ago. 'Doesn't it say in the article who it is?'

'No, just the bloke in front – Jack Silverman. He owns a big construction company, Abbott Construction. But the one behind him looks as though he's with him, don't you think? Sort of attached.'

'What was the story?'

'Davy Lane's a rundown area that needs reviving. It's been going on for years – since before my time. One of those things where there's a new scheme put forward every few years, but nothing comes of it, because the money's not there. Obviously this one—' she tapped the picture – 'didn't take off either, because nothing's happened, as far as I know.'

'Jack Silverman,' Slider mused. 'Any relation to Myra Silverman?'

She frowned. 'I know that name . . . Wait a minute, isn't she that woman who got in trouble a while back over some kids' charity? KidZone, that was it. Well, I don't know, but he could be. Easy enough to find out, anyway. What's she got to do with it?'

'I don't know. Nothing, probably,' Slider said. She had a connection to Rathkeale and Rathkeale had a connection – involuntarily – to Kimmelman, but beyond that . . . Still, the name was not all that common. Coincidence?

'Well, thanks a lot for this,' he said. 'It gives us another avenue to explore, try and find out more about this bloke. He's a bit of a mystery man.'

She stood up to go, smiling, pleased with herself. 'If I find any other references to him, I'll let you know. And anything else you want . . .'

'I won't forget.' He shook her hand heartily and guided her out.

'And you'll keep me in the loop over this murder? It'd be great to scoop all those big boys with the first news of an arrest,' she said wistfully.

He didn't like to tell her that the big boys weren't interested in the death of an unnamed nobody; or that they were desperately keeping the Rathkeale connection away from everyone. 'I'll do my best,' he said.

'Jack Silverman, Abbott Construction,' Swilley said as her fingers rattled over the keys.

'Why Abbott when his name's not Abbott?' McLaren objected.

'Position in the alphabet,' Swilley said impatiently. 'Keep up!'

'What're you talking about?'

Atherton took over. 'If your name begins with an "A", you're the first on the list in *Yellow Pages*. "Ab" is good, and "Abb" is even better. The only person who'll beat you is Mr Aardvark.'

'I know that,' McLaren said contemptuously. 'It's still stupid. Who picks a builder because he's the first on the page?'

Atherton looked at him admiringly. 'You know, Maurice, I think you've got something. I hand it to you.'

'And his name's *not* Abbott.'

'Ah, I'll have it back, please.'

'Here we are. Jack Silverman,' Swilley interrupted.

'Interesting – his name apparently *is* Jack, not John. Age fifty-eight – he doesn't look it. Hmm. Hmm. Yes, he *is* married to Myra. No children. Abbott Construction, formerly AA Construction – old habits die hard. Let's have a look at the website. Here we are – pretty glossy. Quite impressive.' There were photographs of large-scale construction sites, people in yellow jackets and hard hats consulting over blueprints, a shot of a boardroom with serious men around a shiny table with a glimpse through the windows of a skyscape that could be any modern city's downtown.

'Do they look like generic pictures to you?' she said, frowning.

'Culled from the Internet, from Shutterstock?' Atherton said. 'You could be right. It has that feel. I can't see anyone who looks like Silverman in there.'

Swilley scrolled to the copyright line, very, very small down the bottom. 'And it hasn't been updated since last year.'

'What does that mean?' Slider asked.

'Maybe nothing. Maybe that they're not very busy.'

'Or it could mean the exact opposite,' said Atherton. 'Maybe they've got so much work on the books they don't need any new stuff coming in, so it doesn't matter whether the website's kept fresh or not.'

'Helpful,' said Slider. 'Well, given that it's the first new thing we've learned about Kimmelman, I think we'd better go and have a chat to Mr Silverman. Where's the office?'

'Fulham Palace Road.'

'Nice and handy. Give them a bell, see if he's in.'

The office was in a newish building of red brick and glass, at the Hammersmith end of the Fulham Palace Road – very nice, but you'd have needed a satellite link to get the window view in the website picture. Slider mentioned this to Silverman to break the ice, and he said, 'You misunderstand. Those pictures represent jobs we've done – offices we've built.' And he looked worried. 'Did you really not get that?'

'I'm sorry. My mind works a different way,' Slider said.

Silverman reminded him a bit of Porson, not to look at, but in his air of contained restlessness. He was obviously so full

of energy, or nerves, or possibly caffeine – there was a tall
mug steaming on his desk – that standing still was a penance
to him. His lean dark face was vivid, his hair seemed to have
a life of its own, and his hands were never still. They spent a
lot of time pushing his glasses up his nose and sliding them
down again, for near and remote vision. Well, Slider thought,
some people can't get on with bifocals. In the flesh, and with
the sunlight coming in from the window, he looked his age,
but not in a bad way. He was an attractive, mature man. He
offered coffee, which Slider refused.

'How is business?' Slider asked.

'Booming,' Silverman said promptly. 'Books full – amazing
how things have picked up. We had a tough time during the
recession, like everybody else, but it's all systems go, now.'
He gave Slider a curious look. 'Is that what you came to ask
me?' And he glanced at his watch, to let him know he was a
busy man with no time for wasting.

'No,' said Slider, and passed the *Telegraph* picture across.
'I wanted to ask you what you know about this man.'

Silverman looked at the picture for a long moment, frowning.
'Well, that's me at the front, so you must mean the person
behind me? I don't know him, I'm afraid.'

'He seems to be with you,' Slider said.

Silverman shook his head. 'He looks vaguely familiar, but
I can't place him. What was the occasion?'

'You don't remember?'

He smiled pleasantly. 'I'd need a few more clues than a
door in the background. Obviously a meeting of some kind,
but I go to plenty of those.'

'"Davy Lane Hopes Crushed",' Slider gave him the headline.

'Oh,' Silverman said, enlightened. 'Well, there were lots of
meetings – residents' associations, councillors, planning
committees. It could have been any of those. That must be
why the man looks slightly familiar – if he was at the meetings and I caught sight of him.'

'His name's Leon Kimmelman.'

Silverman shook his head slowly, looking at the picture.
'Doesn't ring a bell. Could be one of the residents, or a
solicitor or surveyor.' He smiled briskly and passed the picture

back. 'Sorry. Was there anything else?' He glanced at his watch again.

Slider didn't like being dismissed by people who thought they were busier than him, but there was no point in flogging a dead end, as Mr Porson might say.

'Not at the moment, thank you,' he said. He didn't mean anything by it, was only saving face, but was pleased to see a faint look of consternation at the thought that he might be bothered again slip across Silverman's good-looking face.

DC Phil Gascoyne had come up to the Department via the uniform side, much to the amusement and derision of his colleagues. The detectives called the uniforms woodentops, and the uniforms called the detectives bananas – yellow, bent, and go round in bunches. They thought Gascoyne in particular had a lot to betray, since he came from a long line of policemen. His grandfather had been in the mounted police working out of Hammersmith stables, his uncle and younger sister were in the Job in other parts of London, and his father, Harry 'Bob' Gascoyne, was an instructor at Hendon and had been a beat copper in Shepherd's Bush when walking the beat really meant something.

Gascoyne, however, was one of those serene people who know their own mind and go their own way without worrying what others think. He'd developed the desire to become a detective over a long period, and had achieved it. They could tease him all they liked – he just smiled genially as it rolled right off him.

It didn't mean, however, that he wasn't ready to use his contacts. His father, in particular, seemed to know everyone who had ever lived in and around the borough, and soon put him on to Tommy Rylance, who had been a trainer and fight promoter thirty years ago.

Gascoyne met him in the Stonemasons, just off Glenthorne Road. Like most Hammersmith pubs it had been, in Tommy's words, 'ponced up', but 'at least it was Fullers', he said, so young Phil could buy him a decent pint.

It was only just past opening time, but a retired man often found time hung heavy on his hands. At least the pub was quiet at that time of a Tuesday, so they could keep their conversation private. Like most pubs visited too early in the day, it had a hollow, echoey feel to it, an unrealness, like a theatre during daylight hours. In the old days it would also have had a smell of stale beer, but they cleaned everything with anti-germ spray these days, so it didn't really smell of anything at all.

Tommy Rylance had been a big man, but age had shrunk and bent him, giving him a curious shape inside his inevitable camel overcoat, as if he were concealing a lot of awkwardly-stuffed shopping bags under there. In deference to the poncing up, he removed his brown trilby inside the pub, revealing sparse hair carefully eked over his scalp, two cauliflower ears, and a face whose bumps and lopsidedness confessed a life in the ring before his life managing it.

He downed half the pint in one seamless action, put down the glass, wiped his watery eyes, and said, 'Aah! I was due that. Lovely! Now then, young Phil, whatja wanta know?'

Gascoyne produced the picture of Kimmelman. 'I've got a feeling this man might have been a boxer. Or if not, you might know him anyway.'

Rylance took the photo, felt inside his coat for his glasses, wiped them carefully, put them on, adjusted the picture to get the best light, tilted his head around for the best focus, sniffed, and said, 'Right then, let's have a gander.'

Gascoyne waited patiently. Patience was one of his best qualities as a policeman.

Rylance spoke at last. 'Maybe, maybe. Difficult with the eyes shut. You got a name?'

'Kimmelman. Leon Kimmelman.'

'Gor Blimey, yes, Kimmelman. I remember that name! No name for a fighter, that's what I told him back then. Lime Grove Baths, that's where I met him. Quiet chap, sort of brooding, if you know what I mean. Ex service.'

Well spotted, LaSalle, Gascoyne thought.

'Done his time in REME, got a useful trade,' Rylance went on, 'but when he come out, he couldn't settle to it. Seen a lot like that. Done a bit of boxing in the army, thought he could make his living that way. Change the name, I told him.

Something punchier, pardon my pun. So he went for King, on account he lived in King Street. Lennie King, the King of King Street.' He chuckled.

'*Lennie* King?' Gascoyne queried.

'No, I tell a lie. It wasn't Lennie. No, it was Leo – Leo the Lion, see, king of the jungle.' He shook his head. 'He thought too much, that was his trouble.'

'So, did you train him? Manage him?'

'Not as such. He had a trainer – Puggsy Littlejohn, at Lime Grove. Old Puggsy got me to look at him. I put him in a couple of fights, but I could see right away he wasn't going to work out. Nice lad, and he had the technique all right – the army's good for that – but he didn't have the drive, know what I mean? The killer instinct. You gotta be hungry when you go in the ring. Technique'll keep you from getting bad hurt, but you need fire in your guts to win and keep winning. I told him, you're never going to make it, professionally. Pure skill's all very well, but people pay to see a fight, not a points contest.'

'Do you know what happened to him?' Gascoyne asked.

'Well, he gave it up, that I do know. Yes, as I remember, he got himself a job driving. That's the other thing they teach you in the army – that, and how to shine shoes properly.' He grinned at his own jest. 'Yeah, he got a job driving for some limo hire company. And that's all I know. Never seen him from that day to this.' He met Gascoyne's eyes, his own faded and watery, but still direct and sharp. 'This photo – something happened to him? Looks like a whatjacall – corpse shot.'

'I'm afraid someone did for him.'

'Murdered?' Gascoyne nodded. Rylance studied the picture again. 'Shame. He wasn't a bad bloke. Quiet. Read books, as I remember. The sort of bloke that's good to his mother. Not that he ever mentioned a mother, mind you. Never mentioned any home life. How'd they do it?'

'A heavy blow to the back of the neck.'

'Ah,' said Rylance. 'Well, technique won't help you there. Can't guard against that.' He handed the picture back. 'I'll keep an ear open, and if I hear anything, I'll let you know. But don't hold your breath. Like I said, I never seen or heard of him since he left the ring, and that's gotta be – what? Thirty, forty year. How's your dad?'

'Just the same. You know Dad.'

'And your mum? Gor, she was a smasher when she was young! Gold hair and blue eyes and a smile that made your knees go wobbly. You look just like her, some lights. Old Bob was a lucky bloke, I always said. She all right?'

'She's fine. Still beautiful – *we* all think.'

'Well, give her my best.'

Atherton went up to the canteen for a quick lunch, grabbed a salad, looked around for somewhere to sit, and saw Hart on her own in a corner. She looked up as he approached and waved him to the seat opposite.

'You don't mind?' he said, sliding his plate and bottle of water off the tray.

'Solidarity,' she said. 'All sergeants togevver.'

'I see you've picked the salad, too,' he said, just to make conversation.

'Yeah, they was all out of ackee an' saltfish,' she said imperturbably, spearing a mini tomato and popping it in her mouth. 'I hate these buggers,' she remarked. 'Bite too soon an' they burst all down your front. So what's on your mind?'

'Why should there be anything on my mind?'

'It's not rocket science, is it? Pardon my pun. You didn't single me out to discuss my dietary choices. What's up?'

Atherton hesitated. 'Well – you're a woman,' he began.

'Thanks for noticing.' She grinned. 'It's going to be one of *those* conversations, is it?'

'I just wanted some advice,' he said huffily, 'but if it's a problem . . .'

'Oh, get over yourself!' she said with rough affection. 'Spit it out – I gotta go make some calls.'

He eyed her expression, but it didn't seem more than usually derisive. 'I just wondered,' he said cautiously, 'what it means when you catch a woman looking at the Mothercare website. Whether it's an ominous thing.'

'Nah. My mum does it all the time,' Hart said cheerfully. 'Mind you, she has got eight grandkids.'

'You're obviously not going to take this seriously,' he said.

'Women like looking at baby things,' she said. 'Doesn't mean anything.'

'Do you?'

'Me? Nah. I hate that stuff. Bleedin' goldfish mobiles and little romper suits. When I have a kid, I'm puttin' it in a sack in a drawer till it can dress itself an' hold a rational conversation.'

Atherton felt his way through this. 'But you do want to have kids?'

'Some time. Maybe. Probably. If I find the right bloke. What about you?'

'Me?' he said, alarmed.

Another eye roll. 'Not to father my children, dorkus. I ain't *that* keen on sergeants. I mean, d'you want kids?'

He thought a moment – sign, Hart thought, that it was a serious problem. 'I like the idea of, say, having a son, if he was about eight or nine, and I could take him to cricket matches and watch rugby with him and so on. It's the bits before that that worry me. And the bits after. If you could keep them between, say, eight and thirteen . . .'

'Yeah, but it don't work that way. I reckon you've got a problem, Jim. Who's freakin' you out? You got a girl up the duff?'

'No, but – I'm afraid that, if it's serious, I may get an ultimatum.'

'What, water my garden or piss off?' She nodded sympathetically. 'It could happen. And which way would you jump?'

'I don't know,' he said, staring at his plate.

She watched him for a moment, then got up, loading her empties onto her tray. She came round the table, and paused beside him. 'Comes a time,' she said, not unkindly, 'when pure bonking loses its charm, and you start to wonder if that's all there is to life. Females tend to get there first.' She patted his shoulder. 'Comes a time when you can't attract the females any more with nothing but your manly bod. Think about that.'

'I'm not there yet,' he said firmly.

'Course you're not.' She took a step past him, then paused and said, 'Here, you're startin' to go a bit thin on top, ain't you? Little bald spot startin' up here.'

'*What*! Where?' His hand flew up to his head, his startled face tilted up to her. 'God, I can't be! I'm not, am I?'

She grinned. 'Nah. I'm just messin' wiv your head.'

'You!'

'Made you think, though, didn't I?' she concluded, and went off, whistling.

LaSalle was pleased that his hunch about Kimmelman being in the army had turned out right.

'And he was trained in electronics,' Swilley said, 'so that explains him knowing how to set up the camera and stuff on the boat.'

'And seeing the house Rathkeale lives in,' Hart added, 'it looks as if he might have enough money to make him worth blackmailing.'

'But it doesn't get us any closer to who killed him,' Slider said.

'What about going through the pro boxing association – what's that called? Seeing if he's in their records?' Loessop said.

'British Boxing Board of Control,' Gascoyne supplied. 'But I don't suppose they go back that far.'

'Or the army,' said LaSalle.

'What could they tell you?' Swilley said impatiently. 'His address thirty-plus years ago? It's last week we want to know about.'

'Might get a next of kin out of it,' LaSalle said, a little sulkily.

'It might come to that,' Slider intervened, 'but I don't think we're that desperate yet. How are our other lines coming along?'

'I'm still going through the camera tapes, Hammersmith Road,' McLaren said. 'It's a slow business.'

'I'm still waiting for the bank records. I'll goose them up,' said Swilley.

'I've got Rathkeale's phone log, I'm going through it,' said Hart.

Fathom had been out to the Cheyne Walk moorings. 'There's not a security camera there, guv,' he said. 'I talked to the girl in the office and she said the gates are always locked, and anything else is up to the owners, security-wise. But she

did say there's no way the key to the *Rosita* could have been
stolen from the office. She says they're kept in the back room,
not on display, and the office is never left alone. I said,' he
looked slightly red, 'what about when she went to the bog,
and she said she'd lock the outside door, because they've got
a cash box in there as well.'

'Doesn't prove she'd necessarily remember to do it every
time,' McLaren objected. 'Women are always going off to
the lav, every five minutes. Don't tell me she never forgets,
or doesn't bother.'

'Honestly, Maurice! Who ties your shoelaces for you?'
Swilley said impatiently. 'How would Kimmelman know
which occasion she didn't lock the door, so as to be on hand
just at that one moment?'

'He could be hanging around watching,' McLaren defended
himself. 'He's only got to be in there long enough to take an
impression. Slip in and out in seconds. And I bet it wasn't
one moment. I bet she left it open lots of time.'

'We're not here to bet,' Slider said. 'Evidence is what we
want.'

'Guv, there is a traffic camera on the corner of Blantyre
Street that might cover it,' Fathom went on. 'Trouble is, there's
a lot of trees along there, and with the leaves still on, they
may get in the way.'

'Worth having a look, anyway,' Slider said. 'We've precious
little else.'

'What about this Davy Lane thing?' Atherton asked. 'It seems
to have been a couple of years ago, but that's better than thirty.
May be able to find some contacts of his through that.'

'Where *is* Davy Lane, anyway?' Gascoyne asked. 'I've never
heard of it.'

'Must be local, if it's in the *Telegraph*,' Atherton said.

'LaSalle, you're the local boy,' Slider prompted.

'I don't know any Davy Lane,' LaSalle admitted. 'I could
ask my mum.'

'You do that,' Slider said. 'And I'll ask Penny Duckham to
drag out anything she's got on it. There must be a history: if
it was "Davy Lane Hopes Crushed", they must have been rising
at some point.'

'You could ask Jack Silverman,' Atherton pointed out. 'If he was at the meeting, he must know.'

'Yes,' said Slider neutrally. 'But I think I'll try Penny first. Jack Silverman made it clear he was a very busy man. And I'd like to encourage her. She could be useful to us one day.'

ELEVEN

The Name of the Roads

LaSalle was back, just before home time. 'My mum's never heard of Davy Lane, either. And it's not in the A to Z. Maybe it's not local after all.'

Swilley followed him in closely. 'Boss, I think you'll want to see this.'

And Fathom nudged her out of the way. 'Guv, I've had an idea.'

Swilley looked at him without affection. 'Careful, Jezza. You know they give you headaches.'

Slider sorted it out. 'All right, LaSalle. Penny Duckham's looking into it for me. Yes, Fathom?'

Fathom gave Swilley a look of triumph, not appreciating that Slider had judged her offering as worthy of the most attention. 'Well, guv, that Blantyre Street camera, you can't see the actual boats through the trees. You can see cars coming along, but not which ones stop. So I thought, we know Kimmelman had a car outside Ivanka's to pick up the jolly-boys, and we know about what time, and there's a shit-load of cameras all over Soho. So what if I—?'

'Absolutely. Good thought,' said Slider. 'Go to it.'

'Tonight, guv? Overtime?' Fathom wheedled. 'There's never anybody there during the day.'

'All right, but don't push your luck. Now we've more or less cleared Rathkeale, Kimmelman's gone back to being a nobody, so we can't splash out on the budget.' Fathom went away, and Slider said, 'Now, Norma?'

She came round his desk to lay some sheets before him, giving him a whiff of her perfume – light and floral. Better than Fathom's mule-kick aftershave. 'Kimmelman's bank statements,' she said. 'The last twelve months.'

'That was quick. Your goosing obviously worked.'

'I know someone,' she said modestly. 'They ran it off for me. Anyway, look here – regular payment in, looks like salary from the amount. I'd have to go back further to be absolutely sure, and to see how long it's been going on. But you see who the payment is from?'

'Yes,' said Slider. 'Target. That is interesting.'

'And Target owned Jacket's Yard, so there's a connection there.'

'I wonder what they paid him for. You're going to have to have a look at them.'

'Yes, boss. There's nothing much else here to get hold of. The ground rent to Wiley's, and a regular sum into a savings account – he really *was* saving up for something, maybe his retirement – and a large withdrawal of cash every week. I suppose he paid cash for most things. Old habits die hard – some people just don't like credit cards. There is a direct debit payment to a NatWest credit card, but it's not very large. I can try and get hold of the statement and see what he spent on.'

'Yes, all right, do that,' Slider said, in a dissatisfied tone. 'May not help much. It would be better to have his phone and email records.'

He was just finishing up a couple of reports when his doorway darkened again, and Atherton's voice said, 'We have a visitor.'

'We?' he queried, looked up and saw Emily standing beside Atherton.

'I've got to go off to Paris tomorrow to cover the run-up to the French primaries,' she said, 'so I thought I'd better report to you before I go about what I've been doing.'

'As far as I'm aware you haven't been doing anything,' Slider said sternly, 'and "report" suggests some kind of formal arrangement, which there is not one of.'

Atherton grinned. 'Relax. Everyone's gone except for McLaren, and he's eating cheese and onion crisps. You can't earwig and crunch at the same time.'

'I'm establishing a principle,' Slider said with dignity. 'So, you've dropped in to see Atherton, have you?' he addressed Emily. 'How nice.'

'To pick him up. We're going out to eat, and then some late jazz,' she said. 'And you'll never guess what I've been doing, completely off my own bat and purely for my own interest. I've been looking into the background of a couple of chaps who, it turns out quite by chance, you might be interested in.'

'I can't guess who. Please go on,' Slider said politely.

She perched on the edge of his desk. She had gussied up her usual pleated cargo pants with a moss-green silk blouse and a chunky green necklace, and had her coarse black hair piled up messily on top of her head with combs, which softened the firm and characterful elements of her face, and allowed her warm brown eyes and sensationally sensual mouth to take the attention. You wouldn't call her pretty, and she probably wouldn't have wanted you to, but you could see why Atherton had fallen instantly in love with her and, being Atherton, had been fighting it ever since. Slider was married to a woman of purpose and character himself and was perfectly content with the situation, but Atherton seemed to think falling in love was the same as sinking into quicksand and had to be resisted *de tout coeur*. He had also been a bachelor for a long time and had got used to shooting from the hip, so to speak, when confronted with any sexually available woman, which a partner of purpose and character could not be happy with. But they seemed for the moment to have reached an accommodation – how long it would last, Slider couldn't guess.

'Leon or Leo Kimmelman or King I couldn't get anywhere on,' she confessed. 'There are plenty of people who fly under the radar despite the computer age, and he seems to be one of them. Sorry about that.'

'Don't apologise to *me*,' Slider said.

'Of course not. So I had a look at Rathkeale. You probably know most of it – his career and various brushes with contro-versy are well documented. I've compiled a digest, in case it's of interest to you.' She handed over a slim manila file. 'One thing you may like to know is that he's not in any financial bother, as far as one can tell. Apart from his salary from the GLA, he does speaking engagements – not in the Tony Blair league, but adequately lucrative – and he owns two properties in Leeds which he rents out, as well as a pretty spiffy house in Regent's Park. Despite living in Regent's Park, he bought a house in Hackney when he was an MP, got it done up on Parliamentary expenses, and then "flipped" so as to sell it tax free – this is one canny operator. Before he got elected to the Assembly he had a couple of directorships, which he had to stand down from as a requirement of the job, but they'd have brought him in money. He has an ex-wife and two children on partial support, but his current wife is a well-paid solicitor and they have no children to drain the purse. On the negative side, you now know he has a drug and rent-boys habit which must cost him, but he seems to have kept that quiet so far – I couldn't find any references to it in the media. I did manage to get hold of his agent, who happens to be someone who owes me a favour, and he put me on to a financial advisor who knows where Rathkeale's money is invested. He wouldn't tell me the details, but he reckons he's got non-real-estate assets in the million to million and a half region, and that there have been no recent, sudden, unexpected draws on them.'

'Which means,' Atherton put in, 'that he's just about worth blackmailing, but hasn't been yet.'

Emily said, 'A million surely isn't worth murdering for?'

And Slider said, 'Depends on your point of view. People commit murders for the most deeply inadequate reasons. My first case was the murder of an old man by his neighbour for his Post Office Savings account, which contained seven pounds fifty-three. It was worth it to her. She called the police herself, claiming she'd found him dead, but the bloody poker was lying on her kitchen table for all to see, and she had the savings book in her pocket.'

'Ah, life!' said Atherton. 'Hate it or ignore it, you can't love it. Well . . .' He straightened and stretched, preparatory to leaving.

'I haven't finished yet,' Emily stopped him. 'I got frustrated with not finding out anything interesting, so I had a go at your sinister boat owner, Charles Holdsworth.'

'In what way sinister?' Slider asked. 'As far as we know, he's got nothing to do with it. It's not a crime to own a houseboat.'

'It ought to be,' Emily said firmly, 'when you don't live in it, and it sits empty in a city with an intractable housing shortage.'

'Ah, there speaks my social conscience!' Atherton said, patting her.

'Remove that hand, or lose it,' she said. 'As I was saying, I was frustrated, and happened to remember the name from what Jim was wittering on about—'

'I *never* witter!'

'So I stuck him in. And that was quite interesting. Not that your Charles Holdsworth seems to be a criminal character, but there were a lot of references to a Charles Edward Holdsworth, who turns out to be his son, and he's a bit of a live wire. Drugs – possession mostly, but with the change in the law a couple of dealing charges as well. Shoplifting. Breaking and entering. Breaking bail – that must have cost dad a bit, because he'd stood bail for him. His last drugs bust they changed tactics and spared him gaol if he went into rehab, and the court records show he was registered at the Bishop's Palace centre in Hertfordshire, one of the most expensive and exclusive clinics there is. A lot of stars go there. I'm guessing C.E. Holdsworth didn't pay for that himself. And in between the official legal tangles, who knows what private money had to be dished out to support the lad and get him out of trouble. Well,' she stopped herself, 'I say "lad", but he's well in his thirties. A hopeless case, one would guess.'

'Hmm. Interesting,' Slider said, 'but I'm not sure how it affects our case.'

She shrugged. 'Only that people who are badly short of money can teeter on the edge of criminality. The house in Luxemburg Place is worth a good bit, but it's mortgaged up to the hilt – a second mortgage was taken out to cover the increase in value just fourteen months ago. And even the boat's got a loan against it, which means he couldn't sell it if he wanted to. So big Chaz is up against it, financially. A good fat blackmail could look like a tempting prospect to a man with a grown-up son to put through finishing-school – and he does own the boat where the naughty film was taken.'

'Yes, you're right. It *is* interesting,' said Slider, thinking hard. 'But we haven't yet got any evidence of a connection between Holdsworth and Kimmelman. I suppose you're suggesting Kimmelman was doing the blackmail on Holdsworth's behalf?'

'I'm not suggesting anything,' Emily said blandly.

'Yes, you are,' said Atherton. 'But don't forget, if Kimmelman was doing the deed *for* Holdsworth, Holdsworth would be unlikely to kill him. And it's the killer we're after. And that keeps bringing us back to Rathkeale, who's the only one with a motive.'

'But as far as we know, he didn't know he'd been filmed, hasn't accessed any big money, and has an alibi for the Sunday in question,' Slider said with dissatisfaction.

'On which note,' Atherton said, 'we'll bid you adieu. Top nosh and hot jazz awaits.'

'Want to come with?' Emily asked, hitching herself off the desk.

'Tempting,' Slider said, 'but I've got supper in the oven and a whole box of *Mad Men* I haven't watched yet.'

'Which means you'll spend the evening going over the case,' Atherton said. 'But you can stare at your notes until your eyebrows hurt, without getting any further forward. Much better come out and refresh yourself.'

'Joanna's working,' Slider said. 'I'm babysitting. Thanks all the same.'

'Well, if you change your mind, we'll be at Ronnie's. Bring George with you – it'll do him good to start him early on the good stuff.'

Atherton was right, of course, that not much of *Mad Men* got watched. Slider couldn't follow it, anyway. There was always too much of a hiatus between his watchings, so he could never remember who anyone was. And Atherton was right that reading and re-reading his notes didn't make any conclusions leap, salmon-like, up the falls of his consciousness. Joanna

– or more likely Dad, since she'd had a double session, two-till-five and six-till-nine – had left him shepherd's pie in the oven, and there were vegetables ready to cook, but he was too lazy, and just ate the pie on its own with a spoon out of the dish. He felt guilty about it afterwards, but knowing that he *would* had not been enough to make him do the thing properly, which of course was always the trouble with guilt – by its nature it operated *ex post facto*.

Joanna got home at a quarter to ten, bubbling with her afternoon and evening. Session work was always fun because you got to play with the best, most professional – and often the most irreverent – musicians on the circuit. There was always a great atmosphere. But she took one look at her husband's aspect, grey and brooding as a large heron on a cold lake, and sat down meekly with him to watch the ten o'clock news and then go to bed. Once in bed, the proximity of her warm and pliant body dragged him back from his thoughts, so the evening ended well for them both.

In the morning, he had to face a meeting with Mr Porson, who was facing a meeting at Hammersmith and of the two was the more to be pitied.

'Ten days now,' he reminded Slider, 'and you seem to be going nowhere. You ought to be seeing the light for the trees by now.'

'We have pretty much eliminated Rathkeale from our enquiries,' Slider said, as it was the part that had most exercised his boss.

Porson was not deflected. 'What do you mean, pretty much?' He glared. 'Either he is or he isn't.'

'I mean, we don't think he could have been responsible for the murder. But I still feel there has to be a connection there, though I can't put my finger on it yet.'

'What *can* you put your finger on?'

Slider stared away over Porson's shoulder, working his jaw. It didn't help. 'I can't say,' he admitted at last. 'There's something going on, a link between Kimmelman's blackmail activities and the bigger picture, but I can't see it yet.'

'Bloody hell, Slider,' Porson exploded, though fairly mildly all things considered, 'don't tell me you've got a hunch! What am I supposed to tell 'em upstairs? We've got budget decisions coming up that'd set your hair on edge, more reorganisations in the pipeline, and you've got a *hunch*?'

'I didn't say that, sir,' Slider objected mildly. 'But you know how it is. All the information doesn't come to light at the same time, but you know it's there.'

'*I* know how it is,' Porson said. 'The buggers who pay our wages don't. You may have got Rathkeale out of it, but that just leaves us with Kimmelman, who's nobody.'

'Murder is always a priority,' Slider reminded him, daringly.

But Porson only muttered, 'Tell your grandmother.' He did a couple of brisk turns to settle his mind, and said, 'All right, I'll think of something to tell them. But if this does turn out to be nothing, Gawd help us all. You've got our entire Department on it, and everything else piling up behind like a blocked lav.'

Graphic, Slider thought, as he went away.

He met Nutty Nicholls, one of the relief sergeants, coming along the corridor. Nicholls, a handsome, polyphiloprogenitive Scot from the far north west, had an accent as soft as sea mist and eyes as blue as hyssop flower. He was a star of the Hammersmith police am-dram society, and much in demand when they did musicals as he not only had a fine tenor but could also sing in a true falsetto, and sopranos were scarce in the Met. When they'd done *The Sound of Music*, he'd played Maria. When he sang 'The Hills Are Alive', there wasn't a dry seat in the house.

Slider paused in front of him. 'You've lived round here a long time, Nutty. Ever heard of a place called Davy Lane?'

He considered. 'It rings a bell, but I can't remember why.'

'It's not in the A to Z.'

'Roads have their names changed sometimes. I tell you what, now: one of our volunteer ladies at the Dramatics is president of the local history society. Ada Forster is her name. She's lived here all her life. Knows every inch. Would you like me to ask her to give you a ring?'

'Thanks, Nutty. That'll help.'

'Well, I'll just be doing that, then,' he said, at his most

lyrically Gaelic. He sounded like Duncan Macrae as Pipe Major Maclean in *Tunes of Glory*. 'As a favour to you.'

'Uh-oh,' said Slider. 'Favour?' He narrowed his eyes. 'What were you doing up here, anyway?'

Nutty smiled caressingly. 'Just selling the tickets for our next endeavour. An operetta based on the works of Beatrix Potter. A delight for the whole family. Some children from the Barbara Speake will be dancing in it, in animal costumes. And all for a good cause, Bill, as you know fine well.'

Nutty was too good at this, Slider reflected. He seemed to bypass your mind and go straight to your inside top pocket. He'd bought two tickets before he knew what he was doing. Well, he could always make Dad and Lydia go. Although it could often be worth the pain, to see Nutty in a dress and bonnet.

'So what part are you doing in it?' he asked, as they were parting.

Nicholls paused. 'I shall be playing a certain Mrs Puddleduck.'

'Jemima?'

'No, I'm doing the voice as well,' said Nutty.

Slider couldn't help feeling he'd been manoeuvred into that.

But Nicholls was as good as his word, and only ten minutes later his phone rang, and a very fruity voice asked for Chief Inspector Slider.

She introduced herself as Ada Forster.

'Our most talented Mr Nicholls said that you'd be interested in learning something about Davy Lane. Is now a good time?'

'Yes, indeed. Please go ahead. I couldn't find Davy Lane on the A to Z.'

'Ah, well, you wouldn't,' she said. 'The name was changed in the nineteenth century, when the railways came. It's called Coal Sidings Road now.'

Enlightenment. 'Oh, yes, I know where that is. Round the back of the station.'

'Quite so. Not such a pretty name, is it? It's no wonder the residents want to change it back.'

Having placed Coal Sidings Road in his mental geography, he was trying for some context. He didn't think he'd ever been down it, but had he heard anything about it? Had there been trouble there, or a recent case, or an historic murder?

While he was thinking, she had taken the pause as an invitation to continue. 'The road didn't exist at all until the 1780s,' she explained. 'At that time, Shepherd's Bush was little more than a village, though it was on an old droving route. But London was expanding, and there were new houses springing up as far west as Kensington and Notting Hill. So a speculative builder called Horace Davy decided to buy a piece of land at the edge of the village and put up some houses.'

'Hence the name,' Slider said intelligently.

'Just so. It was called variously Davy's Lane and Davy Lane on old maps. But an apostrophe "s" often gets lost, and by the 1820s it was always written as Davy Lane. He built ten rather handsome terraced houses, five on either side, of three storeys plus semi-basement. Meant for the aspirant middle classes. That is to say, people with two or three servants, who did not keep their own carriage but hired one when required. Prosperous people, but not upper class.'

'I understand.'

'It must have been rather a pleasant lane, just off the Green. The Green was already there, of course, and regarded as a valuable local resource, making Shepherd's Bush an attractive place to live.'

'And then the railways came?'

'Indeed. In the mid-nineteenth century. It was a brutal time, architecturally. The whole of the east side of the road was demolished for sidings and railway sheds. By then, of course, Shepherd's Bush had changed, expanded, and the aspirant middle classes had moved elsewhere. The road began to be referred to as Coal Sidings Road, and when the Local Government Act of 1899 put such things into the control of the borough, the name was changed permanently.'

'What a shame,' he said politely.

'I believe it has become rather rundown now,' Mrs Forster

went on. 'There was a move to change the name back to Davy Lane – oh – about ten years ago, if I remember, but nothing came of it.'

'"Davy Lane Hopes Crushed",' Slider murmured.

'I beg your pardon?'

'Nothing – just something I heard recently. Well, thank you very much for your help, Mrs Forster.'

'Not at all. Our little society, Friends of Hammersmith Local History, has produced a series of pamphlets, rather attractive and informative if I may say so. I could send you a copy of the one on Shepherd's Bush.'

'That's very kind. Thank you. I'm sorry, I must go – my other phone's ringing.'

He actually didn't have another phone, but Gascoyne was standing enquiringly in his doorway making the telephone gesture with his little finger and thumb. And it got him away from someone with more detail than he needed at the moment.

'I've got one on hold for you, sir,' Gascoyne said as he put the phone down. 'I'll switch it through.'

Wednesday was steak and kidney pie in the canteen, one of the few things they did well. They did a proper pie, not just meat with a circle of industrial heat-expanded puff pastry laid on top of it at the point of serving. It came with mashed potatoes, carrots and cabbage. 'I give you extra steakankidney, love,' said Marge, the canteen cook, with a motherly look, as she handed over his plate, her thumb planted firmly in the gravy. He found an empty table and ingested slowly, letting his mind float. Things sometimes joined up if you didn't strain after them. The glorious juices had soaked into the underside of the shortcrust pastry lid, so it was crisp on one side and decadent on the other. Davy Lane till the railways came . . . Leo the Lion, King of King Street . . . Jacket's Yard and the *Anna Rosita* . . . Jemima Puddleduck . . .

He jerked back from the brink of sleep. That was the trouble with eating when you were hungry, your blood all decamped to your stomach on detached duty. He had the feeling he'd been on the brink of a breakthrough, but it was probably just the beginning of a dream. He finished up and headed back to the office where he wouldn't be left alone for long enough to fall asleep.

Penny Duckham rang him shortly after his return. 'I know where Davy Lane is now,' she began triumphantly.

'So do I,' Slider said. 'I had a chat with a local historian this morning.'

'Oh,' she said, disappointed. Then, hopeful that he might have got it wrong, 'It's Coal Sidings Road, you know.'

'Yes, I know.'

'So you know all about it?'

'Only up to the mid-nineteenth century. It's the last few weeks or months I want to know about.'

She cheered up. 'Oh, right! Well, in that case – I've got hold of the chair of the Davy Lane Residents Action Committee.'

'Only one chair? The rest of them stand up at meetings, do they?'

'Ha ha,' she said sourly. 'You know what I mean. Anyway, she knows all about what's been going on. I've told her about you, and she said she's happy to talk to you, and either she'll come in, or you can go and see her, whichever you like. She said she'd meet you at Coal Sidings Road if you prefer. I've got her mobile number – you got a pencil?'

He wrote it down, thinking that perhaps he would go and meet her, for the chance of seeing the road. He was interested in architecture, and there weren't many eighteenth-century terraces left in Shepherd's Bush. Also there weren't many roads on the patch that he hadn't walked down at least once, and this was one of them.

'So – what's this got to do with the murder?' Penny asked in a hungry voice.

'I don't know. Probably nothing. But if Kimmelman went to a meeting about it, maybe this committee will know something about him, and give us a lead.'

'Gosh, that's tenuous,' she said.

'Welcome to my world,' said Slider.

TWELVE
Winsome, Lose Some

S lider must have driven past the end of Coal Sidings Road hundreds of times, but had never noticed it one way or the other. Approaching on foot, he saw why. It was a narrow road, and on its right side, the eastern side, was defined by the long blank wall of the rebuilt and enlarged underground station. On the left, western side, the corner plot was occupied by the Victorian building which was the end of the terrace fronting the Green: red brick with white copings, and a sort of decorative turret on the upper floor where the building went round the corner. There had been a shop on the ground floor, but it was boarded up – the whole ground floor was boarded up – and the upper floors appeared to be empty, another reason one wouldn't notice it in passing. It gave the place a forlorn look, as unused buildings always do.

He turned into the street, and saw that it ended in the blank grey wall of the vast shopping centre that reared a hundred feet up into the sky, dwarfing everything around it and blighting the view. He thought, as he always did when contemplating the massive retail footage of the Westfield centre, *Who could need that many more shops?* The whole of the centre of Shepherd's Bush, all round the Green, was lined with shops, they extended seamlessly for miles all down Uxbridge Road and Goldhawk Road out to Acton and Ealing, and all the way down Shepherd's Bush Road to Hammersmith Broadway and thence on to Fulham, Chiswick and into central London . . . You could walk non-stop from shop to shop without a break, except to cross a side street, for years and not come to the end of them. But apparently no one's life had been complete without the 1.6 million square feet of new retail opportunities – the size, he thought he had read somewhere, of thirty football pitches. No wonder there were boarded-up

shops out here in the real world, where you could get rained
on, and you couldn't park.

And now, beyond the dead shop, he could see the remains
of the original terrace. Five houses either side, Mrs Forster
had said. The eastern side had been sacrificed for the railway,
and of the western side, there were four viable houses left –
the fifth, furthest down the road, had boarded-up windows and
high hoardings all the way round at street level to keep vandals
out. In between, bracketed by the desolation, the flat greyish-
yellow brick Georgian façade with the handsome tall windows
stared patiently at eternity. Two storeys, plus attic, plus semi-
basement, steps going up to the front door. They were occupied,
as was evident from the curtains in windows and the cars
along the kerb in residents' parking bays, but they looked
neglected and shabby, with peeling paint and chipped steps
and slipped slates on the roof. It was a tragedy, he thought,
to let something so venerable and fine deteriorate like this.

'Sad, isn't it?' said a voice behind him.

He turned. 'I was just thinking that,' he said. It was a small
elderly woman in an expensive grey coat, red muffler around
her throat, leather gloves, polished court shoes. Her silver hair
was drawn straight back to a bun at the nape of the neck like
a ballet dancer's, a style only those with 'good bones' could
carry off. Her face was sculpted and elegant, with dark eyes.
She must have been beautiful when she was young, he thought.
'Mrs Fontaine?'

'Isobel Fontaine,' she said, offering her hand. 'Like the
ballerina, but with an a-i-n-e. How did you guess?'

'I was expecting to meet you here. Chief Inspector Slider.'
They turned together to look up at the terrace again. '1780s.
George III,' he said.

'You know?'

'Architecture is a hobby of mine.'

She smiled. It was a lovely smile. 'I didn't think policemen
nowadays had time for hobbies. It would have been better for
it if it had been some other period,' she went on. 'Late Georgian
is too austere for most people's taste. Too unornamented.'

'It's all in the proportions,' he said. 'What more could you
want than complete harmony?'

'You understand,' she said gratefully. 'I've loved these houses for as long as I can remember, and fought for them for . . . oh, a ridiculous length of time.'

'You live here?'

'Not any more,' she said, with a hint of bitterness. 'But if you'd like to see inside one, I do know the occupants.'

'Perhaps another time,' he said. He could imagine what they ought to look like, and was afraid that they might have been let go, like the exterior, which might break his heart. 'I would like to hear the story, though.'

'I'm yours to command,' she said graciously. 'There's a long version and a short version.'

'Long version, please,' he said.

'Then perhaps we could sit down? There's a café round the corner.'

'You have to go back twenty years or so for the root of the problem,' Mrs Fontaine said.

The Italian café was quite new, starkly modern, and smelled so agreeably – and appropriately – of coffee, that Slider, who was not much of a coffee drinker, had ordered it for himself, instead of tea. In his experience, anyway, places like this couldn't make tea properly. They used hot water, instead of boiling, and served it in wide shallow cups so it was cold before you got halfway down it. If tea wasn't too hot to drink, in his view, it wasn't hot enough.

They had some nice-looking Danish pastries at the counter, so he bought two and carried the tray back to the table in the window where Mrs Fontaine was waiting.

'Lovely, thank you,' she said as he put the pastry down in front of her. He honoured her for not saying, 'Oh, I shouldn't really,' or 'Have to watch my waist,' or any of the other whimsical get-out-of-greed-free cards women seemed to feel obliged to play.

'So, twenty years ago – you're talking about the nineties?' Slider asked.

She nodded. 'There was a recession, if you remember, and a period of high interest rates. It pushed mortgage repayments up, people had no spare money, and houses like those in Davy

Lane are expensive to maintain. Things started to get a little
shabby and rundown. The end house was sold and the new land-
lord broke it up into bedsitters. And of course that just accelerated
its decline. There were some railway buildings at the far end of
the street, where the old coal wharf had been, and when their
windows got broken by vandals, they resolved the problem by
concreting them over, which was not a pretty sight. So, by the
end of the decade, the street was not looking at its best.'

'I can imagine.'

'We had a Labour council at that time, and a rather Marxist
element got control,' she went on. 'They disapproved of private
ownership, and seeing that Davy Lane was in need of refurbishment, they took the opportunity to compulsorily purchase
the five houses, with the intention of turning them into council
flats.'

'Pull them down, you mean?' Slider asked.

'That was the original intention. But there wasn't much
money around, if you remember, and when that idea proved
too expensive, the plan was modified, and each house was to
be divided into four separate flats for council tenants. But they
couldn't find the money even for that, and things drifted on
in a state of limbo. Meanwhile, the former owners were allowed
to stay on as tenants.'

'And you were still there?'

'At that point, yes. I had teenage children and my mother
and mother-in-law were both living with us, so I didn't want
the disruption of moving.'

'Of course. So what happened next?'

'A change of council control. The Conservatives got in,
there was a revival of interest in things antique, and the houses
got listed.'

'Grade II?'

She nodded. 'But there still wasn't any money for refurbishment, and the council was trying to retrench, so they sold
Davy Lane to a property company. The hope was that *they*
would do the refurbishing, and we all felt frightfully bucked
at the prospect.'

'But what would your situation have been, in that case?'
Slider asked.

'Oh, you put your finger on it. Of course, we had no security of tenure, and if they *had* brought the houses back to their true beauty, we'd have been moved out and they would have been sold for far more than we could afford to pay for them. But we loved them, you see, and we'd sooner see them made beautiful, even if it meant losing them.'

'*The Little Mermaid*,' Slider commented.

She raised an eyebrow, and then got the reference. 'Oh yes – she couldn't kill the prince, even though it meant her own destruction. Well, I perhaps wouldn't go that far, but I allow the comparison. In the end, of course, it came to nothing.'

'"Davy Lane Hopes Crushed"?'

'I beg your pardon?'

'A newspaper headline.'

'Ah. Yes, well, nothing happened for a long time after the sale, and eventually we residents got together and demanded a meeting with the owner, and it turned out that they'd never had any intention of refurbishing. They bought the houses to knock them down and build a new block of luxury flats, but they'd run into trouble with the listing. They'd assumed they could get it overturned, but at the meeting they revealed that the council was refusing to budge. And in fact, a few months later the council added Davy Lane to the Conservation Area, which laid even greater protections on it.'

'You must have been happy about that.'

'Well, yes and no. It meant there was less chance of the owners developing the site, but if they weren't prepared to put the money into refurbishment – which apparently they weren't – we were no better off. And if they sold it with the protections in place, what chance was there that the new owners would want to refurbish? We were trapped with our unsympathetic landlords. It was at that point that I moved out.'

'But you stayed on as chairman of the action committee?'

'For what good it did. The houses were continuing to deteriorate, and in fact number five, the end house, got so dilapidated that it had to be vacated. When the owners boarded it up, we saw what they intended to do – let the whole row get so bad they'd fall down, and then the council would *have* to allow them to develop. It happened in Camden some years ago, if you remember. There was a big scandal about it at the time.'

'I remember. So the council didn't help at all?'

'Well, we protested to them, as well as to the owners, but they weren't really interested. By then they were getting excited about Westfield and the station rebuild, and I think they thought that if our terrace got fatally damaged in the mean time, it would be a problem solved.'

'And what is the situation now?'

'We're in limbo. The council have reaffirmed their commitment to the listing and the conservation zoning, but they say day-to-day repairs are not their business and it's up to us to pressure the owners. They won't let the houses be knocked down, but they won't do anything to help us keep them up. And of course you never talk to the same person twice, so every time, you have to tell the whole story all over again. Then that person says they'll look into it and get back to you, and of course they don't, so you send more emails, and telephone again, and a new person picks it up.' She sighed. 'It's like walking up a down escalator.'

'And the owners?'

'They're even worse. At least the council has an official duty and a stated aim to reply to you within a certain period, even if they fail to live up to it. The owners don't have to talk to you at all. And they don't. Complete absence of communication. Letters and emails go unanswered, and the phone is always on an answering machine. The only reason the other occupants are still there is sheer stubbornness. They know that if they move out it will delight the owners, because then they can leave the houses empty until they fall down. We're all determined not to be beaten, but we haven't anything else in our arsenal now.' She sighed again, and cut the last of her pastry in two with her fork. 'I'm afraid unless we get another change of council we're doomed. Labour's in again at the moment, and they don't care as much for antiquities – not deep down. And with all this public clamour for more housing, they might find it in their hearts to get rid of the protections in a good cause.'

There was a silence as they both finished off their pastries. Then she said, 'Can you tell me why you wanted to know all this? You mentioned a newspaper headline – what made you think of that?'

He brought out the newspaper picture and passed it across. 'It concerns this man,' he said. 'We're trying to find out more about him.'

'Oh, I remember this,' she said. 'Yes, our hopes *were* crushed. That was the meeting I mentioned, when we got the owners to talk to us at last, and they revealed they wanted to demolish and redevelop.'

'Is that the owner – the man in front?'

'No, he was from the building firm, the one that was actually going to build the new block. A very sharp operator, I thought him. I'm sure his firm was going to do well out of it. Silverman, his name was. AA Construction.'

'They've changed the name now to Abbott Construction,' Slider said. It didn't seem to mean anything to her. He reached across and tapped Kimmelman. 'What about this man? Was he with Silverman?'

She peered, then straightened. 'Oh, I recognise him. No, he was there with the owner. I don't think he was anyone important – I think he was just the driver. We saw him a few times, when they made visits to the street. He'd be sort of following them about.' She smiled. 'Rather like a bodyguard. In case we started throwing bricks, I suppose. I don't think I ever spoke to him, but he looked rather a tough.' She looked up. 'What's he done?'

'I'm afraid he's got himself killed.'

'Killed? In an accident?'

'It wasn't an accident.'

'Oh,' she said. She thought a moment. 'I'm sorry – you can't be thinking any one of us – on the Action Committee, I mean – could have had anything to do with it? We're desperate, but not to the point of committing murder.'

'No, I wasn't thinking that,' Slider said. 'This man – Leon Kimmelman is his name – is a bit of a mystery, and we're having difficulty in finding out anything about him. This picture was one of the few records we found of him, so we hoped if

he was involved with the Davy Lane project, one of you might
have known him.'

She shook her head. 'Only by sight. He was just a figure
at the back of the hall, if you know what I mean. Gave the
impression of being a loyal bulldog, that's all.' She looked at
the picture again. 'You can just see, in the shadow, his boss
coming out, and he's walking in front.' She looked up and
smiled. 'Like those FBI chaps who walk in front of the
President of America, in case anyone shoots at him. Absurd!'

Whether the absurdity was hers, or Kimmelman's, he wasn't
sure. 'And who was the owner?' he asked.

'A property company called Target,' she said. 'In the person
of somebody called Holdsworth, Charles Holdsworth. One of
those people who is all charm, except that their smile doesn't
touch their eyes. A real politician.'

'He was an MP?'

'No, I mean he was practiced in the political arts.'

'A schmoozer?' Slider tried.

'Yes – good word.'

'And Kimmelman was his driver?'

'Yes, driver. Bodyguard. General bag-carrier, something like
that. The man at his elbow.'

'Interesting,' said Slider. It explained why Kimmelman was
paid a salary by Target. It didn't explain why Holdsworth said
he didn't recognise him.

'So who on earth would want to kill him?' Mrs Fontaine
went on. 'Are you sure it wasn't an accident?'

'It's certain that someone hit him. Whether they intended
to kill him we can't tell, but they certainly intended to do him
serious harm.'

'And you think it was something to do with Target?'

'We don't know that.'

'Well, if they behaved over other properties as they did over
Davy Lane, they'd have made plenty of enemies,' she said.

Slider decided to round off the day with a visit to Abbott
Construction. Jack Silverman was not in the office, but he
spoke to a very helpful young woman who evinced a refreshing
lack of suspicion when he showed his warrant card – indeed,

she brightened up, as though her day had been dull so far and she hoped Slider might represent a change of speed.

'Coal Sidings Road? Oh, that's one of the zombies. That's what we call them,' she explained with a grin. 'The living dead – stuck in limbo waiting for planning permission. The planning system in this country's a nightmare,' she offered, free of charge. 'They're always complaining about not enough houses being built, but it can take a couple of years to get a new development through planning, which plays havoc with your cash flow.'

'I imagine so,' Slider said encouragingly. 'But Coal Sidings Road – is there a particular problem with that?'

'Some old listed buildings,' she said promptly. 'Hopeless case. I always say it's not the living dead, it's the dead dead.'

'So there's no chance of getting the listing removed?'

'Not an earthly. I don't think the owner's even trying any more. That one's dead in the water, believe me. It'll never get built. Which is a shame, because it was a good plan. A youth outreach centre on the street level, with a gym and theatre and *everything*, and luxury flats on the floors above. There was some question about the roof line being too high, but there's always ways round that – parapets and set-backs and so on. And anyway, Westfield has made that sort of thing moot anyway.' She shrugged.

'It must be a disappointment for your boss,' Slider suggested.

'Well, yes,' she allowed, 'because we're not exactly snowed under with work, but there you are. You win some, you lose some,' she concluded with a perky smile, and the ease of someone happily on Schedule E for whom profit and loss was someone else's problem.

Abbott had some parking down a service road round the back of the building, where Slider had left his car, and as he was driving out he passed an incoming black Mercedes. The driver, as Slider saw when they were still approaching each other, was Jack Silverman, but he decided on the instant not to stop and talk to him – time was getting on and he had a meeting to go to this evening. Silverman didn't seem to register him until they were actually passing, when he glanced sideways at him and then did a double-take. Slider kept looking ahead, rather than have to acknowledge him, and was past and out into the side street in a jiffy.

Back at the factory, he relayed his information about Davy Lane to his assembled troops.

'Target again,' Atherton said. 'Everywhere we go, we stub our toes on them.'

'It gets better,' said Swilley. 'I'm still looking into them, but you know the chap at Blenheim said they'd been divesting? Well, he wasn't wrong. It's just a shell company now – no economic activity for nearly two years. And what I was going to tell you,' she interrupted Atherton, who had opened his mouth to speak, 'is that the directors of Target are Charles Holdsworth, Mrs A Holdsworth, and C.E. Holdsworth.'

'A family company,' Gascoyne remarked, scribbling on the whiteboard.

'So Holdsworth owns Target, which paid Kimmelman a salary, and he didn't know about it,' said Atherton. 'Very lax accounting practice.'

'I'd like to find out who Target sold Davy Lane to,' Swilley went on. 'Because if it's such a dud, who would buy it? Wouldn't it be interesting if he sold it to Farraday?'

'But he owns Farraday,' McLaren objected. 'He'd be selling to himself. What's the point of that?'

'If he sells it for less than he bought it for, he consolidates the loss,' Swilley said impatiently. McLaren continued to look obtuse. 'Tax dodge,' she translated.

'Oh!' he said, enlightened.

'That's pure speculation,' said Atherton. 'And, if it were true, peculation.'

'What are you talking about?' Swilley asked impatiently.

'He's blinding you wiv vocab – pay no attention,' said Hart. 'What I want to know is, what's the point of all this property development bollocks anyway? What's it got to do with Kimmelman? It's his murder we're interested in, not some trashy old buildings.'

Slider managed not to wince, and merely murmured, 'Georgian.'

'Holdsworth said he didn't recognise Kimmelman or know

his name,' Atherton pointed out. 'He denied him thrice before cock-crow.'

'That's only twice,' Swilley objected.

'Give him time,' said Atherton. 'I'm prepared to allow that a director doesn't necessarily know all the people he employs, but when it comes to his own driver, surely even the biggest egotist would have a vague feeling he'd seen him somewhere before?'

'Certainly friend Holdsworth is becoming more interesting,' said Slider.

'But what's it got to do with the *murder*?' Hart said irritably. 'And the blackmail on Gingernuts Rathkeale?'

'How d'you know his—?' Fathom began, and Atherton cut in hastily.

'Maybe nothing,' he said. 'Maybe Kimmelman was just an annoying bloke and somebody got fed up with him and clobbered him. But we can only go on what we know, and we know Holdsworth lied about knowing him.'

'Can we go after him, boss?' Swilley asked eagerly. 'Holdsworth?'

'Don't get carried away,' Slider said. 'Remember we don't have any direct evidence against him. I don't see any harm in popping round to ask him why he doesn't know someone who worked for him, but we don't want to frighten the horses. If he *is* guilty of something, I'd sooner he thought we didn't know about it. He's more likely to give himself away if we don't put him on his guard.'

'Be subtle, you mean,' said Atherton.

'Well, that lets you out,' Swilley said.

'What are you talking about? Subtlety is my USP.'

'You kidding me?' Hart broke in, out of solidarity. 'You got copper writ all over you from your face to your size elevens. Honest but stupid, that's what the guv'nor wants.'

'Let me go, boss,' said Swilley.

He smiled at her. 'No one's ever going to think you're stupid.'

'She's got the tits for it,' Hart answered for her. 'You'd be amazed how many men never look above or below the bust line. I'd offer to go, but my suntan might upset him.'

'You can go,' Slider said to Swilley. 'I don't mind you using your assets.'

'She can swing that, an' all,' Hart commented.

'Just don't overdo it,' said Slider. 'We don't want you pounced on. Meanwhile—' he turned to Atherton – 'see what you can find out from the council about Davy Lane and the whole development issue. I'm remembering that Rathkeale was a councillor—'

'Not in Hammersmith. That was Leeds.'

'I know. But I'm stuck with the nagging feeling that Rathkeale comes into it somewhere. Maybe he had connections with more than one council. The one thing we know about Kimmelman is that he was involved in blackmailing Rathkeale.'

'Thank Gawd,' Hart said, rolling her eyes, 'someone's remembering where all this started.'

'Where it started was Jacket's Yard and Gypsy Eli,' Atherton objected.

'Pick, pick, pick! Rathkeale is still number one suspect, an' the fact his motor never moved that Sunday just makes him look tastier to me.'

'You have an untutored palate,' said Atherton.

She grinned. 'Yeah, it's all that curry goat and okra. Gawd, you're a right old colonialist sometimes!'

THIRTEEN

In Which We Swerve

There were still two cars parked on the frontage, suggesting the occupants were in. After she rang the bell, there was such a long hiatus that Swilley thought the door wasn't going to be answered, but at last there was a shadow on the glass, another long pause, and then it opened. She would have expected a cardigan and carpet-slipper aspect, but the man – Charles Holdsworth, from Atherton's description

– was fully dressed in suit and tie, hair neatly brushed, clean shaven with a whiff of aftershave. His face looked worn and there were bags under his eyes, but at the sight of her he put on the sort of lizard smile that men of that age and class always have available for attractive women they think slightly beneath them. It was meant to be roguish. The words, 'what's a lovely young lady like you doing, visiting an old fogey like me?' seemed to hover in the air above him. If he says, 'what a lucky chap I am', I'm going to deck him, she thought.

'Mr Holdsworth, I'm Detective Constable Swilley. From Shepherd's Bush,' she said.

His mouth kept smiling, but the rest of his face didn't want anything more to do with it and moved pointedly away. 'Ah,' he said. 'And what can I do for *you*?' There was just enough emphasis on the 'you' to indicate that she was one of a long line of people bothering him, and that they had used up her share of his patience before she even got there. His eyes inside their pouched and wrinkled lids were like a chameleon's, and his mouth had as much humour. At any moment a long and muscular tongue might flick out, stick itself to her forehead and reel her in.

'I'm sorry to bother you,' she said, trying to sound as if she meant it, 'but I wonder if I could ask you one or two questions.'

He seemed to consider his answer a moment, before saying, 'Certainly.'

She paused, expecting him to ask her in, but he didn't move. She must interview him on the doorstep. Lucky it wasn't raining. She got out the picture of Leon Kimmelman and proffered it, but he didn't take it, and only gave it enough of a glance to see what it was. 'It's about—' she began.

'Not this again!' he said with a heavy sigh. 'I told the other person who came here last week that I don't know this man. Surely he must have told you that? Don't you people communicate with each other *at all*? Who is your senior officer? I shall have a stiff word with him. I am not prepared to be badgered day and night with pointless questions that I've already answered.'

'We do communicate everything, of course, and Mr Slider

is quite well aware of your previous statement,' she said, with a faint emphasis on the word 'statement' to remind him that what was said to the police was always and everywhere official. At the same time, remembering her injunction not to scare him off, she gave him as winsome a smile as she could manage. It would have frightened a sensitive man, but she wasn't worried about this gender-wars fossil. 'But you see, new information has come to light, and I *have* to follow it up.' She hoped to give the impression that it *was* a pointless job, and that was why they gave it to a poor little girlie, so he should go easy on her.

He seemed to thaw just slightly. 'New information. What new information?'

She smiled hopefully, and would have liked to smile upwards at him so that she could be appealing, but even with the advantage of the doorstep he was no taller than her. 'We have discovered, you see, that Mr Kimmelman was paid a monthly salary by a company called Target.'

He toughed it out. 'And this concerns me because . . .?' he asked impatiently.

'Well, sir, you *are* a director of Target.'

There was a breath of a pause as he regrouped. Interesting, she thought. Did he think she didn't know that? Was it meant to be a secret? Or did he genuinely not see the point of the question?

'My dear young lady,' he said, and he sounded quite relaxed now, 'you surely cannot expect me to know every one of the company's employees by sight.'

'I'm sure not, sir. But we have information that this man was your driver.'

His face did not change. 'It's possible that he has driven me on one or two occasions. I couldn't say. It would have been a long time ago, and I would not particularly be paying attention. I have been driven by many different people over a long career, and I'm sure I could not pick any of them out if you paraded them in front of me.'

She nodded sympathetically, leaving him a space to drop himself in it, if he was inclined.

But he only said, 'In any case, I have very little to do

with that company any more.' He hoisted the smile again. It looked as though he'd read about smiling in a book and was trying it for himself for the first time. 'I am more or less retired.'

Well, it was possible that he *was* retired from Target, as there was no commercial activity in that business. She tried him with: 'What about your other company?'

She would have put money on his saying, 'My other company?' – and he did.

'Farraday,' she said baldly.

'That's really more of a convenience for holding assets. Tax management, that sort of thing. A financial device – I won't bore you with the details,' he said, giving her a 'you wouldn't understand, dear' look. 'I am, as I said, more or less retired from commercial life. My days revolve around the golf club and the bridge club, ha ha. Perhaps a little consultancy now and then, but nothing more exciting. I'm very much the – er – elder statesman, I'm afraid.' He tried the smile again. She flinched. It still needed more time in the nets.

'I see,' she said.

He seemed reassured by this meaningless phrase. 'Well, if there's nothing else?' he said, stepping back, preparatory to closing the door. 'If you'll excuse me . . .'

Given that the boss didn't want him put to flight, she said, 'Thank you for your time, sir,' and let it go at that. She had given him the opportunity to know Kimmelman, and now he *had* denied him thrice. That went on file. But she didn't quite know what to make of him. Given his age and the stiffness of that generation of businessmen, he could be just what he seemed – a harmless boring old fart. The sort that saw an unbridgeable gulf between the proper occupations of men and of women. The sort that viewed the police rather as paid servants. The sort that always said, 'I don't have to divulge my private business to anyone,' even when their lives depended on full disclosure. And, yes, it was perfectly possible that someone who looked down their nose so much would not register the features or name of a minion even when they were under it.

Or . . .

She turned away and heard the door snick shut behind her. She walked back to the car, and as she reached it, turned in opening the door, and looked back at the house. Someone was standing at an upper window, looking out at her: a little old lady, with white hair. It was the anxious and sorrowful expression that attracted her attention. There was something, in any case, about a person staring from an upper window that always made you think of false imprisonment. The mind naturally wanted to supply the hastily crayoned notice pressed against the glass, the slashed and uneven capitals shouting HELP I AM BEING HELD HOSTAGE. As she looked, the woman disappeared abruptly from the window, as though yanked away by a hidden hand.

Overactive imagination, she told herself. As for sorrowful – with a son always in trouble, who wouldn't look that way? Looking at her watch, she saw that it was nearly home time. So it was back to the factory, write up her report, and then dash to the Tesco in Shepherd's Bush Road on her way home. Tony would have collected Ashley from pre-school, but it was his darts night at The Clarence in North End Road so he'd want his supper before he went. And she'd have a nice quiet evening with the telly and the ironing. She liked ironing: the clean smell, the soothing repetition, plus the satisfaction of seeing everything crease-free and folded and put away. And it was the perfect excuse to watch some TV: she had three episodes of *Suits* to catch up with.

Joanna was in, but Slider was out – one of the frustrations of their respective lives was trying to schedule a time when they could both be at home to enjoy each other's company. At least Joanna, with an unpredictable job herself, understood: Slider's first wife, Irene, had been a stay-at-home, and his frequent and long absences from the hearth had led her in the end to find another man. It was a common fate for policemen. Of course, many of them hastened the process by embracing the many opportunities of infidelity offered by the Job: put red-blooded men, teeming with adrenaline, in a situation where no one could check up on their whereabouts from hour to hour, and it was not surprising if some of them went astray.

Slider, being both faithful and uxorious, would much sooner have been at home and thoroughly accountable, even had his evening promised him any pleasure. As it was, it was a meet-the-constabulary drinky-do for social workers, being held in one of the less lyrical rooms in Hammersmith Town Hall. There was cheap wine and rather limp canapés, and a lot of really earnest people, mostly women, all trying at once to get across the difficulties of their job, resulting in a level and pitch of noise that made it impossible to do other than smile sympa-thetically and make reassuring murmurs. The only good thing about it was that it was not a dress-do. Lounge suit and tie was required, of course, but Slider had been in that all day and had ceased to notice it.

Slider would have made his escape as soon as the numbers began to thin, but he had been buttonholed by a woman with desperate eyes who, he gathered, really just needed someone to talk to. She had been recounting her most distressing cases for half an hour when finally one of the few men among the social workers came up to her, clutching a motor-bike helmet, and said if she wanted a lift he was leaving right now. She abandoned Slider in mid-sentence and apparently without regret, and trotted off with her companion as though she hadn't a care in the world, leaving Slider feeling somewhat had.

'Thank Gawd for that – I thought she'd never leave,' said a voice at Slider's elbow. He turned to find DI Dave 'Oggy' Ogilvy standing there. Oggy was a bread-and-butter detective much like Slider, who had known him as a uniformed constable in Central, back in the days when dinosaurs roamed the earth. 'Come and have a proper drink. This wine muck'll rot your innards.'

Oggy was a good sort, and a sharp copper, despite his flabby waistline and red sweaty face, but between a pint with him and an early-ish night with Joanna there wasn't even a contest. Still, in making his excuses, he couldn't do less than stay long enough to have a bit of a chin with him. Oggy was not the sort to have many friends among the new breed of university-educated, highly laminated young officers that surrounded their new Commander Carpenter. And if Slider remembered right, he was divorced and didn't see much of his kids. To avoid

setting off a litany of complaint about Policing Today, Slider
got in first and mentioned the Kimmelman murder. Oggy had
heard of it. He spread his feet wide and asked for details, so
the following fifteen minutes was enjoyable to both of them.
Oggy said he'd keep an ear to the ground, Slider said they
must have that drink some time, and they were able to part
with honour satisfied on both sides.

It did mean Slider was almost the last leaving, and he
clattered down the stairs to the fire exit onto Nigel Playfair
Avenue alone, Oggy having gone the other way, to an exit
on the other side.

He pushed out into the crepuscular street light, to hurry
across the road to the car park, his mind on home and possibly
a little late supper and definitely a late but not little malt
whisky – he thought he had some Scapa left in the cupboard
– so he was not paying full attention to his surroundings. But
an instinct buried deep in the brainstem of all coppers, the
primitive bit that would prefer them to survive attacks by
sabre-toothed tigers or ugly blokes with coshes, thank you
very much, made him jump *before* he heard the roar of the
engine or saw the black shape rushing at him. Something hit
him a glancing blow and flung him forward; his feet scrabbled
for balance and a toecap hit the kerb, sending him on what
would have been a beautiful salmon-leap arc had be been a
rugby player scoring a try. He hit the pavement, hurting his
hands, banged his elbow, and managed to roll over, heart
pounding, scrambling defensively to his feet, brainstem
expecting the attack to continue.

He was aware of a number of images that might have been
successive or simultaneous, looming largest the black SUV
that had screamed at him, laying rubber. A passing cyclist had
been knocked off his bike, whether by contact or simply over-
balancing while trying to get out of the way he didn't know.
Two young people arm in arm further up the road had shrieked.
Someone on the far side of the car park – his mental snapshot
had shown their head arrested above the roof line of the car
as they paused in the act of getting in – was hurrying over.

The car was gone. The danger seemed over. Now survival-
brain had gone off duty, he was free to register pain – hip, palms,

shin, elbow – and the aftermath of adrenaline – thundering heart and shaking hands. Outposts reported back: no serious harm done; oh, and we did see the car, didn't we, parked at the near side of the road with the engine idling, because we registered in the split second as we passed it that it was on a double yellow and facing the wrong way, and thought that as the engine was running it was probably waiting for somebody and we didn't have to make it our job to tell it to push off.

Now people were reaching him. The young people turned out to be a pigeon pair – hard to tell at a distance, both being in trousers, jackets and hoods. Car park man was elderly and concerned, probably lonely and longing to be useful to someone. The cyclist was late twenties, muscular, professional-looking, with one of those pointy racing helmets full of holes and a hi-vis jacket over his own. The cyclist got there first, took Slider's arm in a strong, supporting grip and said, 'Are you all right? Hurt anywhere?'

'Bruises,' Slider said. 'Nothing serious.'

'You were lucky,' he said, his voice taut with reaction. 'That was deliberate. Just as I was passing, he accelerated, swerved straight at you.'

'Did he hit you?'

'No, I sort of twisted out of the way, lost my balance. I was too busy looking at you. God, that was . . .! I've never seen anything like that before.'

The youngsters arrived, saying things like 'Cool!' and 'Did you see that?' to nobody in particular. Now the old man arrived, fluttering and concerned, and wanting to insist on driving Slider to the hospital, 'Just in case. You can't be too careful, you know. Internal injuries.'

Slider, who knew that a policeman *could* be too careful, concentrated on the cyclist. 'Did you see who was driving?'

He shook his head regretfully. 'No. It was all too quick. I wasn't really looking, not to notice – you know how it is.'

'Tinted windows. You couldn't 'a' seen,' said one of the youngsters – the male half. They were still arm in arm, welded together from shoulder to knee.

'Are you sure?' Slider asked.

'Yeah,' he said eagerly. 'I looked as it went past. It was a

BMW X3. Super cool! It went down the end, and straight out left onto King Street, like a . . . a . . .'

'Arrow,' the girl suggested.

'Bat outta hell,' the boy corrected.

'Did you get the registration number?'

'Nah. Sorry.'

He looked at the cyclist, who shook his head too.

The boy said, 'It was a man driving, though. It's only the side windows are tinted. Coming straight, I could see it was a man.'

'Would you recognise him again?'

'Nah,' he said with genuine regret. 'It was just, like, a glimpse, like a shape, that's all. *Wish* I'd got the number,' he concluded wistfully. 'That would've been *mega*.'

The old man was still burbling about hospital. The cyclist said, 'I've got to go. But if you want a witness, I'll give you my card. Not that I can be much help.'

Slider took it anyway, and wrote the name and number of the young boy on the back, and then made his escape. His bruises were throbbing now, and one part of his mind was urgently asking him to consider which one of his many enemies might have tried to run him down, and how they had known where he was, while another part was suggesting that the malt whisky be urgently advanced several places up the agenda.

Joanna was not one to flap, or, indeed, to show much concern, but he knew how much she was upset by the tremor in her voice as she cleaned the grazes on his palms and rubbed arnica into his bruises and said, 'Was it definitely deliberate? I don't like to think of someone trying to kill you.'

'Oddly enough, neither do I. And it does pose some troubling questions.'

'The question uppermost on my mind is whether you need an X-ray. This wrist looks awfully swollen. It could be a fracture.'

'Everything moves about all right,' he said. 'I think it's just a sprain. I'll put some ice on it and see how it is tomorrow.'

'Typical macho man. Talking of ice . . .' she said, and topped up both their glasses. Then, 'Have you eaten?'

'Only fiddly bits. Canned apes.' It was what she always called cocktail food. 'I'm starving.'

'Cheese on toast?'

'Please.'

He followed her to the kitchen, and sat at the table with an ice pack on his wrist, watching her moving about and waiting for the question.

'Did you see who it was?' she asked.

'No, there was no time. And the car had tinted windows.'

A long pause. 'It's not going to be Trevor Bates all over again, is it?' she said at last, with her back to him.

There, that was the one. Trevor 'The Needle' Bates had escaped from prison after Slider had helped put him there, and had made determined efforts to kill him. Joanna had been pregnant with George at the time, making them both doubly vulnerable. But Bates was dead, having slipped and fallen off a roof during a wild, adrenaline-fuelled chase through Shepherd's Bush. Slider had seen the body. He wasn't coming back.

However, he had put many people away in his time, some of whom might well feel resentful – though actually to try to kill a policeman required not only industrial-strength resentment but also a detachment from reality that in most cases prevented the task being carried out with efficiency. Bates had been intelligent and resourceful, but two minutes in his company told you he was only hanging on to the world you inhabited by his fingertips. The combination was rare, fortunately. Normal precautions were usually enough.

'It's not like that,' he said.

She said nothing more until she had placed the plate in front of him and sat down opposite. Then she said, 'How did they know where you were? Did they follow you?'

'I don't know,' he said. 'I made sure they didn't follow me afterwards, though. Nobody followed me here, I promise you.'

She gave half a smile. 'Horses and stable doors jump to mind.'

'I'll be more careful in future. Try not to worry.'

'Of course not. Things like this happen all the time, right?' She took a sip of whisky. 'You've got some high-profile enemies. People who could afford to hire a hitman.'

'Hitman,' he scoffed, for her sake.

'People like Millichip. If an Assistant Commissioner doesn't know where to get hold of a bad hat—'

'I never thought of Millichip! Of course, he'd find some low-life he's got a hold over and put him on my tail. He'll be gutted when he finds out it went wrong.'

'You can joke, Bill—'

'I can.' He reached across and laid his hand over hers. 'It was a very amateur attempt and if I'd been paying attention – which I will from now on – he wouldn't have got anywhere near me. In fact, I should really have taken his number for parking on a double yellow. Whoever he was, he must have been a real clot not to think of that.'

'Maybe he *wasn't* trying to kill you,' she said lightly. 'Maybe he'd just realised he was going to get a ticket and tried to run away.'

'People do stupider things,' he said.

He was required, of course, to make a report on the incident on Thursday morning. Mr Porson looked grave, and said, 'We can't have this sort of thing. Which of your slags is fresh out of the pokey?'

'I'll make enquiries,' Slider said.

'Pity you didn't get the index. Turned left into King Street, did he? Must be cameras along there.'

'My firm's fully stretched—'

'I'll find a uniform to put on it,' Porson said impatiently. 'What worries me is, how did they know where you were? Anyone been making enquiries about you?'

'I'll ask around.'

'Do that. Looks bad, having one of us targeted like that. Looks sloppy.'

It's lovely to know how much you care, Slider thought, as he went away. His wrist was swollen and stiff and Joanna had strapped it tight for him. Luckily it was his left, and he was right-handed. And he had a bruise the size of a saucer on his hip. But Porson couldn't know that.

*   *   *

The puzzle was soon resolved. Slider called his team together and said, 'Has anyone been asking questions about me recently? Any unusual enquiries?'

Everyone murmured in the negative, looking at one another. And then Fathom, with a jolt like someone who's just touched an electric fence, said, 'Oh, guv, I just remembered. Some woman rang last night after you'd left, wanting to speak to you. But she was pukka. I forgot to tell you, cos there was no message, she said she'd ring back.'

'What do you mean, she was pukka?' Slider asked.

'She was from the commissioner's office. Said her name was Hastings, Mrs Hastings, the commissioner's PA. Dead posh voice. She asked for you, and I told her you'd gone, and she said she'd ring tomorrow – today, that is.'

The commissioner's PA? What would the commissioner – who was so high-up they said God called him sir – want with lowly DCI Slider? Even if he wanted to tell him off, he wouldn't do it in person. He'd have people to do that for him.

'And did you tell her where I was going?' he asked patiently.

'No, guv. I wouldn't do that,' Fathom said, injured. 'I'm not daft. Anyway, she already knew.'

Curiouser and curiouser. 'Tell me exactly what she said. What you said, and what she said.'

Fathom creased his brow. 'She asked for you, I said you'd gone for the night, and she said had you gone home, because she could ring you there. She said she'd got the number. I said no, you'd gone to a meeting, and she said was that the one at Westminster Hall and I said . . .' He paused, enlightenment slowly sifting through his brain like water through layers of shale.

'Go on,' said Slider.

'I said no, it was the one at Hammersmith Town Hall,' he said unhappily. 'But wait, guv, she said, oh yes, of course, like she knew all about it, and she said she wouldn't bother you there, she'd call you tomorrow. So I thought . . .' His voice trailed off.

No one, not even Swilley, said anything. If anything, she looked sorry for him.

'I mean,' he went on pathetically, 'she sounded so, you know, pukka, and like she really knew. I mean, I thought . . .'

Gascoyne had been quietly pattering away on the computer, and said quietly, 'There's no Mrs Hastings in the commissioner's office.

Slider said nothing, letting it sink in. He thought the lesson had been learned.

Atherton said, 'I wonder what she was going to say if you were there, and she got put through to you?'

'I'm sure she had it all worked out. Try not to worry about her too much,' Swilley told him sourly.

'Who could it have been?' Someone was bound to say it, and in the event it was Loessop. 'Have you put any uppity females away, guv?'

'Any slag could get a female to make a phone call for him,' Hart pointed out.

'But Jezza said she spoke posh.'

'Anyone can put on a posh accent,' Hart retorted. 'Posh enough to fool *him*, anyway.'

'Let's not have any pointless speculation,' Slider said. 'We've got enough to do. I just want you all to be on your guard from now on. And report anything suspicious to me.'

'And don't tell any hitmen where the guv'nor is,' Hart concluded. 'No sense making their job easy for 'em.'

'Enough,' Slider said firmly. He didn't want internal sniping. And if Fathom's face got any redder he'd set fire to his hair. 'Report.'

Fathom spoke, perhaps hoping to make some points back. 'I was down at Ivanka's yest'd'y, guv. All the clubs along there've got cameras, and I got a lot of stuff for the whole road for that Thursday. I haven't put it all together yet, but I got the rent boys coming out of Ivanka's all right, and getting in a car with Kimmelman. It was parked just along the road. I got the index, and I've run it through the DVLA. The registered owner comes back to Target.'

'So he's got a company car as well?' said LaSalle.

'I wonder where he kept it,' said Loessop. 'There's not any parking round the back of Ruskin House, is there?'

'No, those flats're too old. No garridges, either,' LaSalle

supplied. 'Maybe he's got resident's parking down one of the side roads.'

'Now we got the index,' McLaren said with enthusiasm, 'we can put it through the ANPR, see where he went with it.'

'We don't know that he had it all the time,' Gascoyne said cautiously. 'If it was a company car, he might only have had use of it on certain occasions.'

'Worth following it up, though,' said McLaren. 'What make and model was it?'

'Beamer,' said Fathom. 'Black BMW X3.'

'Not entirely unlike, then, the one that drove at me last night?' said Slider.

'You tosser, Jez, why didn't you say so?' Hart said witheringly.

'We weren't talking about that,' he defended himself feebly.

'Never mind that,' Swilley said impatiently, 'where does it leave us?'

'Apparently with Kimmelman back from the dead,' Atherton said calmly, perched on a desk with his elegant ankles crossed, 'and hoping to wreak awful revenge.'

'Bit of a confused zombie,' Loessop commented. 'We're the ones trying to avenge his death. He ought to be going after his killer.'

'That would make it too easy,' Atherton said.

'It puts Holdsworth slap bang in the middle of it, though, doesn't it?' LaSalle said hopefully. 'Kimmelman's his employee, and his company owns the motor that tries to kill the guv.'

'If,' Slider said, taking a tug on the reins, 'it was the same car. There must be more than one black BMW X3 in the metropolitan area. And if Holdsworth had access to it or even knew about it.'

'I can look into it,' said McLaren. 'Bound to be able to pick it up somewhere down King Street.'

'Mr Porson's putting someone on it. You've got enough to do,' said Slider.

'It's still not making any sense, though,' Loessop said broodingly, pulling at his chin plaits. 'Kimmelman makes a blackmail tape of Kevin Rathkeale but never tries to blackmail him – why? Then someone whacks him and turns over his gaff, presumably looking for the tape – why?'

'And why are we spending all this time looking into Davy Lane?' Hart grumbled. 'What's that got to do with it?'

'It's the only common link,' Swilley said, 'between Kimmelman, Holdsworth and Jack Silverman.'

'I don't see how Silverman comes into it,' LaSalle said, 'just because he was going to do the building on the Davy Lane thing. It could have been any builder. What's his connection with Kimmelman and Rathkeale and everything?'

There was a moment's silence, and then several people said at once, 'Myra Silverman.'

'She was definitely connected with Rathkeale,' Gascoyne said. 'We had his secretary saying she'd been bugging him.'

'I think another visit to Mr Rathkeale is indicated,' said Slider. 'Meanwhile, as a matter of urgency, let's find out where that car was on that Friday, Saturday and Sunday. We need to know who Kimmelman was seeing. Because there's every possibility he was mixing with some tasty characters, and that there were other things going on in his life, apart from the Rathkeale shake-down. Other blackmails, drugs, stolen goods – who knows?' He ran his hand distractedly backwards through his hair. 'I think I may have encouraged too much concentration on one aspect of his life.'

'Not your fault, guv,' Hart said. 'Up till now we had nothing to go on, except Target.'

'That, from you, is magnanimous,' said Slider, 'considering the whole Davy Lane thing is anathema to you.'

Hart grinned. 'Yeah boss. What you said.'

FOURTEEN
Conservation Piece

In the interests of thoroughness, tying up loose ends, and showing generosity to her boss's obsession with real estate, Hart went to see a Mr Meikle in the council's planning department. She had asked the switchboard if anyone had been there for a long time, and was told chippily that he had been there 'for ever', which in the event turned out to be thirty-two years, pretty much the same thing as far as anyone under thirty was concerned.

Meikle turned out to be a bulky man with a well-worn suit, heavy glasses and a comb-over. Hart tried not to stare at it, while thinking, how can any man stand in front of the mirror every morning with the left side of his hair five inches longer than the right, carefully spread the strands over his bald top, and regard the result with satisfaction? Did he really, *really* think it made him look as if he had a full head of hair? What was going on here? Of course, baldness was a touchy subject for men; the younger generation dealt with it by aggressively shaving the lot off, thumbing the nose at cruel nature. But the comb-over was such a forlorn thing, it made her want to give him a big hug, while simultaneously shaking him till his teeth rattled.

He greeted her with a suspicious reserve, which she put down at first to her colour, before realising it was actually her sex that made him nervous. Once she'd twigged, she was able to work on him with a line of gentle flirting until he was so relaxed, he was practically putting his feet up on the desk. *Ha, still got it!* she thought. *Eat your heart out, Norma's bust.*

He knew all about Davy Lane, though he called it Coal Sidings Road, or rather by the jaunty abbreviation CSR. 'It's been political all the way, at every stage,' he said. 'Personally, I was in favour of the council flats plan. Back then, it was thought a disgrace for big houses like that to belong to one family, when there were people queuing up for council properties. Been on the list for years, some of them, and little hope of getting a place. Of course,' he allowed, 'the Bush has changed now. Very different place. There's a lot of rich people have moved in, luxury properties everywhere, we're becoming trendy – we're the new Notting Hill, if you like.'

It wasn't clear from his tone whether *he* liked. He seemed torn between the traditional Labour disapproval of personal wealth, and the pride in his area becoming a desirable destination.

'But one thing's for sure,' he concluded, 'the whole process, viz a viz the CSR, has been a waste of what could have been valuable housing, one way or the other. And nobody's done well out of it.'

'Not even the developers?' Hart tried him with.

He sniffed. 'Won't break my heart over *them*! But as a matter of fact, *they*'ve lost a packet as well. That Target's pretty much gone bust, so I've heard. Well, there was a lot of chicanery behind them buying CSR in the first place.'

'There was?' she asked, with flattering attention. *Enlighten me, oh wise one*!

'Well,' he said, gratified, 'it was the Labour-controlled council that first wanted to put a listing on it, did you know that?'

'I thought they compulsory-purchased it to pull it down?'

'Yes, but they hadn't got the money to carry it through, and when they knew they were going to be chucked out at the next election, they tried to rush the listing through, just to stymie the incoming council, so's *they* wouldn't be able to do anything with it. Land them with a white elephant, expensive to maintain, impossible to develop, see? But as it happened, they couldn't get it done in time.'

'But the new council went ahead and listed it anyway. Why'd they do that?'

He chuckled. 'Oh, that was the worst of all! See, the new council, Conservative-controlled, they knew there was no money, and the CSR was getting to be an eyesore. They always intended to sell it off. But there was this councillor, Mr Holdsworth, he reckoned that if it was listed, it would knock the price right down, because a place like that's only valuable if it can be developed. So he puts pressure on to get it listed. And then, when the listing's gone through, he buys it himself, because he just *happens* to be the boss of a development company.'

'Target.'

'That's right.'

Hart frowned. 'But surely the council would want as much money as possible for the sale. Why would they agree to go ahead with the listing if it would lose them money?'

'Oh, he talked them into it. Talked about heritage and architecture and aesthetics and so on and so forth. Blah blah blah. Made out he was just trying to maintain the last little bits of the Bush's history – tragedy to lose such venerable

buildings – future generation would condemn us for chucking
away their treasure. And so on and so forth. What they didn't
know, of course, was that he was the boss of Target. He kept
that nice and quiet.' He chuckled again. 'People in local
politics, they think they're the bees knees, but mostly they're
just Mr and Mrs Average, wet behind the ears as far as
wheeling and dealing is concerned. So someone really savvy,
like this Holdsworth bloke, can run rings round 'em. Still,'
he drew out a handkerchief and blew his nose, mirth having
led to moisture. 'Still,' he went on, 'they got their revenge
all right. Once they worked out what was going on, how
Holdsworth had done 'em like kippers, they put the boot in.'
Hart noticed that the refinement of his accent and his vocabulary had slipped, the further into his story he got. 'They put
the CSR into the Conservation Area. Now there's double
protection on it, so he'll *never* get to pull it down,' he
concluded with satisfaction.

'But he'd hoped to pull it down with the Grade II listing in
place?' Hart queried.

'With him being inside, on the council, he must have thought
he could do it. But he'd turned people against him, and like
I said, once they found out the full story, that was it. And then
he lost his seat at the next election, and that was that. There
he was with a load of old buildings he couldn't do anything
with. Serve him right!'

'So I suppose now he'll just be waiting for them to fall
down?' Hart said.

'That won't help him,' said Meikle with satisfaction. 'Rules
of listing – if you knock it down, or it falls down, you have
to rebuild it to original spec. Otherwise, the protection wouldn't
be worth the paper it's written on, see?'

Hart saw.

All the same, she reflected as she trotted down the stairs,
there must *be* ways of getting round it, or Holdsworth wouldn't
have bought the property in the first place. Or at least, he must
have *thought* there were ways round it. And it was a fact, as
she knew from the occasional stories in the papers, listed
buildings did get destroyed. Fire was a good one. There was
a block of listed Georgian houses right in the centre of London,

by Vauxhall Bridge, that had got badly damaged in a, hem-hem, accidental fire, and the owners were being allowed to build a modern office block on the site as long as the Georgian façade was preserved. It wasn't that she took a lot of notice of that sort of thing, but she'd driven past the site a thousand times and wondered why there was heavy duty scaffolding holding up a single wall of old bricks – wondered enough to make the enquiry. That development was taking a long time. Presumably, having to pile-drive, and operate modern heavy machinery, without destroying the frail façade slowed things down a lot. But with central London property values as they were, it was obviously worth it to someone.

Kevin Rathkeale was in a committee meeting, but Slider asked that he be informed of their presence, and the message came back with gratifying speed that he would appear very shortly. In the mean time, it was no hardship to wait in the outer office, standing by the window and watching the great, grey river roll by. The sky was too hazy for it to sparkle, but it looked serious and important, a waterway of substance. A pair of cormorants was busily fishing, proving how clean the water was, and a row of gulls, perched along the roof of a jetty-hut, shuffled their wings and contemplated the deep, eternal questions of existence.

Out in the corridor there was the sound of lift doors opening, then rapid footsteps. The soothing background rattle of computer keys stopped as the PA looked up and said, 'Here he is,' and then Rathkeale burst into the room, rolled-up shirt-sleeves, loosened tie, jacket over his arm and a faint smell of sweat and aftershave. He scanned Slider's and Atherton's faces briefly but comprehensively, then said, 'No calls,' and led the way into his office. Atherton closed the door behind them. Rathkeale tossed his jacket onto the sofa, went behind his desk and sat down, folded his pale, faintly gleaming arms on the desktop, and said, 'Well? What is it now?'

Slider studied him. He seemed wary, but not like a man racked with fear, guilt or apprehension. He had bags under his eyes, but his skin was of that loose, thick kind that bagged up nicely without encouragement. He didn't look like a man who had longed in vain for the kiss of peaceful sleep for two weeks. He looked like someone called away from some important task by an annoying unavoidable duty which he was hoping to get out of the way as quickly as possible. Slider didn't like it. He didn't like his interviewees to be too comfortable. Especially when they had been caught on film doing illegal things, and they *knew* they had.

'I take it,' he began, 'that you haven't been contacted by a blackmailer. I take it that if you *had* been, you would have let me know.'

'Of course I would,' Rathkeale said impatiently. 'For God's sake, is that what you've pulled me out of a meeting for? Just to ask me that?'

Slider kept up the impassive look. 'Sometimes people feel they'd sooner go it alone. Pay the blackmailer, rather than risk having the material made public.'

He shrugged. 'I can understand that. But I'm telling you, no-one's contacted me. Maybe they know you're onto them. Or they've changed their minds. Or it was just a silly joke. I can't think of a reason why they'd go to all that trouble and then *not* try to get something out of me for it.'

Atherton said, 'I must say, you're amazingly calm. If I knew there was material like that about me out there somewhere, I'd be a nervous wreck.'

'I *am* a nervous wreck,' he asserted. 'But you know how it is. You wait and wait and nothing happens, you start to relax. And there's work – I can't tell you how busy I've been – and that takes all your attention . . .' He surveyed their faces. 'Why do you keep coming and bothering me? I've co-operated with you. I've given you permission to look at my phone logs. What more can I do?'

There was a film of sweat on his upper lip now. Good. That had softened him up a bit.

'As far as the blackmail's concerned, as there was no actual attempt to extort anything from you, no crime has been committed,' Slider said. 'My interest is in who murdered Leon Kimmelman.'

'I've *told* you I didn't even know the man—'

'And the apparent intention to blackmail you interests me

only as it seems to be connected with the murder,' Slider concluded as if he hadn't spoken.

'So why *are* you here? What *do* you want?' He glanced at his watch. 'I haven't got all day, you know. Can't you just come to the point?'

Slider obliged. 'What are your relations with Myra Silverman?'

The question surprised him. 'Myra? What on earth are you asking about her for?'

'Just answer the question please.'

He reddened. 'I don't know what you mean by "relations". There was nothing like *that* between us.'

Which meant, of course, Slider thought, that there probably had been. 'I don't know why not. She's an attractive woman, from what I've seen.'

'She's too old for me,' he said. 'She must be pushing sixty. Not to be ungallant,' he added with a little laugh, 'but my tastes don't run to grandmothers.' They didn't laugh with him. His face straightened. 'Anyway, I haven't seen her for ages. Things cooled between us after that KidZone business.'

'You thought you needed to put some distance between you,' Atherton suggested. 'She'd become bad news. Not to be associated with.'

He was stung to defence. 'Look, Myra does a lot of good. Sometimes her enthusiasm runs away with her. But better that, than all those people who sit on their arses and do nothing.'

'So you're still friends,' Slider asked.

'No, not really,' he said, scratching his head with a badgered look. 'I mean, I don't see her any more, not socially. Our paths cross occasionally at functions, I don't bear her any ill-will, but our worlds have moved apart, that's all.'

'But she has been ringing you a lot recently. Coming to see you at the office.'

'Once,' he said quickly. 'She only came here once. Yes, she did contact me about a scheme she wanted me to back, but that was a while ago. I haven't heard from her for ages.'

'Three weeks is not such an age.'

'I think it's more like four. But anyway, what's Myra got to do with it?'

'You told her you didn't want anything to do with her scheme?'

'No, I said I couldn't help her. You make it sound as if . . . Look, there was nothing wrong with it, it was a good project, it's just that I've got other things already earmarked for the money. She thought she might change my mind, but I told her I'd made my decision and that was that. I was sorry, but I wasn't going back on it.'

'She wanted money?' said Atherton.

'Not for herself,' he said, with a slight blush of vexation. 'For her scheme.'

'Which was?' Slider asked.

'A youth outreach centre,' Rathkeale said. 'Something like what she's done before, only this one was on a bigger scale. Get the disadvantaged youngsters off the streets, give them something to do, turn their thoughts to more constructive activities. A gym, workshops – a theatre with a movie production studio behind, get them interested in film making. Plus a psychiatric clinic, because a lot of them have underlying mental problems.'

'It sounds wonderful. Very worthwhile,' Slider said.

Rathkeale squirmed a little. 'Yes, it was a good one, and of course she knew I had both government and GLA money to invest in youth outreach *and* urban renewal – it's apparently a very rundown site. But the thing was, it was very similar to a scheme I've already gone public as backing. At the Elephant, where all that urban redevelopment is going on. And there's real poverty there, and community integration problems. I've gone on record as backing it. So I told Myra, I'm sorry, but it's no go.'

'Was that the only reason you said no – because you've given your word to the Elephant?'

'Yes.' Another little squirm. 'Well, and because Myra is still unfairly pilloried by the media. Whenever her name is mentioned, that KidZone business comes up. I've just got myself clear of all that, I don't want it sticking to me again.'

'Quite understandable,' Slider said in sympathetic tones.

'And the Elephant is a more deprived area than Shepherd's Bush, anyway,' Rathkeale said. 'What with the new tube station and the Westfield development, and the BBC Media Village, it's hard to put it across as inner-city-deprived any more.'

'So Mrs Silverman's project, it was in Shepherd's Bush? Are you talking about Coal Sidings Road, by any chance?'

'Yes. Oh, of course, you're from there. You'd know about it,' he said. A thoughtfulness came over him. 'Why are you asking me about all this?'

Slider didn't want him pondering along that route. 'You have a large budget for this kind of scheme?'

'Large enough, including the central government grant. In the region of ten million.'

'And yours is the final word on what it gets spent on?' Atherton asked.

He looked proud. 'Yes. Well, there are other people involved, of course – other committees – and I have to justify the expenditure to them. But basically, yes, I'm the one who gives the final say-so. That's what we're elected for – to take responsibility.'

'And I can see you take it seriously,' Slider said. 'So when you last spoke to Mrs Silverman about this, your answer was no? And what was her reaction?'

'She said she understood. She said, "You can't blame me for trying."'

'She took it well, then?'

'Well, she was disappointed, obviously, but she knew I wasn't going to budge. We parted on good terms.'

'And that was – four weeks ago, you said?'

'About that.'

'And you haven't spoken to her or seen her since?'

'Not that I recollect. No, not at all.' He looked puzzled and was obviously about to ask again why he was being asked.

So Slider stood up and said, 'Well, thank you for your help. I won't keep you any longer – I know how busy you must be.'

'Yes, November's always a busy time for us. Everything galloping downhill towards the Christmas break.'

They left him before he could ask any more questions, and their last glimpse of him was of a puzzled and unsatisfied face, wearing a frown of thought and pursed lips of contemplation.

*   *   *

Outside, Atherton said, 'Are you thinking what I'm thinking?'

'Perhaps. But there are problems.'

'Myra Silverman, married to Jack Silverman. Who was going to get the building job.'

'But where does Kimmelman come into it?'

'Oh, stuff Kimmelman. This outreach centre is much more interesting. Ten million?'

'Not just to be pocketed. Something would have to be built for the money,' Slider reminded him.

'But I'm betting there'd be a substantial profit for someone somewhere. Those officially-backed projects always seem to be funded with sticky money. The sort that sticks to people's fingers on its way through.'

Slider shook his head. 'We haven't any proof. Not even any evidence. Or,' he added with irritation, 'any damn reason for Kimmelman's death.'

Atherton looked at him sharply. 'But do you think Myra Silverman is involved?'

'I think the Silvermans and Holdsworth are the only links we've got with Kimmelman. But I also think he could just as easily have been whacked behind a betting-shop by a bloke who thought he'd looked at him funny.'

'Fat lot of help that is,' said Atherton.

PC D'Arblay was waiting for him when Slider got back to his office. He was a fair-haired, pleasant-faced man who looked like someone's favourite nephew, until you clocked the steel under the smile and the sharp intelligence in the eyes. Slider had always liked him, and would have been glad to have him in the firm, but D'Arblay was wedded to the uniform side.

'Sergeant Nicholls detailed me to look for your black SUV, sir,' he said.

'You've got a result already?' Slider said. 'That was quick work.'

'A partial result, sir. I thought you'd like to know before I went any further. There's a traffic camera for the lights at the junction of Dalling Road, and I looked there first. I've got a BMW X3 coming out of Nigel Playfair at about the right time. It turns left onto King Street then immediately right down

Dalling Road – ran the lights and nearly caused a crash with a car coming the other way. But the thing is, sir, you can't read the index. The front plate's obscured – probably mud, or it could be paint. And the rear plate's missing.'

'I see,' said Slider.

'He could have gone any number of ways from Dalling Road – there's a mass of side streets he can zigzag through if he's camera savvy. And without a number to put into the ANPR . . .'

You could not get a ping without a number, so it would mean viewing every possible tape for every possible direction in the hope of spotting the car again.

'I didn't know how much further you wanted me to go, sir,' D'Arblay concluded. 'I could—'

'No,' said Slider. 'You can leave it there. I'm sure you've got better things to do. Thanks, anyway.'

'I'll put out an alert, in case a patrol stops a car for the number plate violation,' D'Arblay offered. 'But otherwise . . .'

'Quite,' Slider finished for him.

Anyway, if it was the same black SUV as the one Kimmelman was driving on blackmail night, McLaren and Fathom were already looking for it.

James Hadleigh, of Blenheim Property Development, greeting Swilley with a grin and sparkly eyes. 'Couldn't get enough of me, eh? Managed to find another excuse to visit? Jacket's Yard again, is it?'

'Not this time,' Swilley said. 'It's some general information I wanted, if you've got a minute?'

'For you, five of them,' he said. 'Take a pew.'

She sat, smoothing her skirt down and crossing her legs. *The things I do for my country . . .*

'It's about developing where there's a Grade II listing in place. I know it's supposed to prevent the buildings being altered or demolished, but I wondered if there was any way round it.'

'What are we talking, here? Country mansion? Georgian rectory in the Cotswolds?'

'No, in London. Suppose there was a row of protected

buildings, and you wanted to knock them down and redevelop the site. Is there any way to do that? Say, for argument's sake, it was in a conservation zone as well Grade II listed?'

If he knew she was talking about Coal Sidings Road – if he had heard about it – he revealed nothing. 'Depends a lot on the individual circumstances. What the buildings are, how historically important, how much local resistance there is. And what the development will be. But as a general rule, you can find your way round anything if you really want to.'

'Bribery?' she suggested.

He grinned. 'Local councils tend to be incompetent rather than corrupt. There are always corrupt individuals, of course. There are also stubbornly virtuous individuals who insist on doing the right thing no matter what. And the sheer bloody-minded who oppose for the sake of opposing.'

'So how do you get round it, then?'

'The best way forward is to get either the GLA or the government interested. If your development has some element that accords with their strategic plans – well, you're home and dry. They can override local objections and force the planning permission through. Happens all the time.'

'You mean, for instance, if they're keen on youth centres . . .?' she suggested.

'Right. You've got the idea. Stick on a youth centre, find the right advocate at City Hall or the DoE, and away you go.' He looked at her quizzically. 'Am I to understand that an elderly aunt has left you some historic property in a sensitive part of Kensington . . .?'

She smiled and shook her head, thinking out her next question. 'Supposing,' she said, 'you wanted to do this development for reasons of personal gain . . .'

'Is there ever another reason?'

'All right, but *who* gains. Who profits from getting the permission?'

'Well, the owner of the site, of course. You expect to get more from the sale after you've developed, than the cost of the site plus the cost of the work.' She nodded receptively. 'You want more? Well, then . . .' He thought. 'I suppose the builder would benefit from getting the contract. Obviously. I mean, that's what he's in business for – and with a government-backed development, your profit margins are always going to be higher. And, depending on *what* you were actually building, I suppose someone might have a financial stake in the end result.'

'What do you mean?'

'Well, for instance, if it was a sports centre, someone who supplies sports equipment might be very happy about it. I can't really tell you without knowing what it is you're building.'

'I had better not tell you,' Swilley said.

'Part of a case, is it?'

'It may be. But thanks, anyway, for your help. You've given me something to think about.'

'No trouble at all,' he said, his eyes following her up as she stood. 'I never knew it could be so pleasurable to be inter-rogated by the police.' She smiled warily, not liking the look in his eye. 'I don't suppose you'd—' he began.

She interrupted him hastily. 'I must get back, we've got a lot on. Thank you again, very much. I shan't disturb you any longer.'

FIFTEEN
The Road Goes Ever On And On

The catch-up meeting was held over lunch in the CID room. Everyone had sandwiches at their desk. Hart had gone down to Mike's for hers, and brought Slider back a cheese roll – simply cheese, butter, not spread, *no* pickle. McLaren had a giant Cornish pasty which, as the microwave was on the blink, he was eating cold from the cellophane. Atherton was eating something salady out of a tupperware tub with a fork – not even a plastic fork but a real one brought from home. And Mr Porson, who had joined them, had taken over Gascoyne's desk and had unwrapped the greaseproof from an obviously home-made corned-beef-on-sliced-white.

All human life is here, Slider thought. You could write a treatise about how the lunchtime sarnie is a window on the soul.

Hart had made her report.

'So Holdsworth got the place listed so as to get it cheap,' LaSalle observed, 'then got stiffed by his old pals, and got left with a white elephant.'

'You'd need a heart of stone not to laugh,' Hart agreed.

'So he comes up with the Davy Lane project,' said Atherton. 'Can't get an ordinary residential development approved, but with some public interest element—'

Swilley jumped in. 'That's what James Hadleigh said. If it's something that fits in with the government's strategic plan, they can override the local planning veto.'

'So Myra Silverman tries to persuade her old pal Kevin Rathkeale,' Atherton took it back, 'with the added benefit that not only will it get the planning permission forced through, but it will involve a large slice of public money.'

'And she gets involved, why?' Loessop asked.

'Ten million? You kidding?' Hart said.

'But how does she get anything out of it?'

'It's the old *cui bono*,' said Atherton. 'Husband Jack will get the building contract.'

'How did those two get together?' Porson interjected. 'Holdsworth and Silverman? Did they know each other before, or did Holdsworth pick him out of the *Yellow Pages*?'

'I don't know,' Slider admitted. Trust the old boy to shove in a stonker! 'Silverman was to be the builder on the original Davy Lane development, the residential-only, but why Holdsworth chose him . . .'

Porson merely nodded, the point made. Slider made a mental note to find out.

'So,' Atherton resumed, 'there's all this lovely government dosh up for grabs. Holdsworth gets to develop his white elephant and make a fat profit—'

'Yeah, and we can guess he's short of cash.' It was Hart who interrupted this time. 'He's got a kid that's in trouble and costing him an arm and a leg.'

'And his business is doing nothing. Target's just a shell,'

Swilley added. 'And Farraday's just a holding company. So where's his income?'

'What about Silverman?' Loessop asked. 'Is his business in trouble?'

'He said he was doing all right,' Slider said, 'but then he would do, wouldn't he? It didn't seem busy when I was there.'

'Look into that as well,' Porson said.

Swilley nodded. 'Yes sir. And I've had a thought about Myra Silverman. It's a good enough reason for getting involved, that her husband'd get the building contract. But if the rumours are true, she made a lot of money personally out of KidZone. And someone else said she has a lot of director-ships, and they can add up to a pretty good income. Well, if this youth outreach centre did get built, they'd need a director for it, wouldn't they?'

'Can't see her getting it, after KidZone,' said LaSalle.

'Unless old pal gingernuts puts in the word,' Hart said. 'He's the one with the moolah. He could make it a condition of the project that she gets the directorship.'

'What'd that pay, anyway?' McLaren asked.

'A high profile, government-approved job like that could easily fetch eighty or ninety thousand,' Atherton said.

McLaren swallowed a lump of pastry and potato. 'Kidding me!' he managed to splutter.

'Some charities pay their executives a lot more than that,' said Atherton. 'Two hundred and fifty thousand, some of the big ones – basically for having your name on the stationery.'

'I'm in the wrong job,' Loessop mourned.

'We all are,' Hart agreed.

'So, it must have been a disappointment, then, when Rathkeale said no,' McLaren said. Everyone looked at him. '*Big* disappointment,' he went on. 'All them people needing the money, all depending on Kevin Rathkeale to come through. There's three people'd be well pissed off.'

'Steady on, Maurice,' Atherton said. 'You had an idea only a few days ago. Mustn't overdo.'

'Never mind all that,' Porson snapped, making Atherton jump – he'd forgotten he was there. 'You got your motif for blackmail right there.'

'Rathkeale had the final say-so. I been wondering all along what Davy Lane had to do with it,' Hart said.

'It gives us a reason for the blackmail,' Slider said, 'and if Kimmelman was working for Holdsworth—'

'Although he denies it,' said Atherton.

'—it explains why he did the actual graft.'

'Not something Holdsworth would get his hands dirty with,' said Swilley disdainfully. She didn't like Holdsworth. She kept thinking of the sad little woman at the upstairs window.

'As you wouldn't,' Slider said, 'But it doesn't give us a reason for Kimmelman's death.'

There was a silence, and then Loessop said hesitantly, 'Because he knows where the bodies are buried?'

Porson slid the last bit of sandwich into his mouth and hitched himself off the desk. 'Well, you got plenty to get on with,' he said. 'I'll leave you to it.' Slider walked to the door with him. 'Any more on that motor that tried to run you down?'

Slider told him about the concealed index. 'But it's the same make and model as the car that picked up the rent boys from the club.'

'So it could be something to do with the case? Oh, well, that's a comfort.'

'Yes, my heart is bursting with gratitude,' Slider said.

Porson gave him a look so old-fashioned it would have suited a reactionary dinosaur. 'I mean,' he said witheringly, 'you don't want any distractions until you've brought this one home.'

'Yes, sir,' said Slider. He knew what he meant. It was good that it might not be an extra random element out to kill him. *Anybody* trying to kill you was enough to be going on with.

Atherton said, 'Do you really think this Davy Lane project had enough juice in it to make killing Kimmelman worthwhile?' He was standing, because Hart had come in first and was sitting where he usually sat on the windowsill. 'To say nothing of trying to kill you. Which, by the way, is stupid, because it wouldn't stop the investigation.'

'Might slow it down,' Hart said. She was twirling an end of hair round and round her finger in thought.

'Trying to run me down doesn't look like the action of a thoughtful person,' Slider said. 'More a blind lashing out.'

'Someone had to think out a plan to find out where you were,' Atherton said.

'Here, boss, I just thought – maybe Myra Silverman was "Mrs Hastings". Posh voice, Jezza said, and I've seen her on the news, she's dead posh.'

Slider was on the Humpty Dumpty plan, still answering the question before last. 'Ten million, or a share of ten million, would be enough of a driver for most people, especially if they really needed the money. As to attacking me, the imperative only gets sharper when you add in murder. If Holdsworth is responsible for that, and he thinks we're getting close, he may see all that lovely money taking wing, and the prospect of jail taking shape, and get himself into a blind panic.'

'But is Myra Silverman close enough to Holdsworth to get involved in that way?' Atherton said.

'If they are all in on the Davy Lane scheme, I suppose he could ask her to make the call without telling her what he was going to do with the information. But it's all speculation. We need evidence,' Slider concluded restlessly.

Swilley came in. 'I've looked into Abbott Construction, boss. They've had a lot of work, but their profits are way down. Can't say why, but there's a lot of things to go wrong on a building project. Cost overruns, bad weather, clients not paying up. And you can just be unlucky. I wish I could have a look at the Silvermans' personal finances – I'd like to bet they've taken out big loans to keep things afloat.'

'Wish we could just order the banks to give us a dekko at any account we wanted,' Hart grumbled. 'Makes you wonder what side they're on, sometimes.'

'Liberty and democracy, perhaps,' Atherton suggested, with the sharpness of someone whose customary seat had been usurped.

Everyone assembled again for McLaren's exposition. Studying vehicle camera tapes was, to the normal person, brain-bleedingly boring. It helped to have the ability to blank out the other parts of your brain; or, as Swilley unkindly remarked, to have no activity in them to begin with. McLaren was largely impervious to insult, partly because he was used to it, but recently because his new relationship with Natalie had sunk him into a bucolic stupor of content, and the barbs of sarcasm went so far over his head you could have bounced mobile phone signals off them.

He did like an audience, though. He preened his moustache, which had gone beyond Burt Reynolds into full walrus mode. It was so rampant now, it looked as though he could strain nourishment out of the air with it. There were baleen whales that had less to filter with. The growth rate had been astonishing. It must be, Swilley said, why he had to keep eating all the time, otherwise, like a pregnant woman, he'd end up consuming his own bones and teeth to sustain it.

First of all, he explained, he'd fed the index they'd got from the motor that picked up the boys at Ivanka's into the ANPR, and established that there had been no registered movement since the Sunday night into Monday morning when Kimmelman had been killed.

'But o' course, if it *was* the same motor that went after the guv, we know they obscured the number plate, so it wouldn't register a ping anyway.'

But on the Sunday night it had been out and about at a time when by any account Kimmelman was already dead.

'It was a company car,' Atherton pointed out. 'We don't know he had exclusive use of it.'

'Obviously he didn't,' Swilley said impatiently.

'Well, not after he was dead, but even before—'

'Get on with it, Maurice. Never mind those two,' Hart urged.

He gave the three of them a patient look, and resumed. For their purposes, the only ANPR camera in the area that mattered was on the west side of the Green, and covered the junction with Uxbridge Road. 'On the Sunday, we got the motor in question going north up Wood Lane at 11.47 pm, and returning the same way at 11.58 pm, so—'

'North up Wood Lane?' Swilley said. 'So it could have been going to Jacket's Yard. With the body.'

'That's cold, using the bloke's own motor to get rid of his corpse,' said LaSalle.

'What d'you want them to do, hire a hearse and a bloke in a top hat to walk in front?'

'Eleven minutes,' Atherton interrupted her. 'Say three minutes each way to the yard and back, that leaves five minutes to roll the body out of the car and make sure it looks all right.'

'If that's where it was going,' Loessop said cautiously.

Slider intervened. 'I'm sure you've got more to tell us than that,' he suggested to McLaren. 'Please carry on.'

'Yes, guv,' he said gratefully. 'I've looked at a lot of cameras, and you won't want to hear all the details, but the main traffic camera I found that covers the front of Ruskin House, looking straight north up Shepherd's Bush Road, it's too far back to recognise people coming out of the house. But o'course as cars come closer to it, you can read the number plate, so you can track them backwards.'

'Understood,' said Slider.

'So it looks like Kimmelman kept the motor in question—'

'Can you stop calling it that?' Atherton said, pained.

'Yeah, just call it the Beamer,' LaSalle suggested.

'OK,' McLaren said, unrattled. He stroked his gnat-strainer and resumed. 'It looks like Kimmelman keeps the Beamer down Westwick Gardens, because you can see a man who could be him come out the front of Ruskin and walk down Westwick, then you see the Beamer come out of Westwick and turn south towards the camera, and then you can clock the index, all right? And I got other cameras picking up the m–the Beamer at other locations. So I can map the journey, OK?'

'Yeah, we know how you do it, Maurice. Get on with it,' said Hart.

'So Friday night he's come back from doing the blackmail tape on the boat. He's took the boys back to Soho first, then he's come home straight along the A40, and you see him park up and walk in the front of Ruskin at 1.36, that'd be Saturday morning. Next movement is Saturday evening, 6.25 pm, he comes out the flats, goes down Westwick, the Beamer comes out and heads south down Shepherd's Bush Road. Now, there's a school on the corner of Shepherd's Bush Road and the south side of Brook Green, that's got a camera covering the road. The Beamer turns left down Brook Green and then right into Luxemburg Gardens.'

'Oh-ho. The plot thickens,' said Atherton.

'Like Maurice's 'tache,' said Hart. 'Where's he go, Mo?'

'I got no camera in Luxemburg Gardens itself,' McLaren said, 'but there's only four ways he can go from there, and with any of 'em, he's got to exit either onto Hammersmith Road or back onto Brook Green. It's like a triangle with just a few roads crossing it. I've got all those possible exits covered. You don't wanna know how—'

'We don't,' said Atherton, and this time without irony. He could imagine the work involved, and was simply glad someone else was willing to do it.

'And he never comes out anywhere else. And he don't come out of Luxemburg Gardens again until he comes back past the school and goes home. Which is 9.33 pm. Which is as good as to say—'

'He was somewhere in that small triangle of streets all that time,' said Atherton.

'And Holdsworth's house is in Luxemburg Place, off Luxemburg Gardens,' Slider said, 'so it's working hypothesis that that's where he was.' It was not cast iron, but it was good enough for most reasonable people. 'What next?'

'Sunday afternoon. He comes out at a quarter to five and drives to Luxemburg Gardens again. Then nothing more until the trip up Wood Lane and back.'

'You got that off the ANPR,' Slider said, 'but have you got any other camera coverage?'

'Yes, guv. The Beamer comes from Luxemburg Gardens. After it crosses into Wood Lane, I got the camera at White City station confirming it passes there both ways. Then it comes back the same way to Luxemburg Gardens.'

'That's very suggestive,' Slider said. 'Any other movements?'

'It comes back to Ruskin House,' McLaren said, with small, allowable triumph. 'Does a u-ey and parks right outside on the double yellow. It's ten to one in the morning, so there's not much traffic about. Bloke gets out and walks up to the house, lets himself in. It's too far off to ID him,' he said apologetically, anticipating the question, 'but I've kind of got used to the *shape* of Kimmelman by now, if you see what I mean, watching him come and go, and this is a taller, thinner bloke to my mind. So he goes in, and he comes out again 2.42, with two big bags in his hands, look like black bin liners, and he gets in the Beamer and drives back to Luxemburg Gardens. And the Beamer doesn't come out again, not as far as I've looked, which is up to the Tuesday. I could go on further, but it's a lot of work. S'up t'you, guv. I got all this put together in an evidential tape, plus the originals copied and preserved. Sorry it took so long, but—'

'It's a great effort,' Slider said. 'Well done.'

There was a silence as everyone digested the information.

Finally, Swilley spoke. 'So it looks as though Kimmelman went to see Holdsworth on Sunday afternoon and never came back.'

'We know he was killed some time on Sunday and dumped after six thirty on Sunday night, so that all fits,' said Slider.

'And Mrs Greenwood heard someone in the flat after midnight,' said Swilley. 'Holdsworth's got to be the man.'

'It's good circumstantial evidence,' Slider said. 'But it's not rock solid. And juries do like a motive.'

'It's a pity we had to waste so much time on Rathkeale,' LaSalle grumbled. 'We might have been watching Holdsworth and catching him at something.'

'If Kimmelman was killed at his house, maybe there's still some evidence around,' Loessop said hopefully.

'It was a dry killing – no blood,' Hart said.

'We'd never get a warrant, anyway,' Atherton said. 'Not on McLaren's tapes alone.'

'So what now, boss?' Hart asked.

Slider looked at his watch. 'I think we go home, and we all rack our brains as to what more we can do. Holdsworth isn't going anywhere.'

'As long as he doesn't have another go at you. Want me to drive you home?' Hart said. 'I can sleep on the floor outside your bedroom door, keep you safe. I know karate.'

There had been a time when he might have thought she was at least half serious, when – according to Atherton – she'd

had a little crush on him. Now her grin told him there was
nothing there but high spirits.

It was good to see how, even with the case dragging on,
morale remained high, and they all remained quite bucked –
several initial letters of the alphabet short of where the top
brass traditionally liked to keep their underlings.

Working on the assumption that the subconscious is better at
thinking things out than the conscious, Slider put the case
into the back of his mind when he got out of the car. He'd
had long enough for fruitless pondering on the journey, since
it had taken longer than usual.

He was being ultra-careful, going by a roundabout route,
changing direction frequently and watching in the rear-view
for lights that kept following, or other cars hastily turning
when he did. He didn't park in his own street until there was
no other car behind him; he didn't park outside his own house,
and he switched off the lights and sat in the car in the dark
for a while to see who else went past. But there was nothing
to alarm.

It was not international espionage, he reminded himself,
or a CIA operation, or a Jason Bourne film. It had been a
clumsy, amateur attempt either to kill or frighten him. Even
professional criminals were pretty stupid and inefficient, and
civilians more so. So he put everything determinedly to one
side as he let himself into his house.

His father and Lydia were on the sofa watching the television news, having just put George to bed. Mr Slider got to
his feet at once.

'I wasn't expecting you so soon,' he said. 'We'll go down,
leave you in peace.'

'Peace is the last thing I want,' said Slider. 'My head's
like a sackful of ferrets. Stay, have a drink, talk to me. I
don't suppose you know if there's anything for supper?' He
knew perfectly well that Dad would know exactly what there
was in his fridge. He still worried that Slider might not eat
properly.

'There's sausages,' Dad said with a promptness that gave him
away. 'I could cook 'em for you, if you're too tired.' He glanced

apologetically at Lydia. 'We were just going to be naughty and telephone for a take-away.'

'Chinese or Indian?' Slider asked.

'Indian,' said Lydia, filtering information from Slider's expression. 'Want us to order some for you, too?'

'I don't fancy sausages,' he admitted. 'Have it here with me.'

They exchanged another of those looks, that made him wonder if they'd actually invented telepathy and hadn't told anybody, then Mr Slider said, 'Go on up and see your boy. We'll phone in the order and put the plates in the oven. What'd you like?'

George was fast asleep, his tender cheek nestled on the uncompromising bosom of a plastic transformer toy. Slider eased it out, and replaced it with George's battered toy lamb, mentally protested at the hard-edged marks left in the rosy mound, while automatically thinking they would present an interesting forensic challenge.

George stirred, said, 'Splad,' in his sleep, and settled again.

'Don't grow up to be a policeman, boy,' Slider murmured. 'Your mind is never really your own again.'

And left him.

He had a pleasant evening, eating butter chicken and a big fat greasy naan, with Dad and Lydia round the kitchen table. They had a bottle of beer each, and talked about holidays.

Slider was contemplating renting a cottage in Devon or Dorset for a family holiday with Joanna and George and his children from his first marriage. 'And you and Lydia as well,' he invited.

Lydia was doubtful, thinking the West Country would be bound to be wet, and probably as expensive as, say, Spain, when you added it all up. Except that the children could only go in August when the air fares were highest. 'Though you could drive down,' she added. 'Save the fare.'

Slider thought two days in a car with Kate and Matthew was less like a holiday and more like *I'm A Celebrity, Get Me Out Of Here*, only with fewer pan-fried maggots.

Dad mourned over the ridiculous necessity of booking

holidays in the middle of winter, while Lydia opined it was a nice way to banish the winter blues, poring over pictures of blue seas and sunshine. Dad said he never had winter blues, winter was as important as summer, and how would you get a decent crop if the fields didn't get their rest, not to mention the cold killing off the pests?

Upon which cue they naturally discussed the unseasonal warmth of the last few weeks.

And Dad said, 'Joanna's late.' And then, 'It's getting very foggy out.'

He probably didn't mean anything by putting the two statements together, but since he and Lydia left soon afterwards, it gave Slider something unwelcome to think about while he washed up the plates, until finally he heard Joanna's key in the lock.

'I went for a quick supper with the trumpets,' she explained, taking off her coat in the hall. The fog was quite thick outside, and the smell of it had come in with her; there were jewels of moisture in her hair from the brief walk from the pavement to the door. 'Peter White and Archie Paul. It was fun. They send their love.'

'I bet they don't.'

'Regards, then. It's a longer word. I was saving energy. Boy, am I pooped!'

'Hard going?' It had been the rehearsal for Children In Need.

'My arm's hanging off. Three hours' solid scrubbing.'

'But worth it?' he suggested.

'For the money? Need you ask?'

'No, I meant the artistic satisfaction, of course.'

She rolled her eyes. 'Oh my God! I don't know if it's the Albert Hall and its world famous acoustics, or just that they're not used to performing with a live orchestra, but the singers were warbling away in a world of their own. There's only so much you can do to adjust the pitch as you play. To get near *them* you'd have had to retune the entire orchestra every few bars.'

'I expect it'll be all right on the night,' he said soothingly.

'The sound engineers will have their work cut out,' she said.

'You know the old saying, why is being a soprano like staying in a cheap hotel? Because you can come in whenever you like and you don't have to worry about the key.'

He laughed. 'Want a drink?'

'No, thanks. Let's just go to bed. Did you have a nice evening?'

Walking up the stairs, he told her about the curry and the holiday talk, the substituting Spain for Dorset and driving down there.

She opened her eyes wide. 'What a terrible idea. Anyway, kids in the back seat of cars cause accidents. It's a well known fact.'

'Equally, accidents in the back seat of cars cause kids,' said Slider.

She snorted. 'How's your case going?'

'Don't want to talk about that. Let's just go to bed and pretend it's the back seat.'

'Rude!' she said admiringly.

SIXTEEN

Nemesis, Exodus

Swilley was already there when Slider got in on Friday morning. She came straight to him with a cup of tea – from the canteen, the sort you could have spread on bread – and an idea.

'I keep thinking about Mrs Holdsworth. Atherton said she seemed nervous and depressed when he was there, and I saw this pathetic figure at the upstairs window. It occurs to me that she could be the weak link. If I could get her on her own and work on her . . .'

'Work on her how?'

'Well, if Holdsworth's a bit of a domestic tyrant, like Atherton thinks, she might open up to a woman. Might be glad of a sympathetic ear.'

'Hmm. If she knows anything. If there's anything to know,' said Slider.

Swilley shrugged. 'If not, I've wasted nothing but my time.'

'And possibly put him on his guard.'

'If he's not on his guard by now, after trying to kill you . . .'

'There is that consideration,' Slider admitted. 'All right, how are you going to get her on her own?'

'Watch the house until he leaves it, then go and knock on the door.'

'It has the merit of simplicity,' Slider said.

He didn't need to warn her of the difficulties and pitfalls. She was an intelligent officer. And he didn't try to tell her how to direct her questions. It would be a delicate business, needing instant adaptation on Swilley's part to whatever direction the conversation took. The art of the interview was always to let the subject think they weren't telling you anything you didn't already know.

But there also could come a point when you had to apply a little judicious menace. Like the shucking knife inserted into the oyster shell, you had to know exactly where to put it in and how to twist it. A less good boss would have insisted on keeping that for himself, but he knew Swilley had all the steel she needed.

'Go for it,' he said.

It was fortunate that Luxemburg Place had only one exit, and also that there were plenty of cars parked in Luxemburg Gardens. Swilley was able to park inconspicuously among them, with a good view of the only way Holdsworth could drive out. She did a careful recce on foot, just far enough up the Place to see that there were still two cars parked on the forecourt, then went back to her own to wait. There was, of course, the chance that he might not leave at all. But it was a nice day, and he'd said he played golf; and if he really did have no business to conduct any more, he would surely not want to be cooped up in the house all day with his uncharismatic wife. Either Davy Lane concerns or the lure of at least the nineteenth hole would surely winkle him out at some point.

It was a quarter to eleven when the Range Rover came
rumbling up to the junction, paused, then turned right,
bringing it right past Swilley. She bent her head as though
looking at her mobile phone, and out of the corner of her
eye got a good sight of Holdsworth driving. He did not glance
her way; he stared straight ahead, leaning forward and grip-
ping the wheel like one not at ease. He was wearing glasses
– presumably he was short-sighted and they were distance
lenses for driving. She had a small bet with herself that he
was off to the golf course; also, given the time, that it was
the club house that would receive his patronage rather than
the greens. She watched in the rear-view until it had trundled
slowly to the junction of Bute Gardens and turned left, and
then made her way to the house. If he had just popped out
for a pint of milk and came suddenly back, she'd have to do
some quick thinking, but she wasn't afraid of him. She'd
trained in hand-to-hand fighting and he was just a civilian.
The faster beat of her heart was due to the excitement of the
chase, gearing up for the challenge of getting information
out of her quarry.

Her quarry opened the door and looked first blank, and then
troubled.

'Oh!' she said. 'It's you. Charles has gone out. You just
missed him, I'm afraid.' She glanced back over her shoulder
with the automatic guilt of someone who has a naked
lover warming up on the sitting-room sofa, but Swilley
reckoned it was just a nervous tic.

'That's all right,' she said soothingly. 'It was you I wanted
to talk to, Mrs Holdsworth.'

Now the expression segued to alarm. 'I – oh! Um! I don't
think Charles would like that. Not without him being here.'
Swilley gave her the receptive-smile-and-silence routine,
forcing her to go on, to justify her previous statement. 'He
– he doesn't like me to talk to – I mean, I'm not . . .' She
foundered on the sweet innocence of the smile, and concluded,
wretchedly, 'I don't really know anything.'

Swilley said kindly, 'About what?'

The eyes flickered over her face, looking for clues, hoping
for mercy. 'It's about Leon, isn't it?' she asked at last.

Swilley's heart sang. 'Yes, mostly,' she said. 'But can I come in? You don't want to be talking out here, on the doorstep.'

'Well, I suppose – I suppose it's all right,' she said at last. 'Charles does know you.' She stepped back, allowing Swilley across the threshold. Her height in the hallway seemed to bring a fresh anxiety. Outside, Swilley had been down a step. Now she towered. Mrs Holdsworth made a fresh appeal. 'Only – can't you wait until he comes back? I do think he'd want to be here.'

It was a good opening. 'How long will he be?'

'Well, several hours,' said Mrs Holdsworth. *Thank God*! 'He's gone to lunch with some people. But I could call him . . .'

'No, don't do that. I don't want to disturb him. As I said, it's really you I wanted to talk to.'

'I don't know why,' Mrs Holdsworth said bleakly, as though the idea of anyone wanting to talk to her was beyond understanding. Swilley conceived a strange desire to bludgeon Charles Holdsworth with clubs.

Mrs H had reached the door of a sitting room, a grimly tidy room in which a vacuum cleaner stood in the middle of the carpet, and a basket of polishes and dusters decorated a coffee table. She hesitated, and said, 'I was just doing the cleaning. I suppose – would you like a cup of coffee? Or tea?'

Better to give her something to do with her hands, Swilley thought. 'A cup of tea would be nice,' she said. When Mrs Holdsworth turned towards the kitchen, she followed her closely, so as not to be marooned in another room. The kitchen was bright, with large windows overlooking a wide but very dull garden, and was spotlessly clean, though the fitments were dated. It had the feel of something that had been newly and quite expensively done twenty-five years ago and would now have to last. Mrs Holdsworth gave her an unsettled look, as if not knowing what to do with her. Swilley sat herself down at the kitchen table with an air of having been here many times before, and smiled helpfully, leaving Mrs Holdsworth with no choice but to switch the kettle on and go about tea-making.

'So tell me about Leon,' Swilley said, with no particular emphasis.

Mrs Holdsworth gave her a glance. 'Well, we're very worried

about him, of course. Charles has been in quite a state. He doesn't
like to show it, but I can tell. I suppose you haven't found
him, or heard anything? You'd have let us know if you had?'

Found him? *What was this*? Swilley had to be careful. Never
answer a question you don't want to answer: that was Slider's
Rule. Ask one of your own instead. 'When did you last see
him?'

'Well, not since that weekend,' she answered. 'Two weeks
ago tomorrow.' She looked puzzled. 'A young man came
from your station about it *last* Friday. I thought Charles must
have told him all about it then – Leon going missing. Otherwise,
why did he come?'

So she didn't know Kimmelman was dead. That could be
used to advantage, perhaps – as long as Swilley could keep
her talking. She mustn't let her get nervous and clam up. 'Of
course,' Swilley said, at her most soothing, 'but you see,
different people sometimes remember different details, and
it's important for us to know everything possible if we're to
help. That's why I wanted to talk to *you*.'

'But I—'

'Women always have a different perspective on things,
don't you find? Men are so busy with their work lives, they
often don't notice little things that seem quite obvious to us.
They see the big picture, but we see the detail.' Mrs Holdsworth
pondered this doubtfully. Swilley went on, 'And we do want
to do everything we can to clear up this business. I know you
must want that, too.'

'Yes,' she said, fiddling with a teaspoon. 'Poor Leon! I am
so worried about him.'

'You're fond of him,' Swilley tried.

She looked up, her eyes naked. 'He's been so good to
Charlie. Our son?' Swilley nodded. 'Charlie's . . . not well.
He has . . . problems. And Leon's taken care of him, kept him
out of trouble, watched over him. Sort of like a—'

'Nursemaid?'

She frowned. 'Well, I wouldn't put it quite like that. But
he was always there for him, and he could do more with
Charlie than anyone else. I don't know what we'd have done
without him.'

'He does a lot for your husband, too, doesn't he?'

'He's Charles's right-hand man. He's almost like family. And he's so capable, so calm – nothing puts him out. Charles always says, if you want anything done, you go to Leon.'

'So I can see how you'd be worried if he went missing,' Swilley said warmly. 'How did you know that he *was* missing?'

Mrs Holdsworth had just poured water into the teapot, and looked up from it, amazed. 'Well, he hasn't been here, of course. We see him practically every day – Charles does, even if I don't – and he hasn't been around. Or telephoned, or anything.'

'He couldn't just have gone on holiday?'

'Not without saying. Anyway, I don't remember him ever having a holiday. He's not the holiday sort. And he'd never have gone anywhere without telling Charles. That's why Charles told the police – reported him missing.'

'And Charles has tried telephoning him?'

'Of *course* he has. But he never answers.'

So that was what Holdsworth had told his wife, to account for the missing factotum. Then he had behaved just as he would have had he really not known Kimmelman was dead – a clever stratagem, until he panicked when Atherton appeared at the door and denied he'd ever known the man. Big mistake. Big, big mistake.

But she must play Mrs H carefully. She had just brought two cups of tea over, and was hesitating about sitting down. Swilley smiled and pulled out the chair catty-corner to her invitingly, and she sat. She seemed to have warmed up a little, or at least had got used to Swilley's presence. Perhaps it was because she was sitting down, and no longer towering over her. At any rate, she seemed to have resigned herself to the process of answering questions. She sipped her tea and looked at Swilley passively, waiting for the next one.

'So, tell me about when you last saw Leon. On Saturday, was it?'

'Well, he did come over on the Saturday. For supper. Myra was here, and Jack—'

'Myra?' It was the familiarity of the tone she was questioning.

'Charles's sister.'

'Yes, of course,' Swilley said, without missing a beat, though her heart had jumped. So Myra Silverman was Holdsworth's sister! That was the missing link. It explained an awful lot.

'And Jack's his business partner, though of course as his brother-in-law he's really more family. And Leon is almost family, so it was like a . . . a . . .'

'Family gathering,' Swilley supplied. 'What did you all talk about?'

'Oh, nothing in particular. I don't remember. Just – you know – normal things.'

'Coal Sidings Road, perhaps?' She looked puzzled. 'The youth centre they're all so interested in.'

'Oh, you mean the Davy Lane centre,' she said. 'That's what it will be called. When it's finished. But they didn't talk about that. They wouldn't talk about business when we're having supper together. I don't have anything to do with Charles's business affairs, anyway. He likes to keep his business life quite separate from his private life. He doesn't think it's civilised to mix the two.'

Convenient way to keep his wife out of it and give himself maximum freedom, Swilley thought. She wondered if there had been other reasons in the past for the separation of church and state – women, perhaps? She supposed he had been handsome, in a stuffed-shirt sort of way. And a man with his own business always had a certain attraction.

'How is it going, the Davy Lane project?' Swilley asked casually.

Mrs Holdsworth frowned. 'I don't know. I don't really know anything about it. Myra would be the one to ask. It was her idea to begin with.' She sounded as though she didn't quite approve.

Swilley wondered if there were bad feeling somewhere in this big happy family. She tried, 'I expect you see a lot of Myra?'

'Well, she's busy, of course. She has her own career.' There it was again, the slight disapproval. Was it Myra in particular or women's careers in general? As a career woman, she had to be careful.

'She does very good things, though, doesn't she? Important work for children?'

'She has time for it. She doesn't have any children of her own. She'd find things are very different when you're . . .' She ran out of steam.

'In the front line?' Swilley suggested.

Mrs Holdsworth sighed. 'It isn't as easy as she thinks.'

'You have just the one?'

'We have a daughter as well, Andrea, but she's married and lives in New Zealand, so we don't see her, just a letter at Christmas. She and Charles – well, they didn't always see eye to eye.' She sighed again. 'And Charlie – well, it's hard being a parent, that's all I'm saying.'

'He's in a facility now, isn't he?' Swilley said, sympathetically.

'A rest home,' Mrs Holdsworth corrected sharply. 'It's like a country hotel, only with medical facilities. Really nice. Leon found it for him – oh dear! Leon. What will Charlie do when he finds out he's missing? We haven't told him yet. You don't think . . . you don't think something's happened to him?'

Slider's Rule again. 'Tell me about the Sunday. You saw him on the Sunday as well, didn't you?'

'Well, he came over, about five o'clock I think it was. I didn't really see him. He rang Charles and said he wanted to come over and talk business.'

'You didn't see him at all?'

'Not to talk to. I was upstairs. I have a sitting room up there, my television room. Charles doesn't like having a television in the drawing room. He says it isn't civilised.' That seemed to be a favourite word of his, Swilley thought. 'He doesn't care for TV much, anyway. So I watch it upstairs. I was watching the serial when I heard Leon arrive. I went to the top of the stairs and looked down, and he was in the hall. Charles had let him in. Then Charles saw me and said, "It's business. Go and watch your programme. And shut the door."'

'Why, "shut the door"?' Swilley queried.

'Oh, so that the sound of the television wouldn't bother them,' she said, as if it were the natural thing.

'And you didn't go down at all?'

'It was business,' she said simply. 'Charles doesn't like being disturbed when it's business.'

Exiled upstairs. Swilley remembered the little face at the window. How easy some women made it for their cheating, manipulative men. But she had seen Holdsworth in the flesh, and thought that perhaps Mrs H was happier in her little haven with the idiot-box for company. It, at least, would never hurt her, or pose questions she couldn't answer.

'And what time did he leave?' she asked.

'Leon? Well, I don't know for sure,' she said, with a worried look. 'I came downstairs at about seven to see about supper. The drawing-room door was shut and I could hear voices inside, so I knocked and Charles put his head out and said "We're busy, get yourself something and go back upstairs." I asked if they wanted anything, and he said he'd sort it out if they did. He said Jack was there and they'd be talking until late, so not to come down again. So I got myself a sandwich and went back upstairs. So I didn't see when Leon left. Or Jack.'

'You said you heard voices. Did you hear what they were talking about?'

'Goodness, no,' she said. 'I wouldn't *listen*.'

'Of course not. I just thought you might have heard a word or two accidentally, when Charles opened the door.'

'They stopped talking when I knocked.'

'Yes, of course, they would. Did Charles say anything the next day about why they'd had a meeting?'

'Well, he wouldn't, not to me. He didn't discuss his business with me. I suppose it was some problem that had come up.'

'Why do you think that?'

'Well, he looked tired. And rather worried.'

'And has he gone on seeming worried?'

She thought about it. 'No, he seemed to be all right for a couple of days, but then he started worrying about where Leon was, and since that young man from your station came round to tell him that you hadn't found him, he's not been himself at all. Very tense and . . . snappy. It's preying on his mind, I can see – worrying about poor Leon.'

'Yes, I'm sure it is,' Swilley said. 'So, you didn't hear Leon leave? Didn't hear his car start up, for instance? It could be very important, any little clue we have about timing.'

She was shaking her head, but there was a tense, gestational look about her, that suggested there was something on her mind. Swilley tried to think what it might be.

'You didn't perhaps look out of the window, and see Leon's car drive off?'

She shook her head again. 'But I did hear it,' she admitted, guiltily. 'Or I think I did. It was quite late. I'd gone to bed, but I got up to go to the bathroom. That was about half past eleven. And I thought I heard a car start down below. Of course, we have triple glazing here, so you can't hear very much. I looked down from the landing window as I passed, and there were only our two cars down there, so Leon and Jack had obviously both gone by then. It may have been one of them I heard.'

'And your husband – where was he then?'

'Downstairs. I heard him come up a bit later.'

'He came up to bed?'

She looked down in what would have been a blush in a younger person. 'We have separate rooms.'

'I see. And is there anything else you can remember about that night?' Swilley felt there *was* something – something she wanted to impart but was afraid or ashamed to. 'Something you saw? Something you overheard?'

Still she shook her head. Swilley said, 'Mrs Holdsworth, I can't impress on you enough how important any little thing might be. It may seem meaningless or trivial to you, but sometimes something like that can be the one link we need.' Resistance. 'You do want us to find out what's happened to Leon, don't you? After he was so kind to you.'

Now she looked up with tears in her eyes. 'I'm afraid,' she said, in a whisper, 'I'm afraid something bad's happened to him.'

'If it has, even more important that we find out. What was it you heard?' Now Mrs Holdsworth stared imploringly, as if begging to have it guessed, so that she need not be guilty of telling it unprovoked. Swilley had to take a punt. 'Something you heard when Charles opened the door of the drawing room. Something they were saying inside?'

She nodded, tears in her eyes – tears of relief, perhaps?

'I didn't knock,' she whispered, the awful confession. 'I heard the raised voices, and I didn't knock, I stood there and *listened*.'

'*Anyone* would do the same,' Swilley said warmly. 'You're not to be blamed. You couldn't help overhearing, if they were shouting.'

'They weren't shouting, exactly, just talking – *heatedly*.'

'And what were they saying?' Swilley urged.

'Oh, nothing important,' said Mrs Holdsworth. Apparently, it was the confession about listening that had blocked her, not what she had heard. 'Jack said something like, "Why me? Why have I got to do all the dirty work?" and Charles said, "Because I've got children and you haven't," or something like that. And then Jack started to say something, and broke off, and I . . .' She looked ashamed again. 'I sort of guessed that they knew I was there. I put my hand up to knock, and Charles opened the door so quickly I know he must have been trying to catch me. I . . . my heart was pounding. I could hardly speak. I said something about supper. I could see from his eyes he was angry, but he didn't say anything, only told me to go upstairs and stay there. I . . . I was afraid he'd come up later and . . . and have it out with me. When I heard him come up, much later, when I was in bed, I heard him open my bedroom door, and I pretended like anything to be asleep. I thought he might wake me up,' she was almost panting now at the memory. 'I was trying not to tremble. But he went away and closed the door. I suppose he thought I really was asleep. It was awful.'

'I can imagine,' Swilley said. She meant it. She wondered if Holdsworth had been in the habit of hitting his dandelion-headed little wife, or if it was just the other, in some ways worse, brutality of mental torture he used on her. 'How dreadful for you.'

'I didn't sleep very well after that. I was so afraid he'd still come in. But he didn't. I kept sort of dozing off and waking again, frightening myself.' Swilley nodded encouragingly. 'Men can be so . . .' She didn't seem to know how to end the sentence.

Swilley felt there was a tender shoot of trust growing between them. She nurtured it. 'They have so much on their minds,' she said – *God help me* – 'that I sometimes think, although they don't *mean* to be cruel . . .'

'Charles does,' she said abruptly, startlingly. 'He likes to dominate everybody around him. That's why Andrea went so far away, all the way across the world, to get away from him. And I sometimes think Charlie's problems . . . He was always so harsh with Charlie. Said he lacked ambition. He wanted to be a rock star, you know – Charlie. He took guitar lessons – Charles didn't approve. He doesn't like modern music – he says it's decadent. He wanted Charlie to follow him into business. But Charlie and some friends started up a band. Charles didn't know. They used to play in secret in their bedrooms. Not here, of course. I don't know if they'd ever have been any good. But Charles found out, somehow, and . . .' Words seemed to fail her as she contemplated the memory. 'Well, he stopped it. Stopped Charlie, anyway. He found his guitar and smashed it. He kept it hidden in the garage—' She stopped abruptly, her eyes inward.

'You've remembered something?' Swilley tried, after a moment.

Mrs Holdsworth looked up. 'I'm not a traitor. I'm not. I would never . . . give anyone away.'

'Of course not,' said Swilley. 'But you do want to help find poor Leon, don't you?'

'You said, anything I remembered. It was nothing important. Just . . . odd.'

'Yes? Anything at all,' Swilley urged.

'Well, in the middle of the night, that night, the Sunday night, I thought I heard the garage door opening and then a bit later closing. It's one of those up and over doors, it makes a sort of rumbling noise. You wouldn't notice it in the daytime, unless you were listening for it. But at night, when the house is quiet – if you happen to be lying awake . . .'

'Did you get up and look?' Swilley asked.

She shook her head. 'I was afraid to. I thought it had to be Charles, and if he'd found me wandering about . . . I didn't want to bump into him.'

'I quite understand,' Swilley said. She thought a bit. 'I notice your two cars are always out front. You don't ever put them in the garage?'

'No,' she said. 'There's only room for one, anyway. Charles says I'm not capable of backing in or out without damaging something. And he likes his Range Rover out front ready to go. He says they're designed for the open air. And he says cars get rusty if you keep them in garages.'

Swilley had heard that before. There was some truth in it, if you put them away wet and left them there for weeks. 'Have you looked in the garage since then? Is anything different in there?'

Now her eyes were round with fright. 'No,' she said. 'I've no reason to go in there. I don't keep anything in there. Charles has his tool bench and so on. It's his place really. I *never* go in there.'

What was she afraid of? Swilley wondered. This was not just general wariness of upsetting Charles – how would he know, if she took a look when he was out? No, she was afraid of what she might see in there.

My God, she thought Leon might be in there, didn't she? His dead body, hung up on a hook, grinning; or stuffed in a cupboard, ready to fall out on her, pantomime style, when she opened the door. Or tied to a chair, gagged, and making muffled appeals for help that she would not be able to respond to. She was clinging outwardly to the belief that Leon was just missing, had wandered off, perhaps, in a fit of amnesia, but some animal instinct regarding her husband, some instinct of self-preservation that made her super-sensitive to him, told her there had been dirty deeds, and that she really, *really* did not want to find out what they were.

Swilley reached out and laid a hand over Mrs Holdsworth's. It was icy cold, and it flinched at her touch. 'Let's go and have a look,' she said.

'No!' Mrs Holdsworth said quickly, breathlessly. 'I couldn't.'

'You don't have to come,' Swilley said, exuding calm and reassurance as she stood. 'I'll just have a quick look, just to reassure you. I'm sure there's nothing in there to be afraid of.'

Mrs Holdsworth dragged herself slowly to her feet, and as Swilley passed her, she fell in behind – perhaps simply not wanting to be left alone. Swilley could guess the way easily enough, knowing which side of the house the garage was on. There was a door in the right rear corner of the kitchen, which led into a utilities room, with washing machine, dryer and a big cabinet freezer. Another door evidently led to the garage. Swilley reached for the door handle and heard Mrs H draw in a sharp breath. She opened the door, sensing the old lady so close behind her, she could almost feel her tremble. And then Mrs Holdsworth let out the breath again, in a rushing sigh of relief.

There was no corpse in there, of course – Swilley knew, within a drawer or two, where Leon Kimmelman's mortal remains now lay. There was just a big black SUV, with a BMW badge. The front index plate had mud caked on it so that you couldn't read the number, and there were mud splashes on the bonnet and wings too, as if an effort had been made to make it look natural and accidental. And Swilley was fairly sure that if she walked round the back, she would find the rear plate had been removed.

And now Mrs Holdsworth, who had breathed such a heart-felt sigh of relief, said, in a puzzled tone, 'What's Leon's car doing here? How did it get in here? If it's here, where can he be?'

Swilley turned to her. 'I think you had better come with me to the station, and make a statement.'

She looked frightened. 'Am I under arrest? Have I done something wrong?'

Swilley laid a kindly hand on her cardigan'd forearm. 'No, no, not at all. There's no need to be alarmed. We just need to take it all down officially, everything you've already told me.'

Also, she thought, we need to make sure you are safe. She could imagine a scenario with Holdsworth coming back and Mrs H, panicked as a horse, blurting out the question – *what's Leon's car doing in our garage?* And the subsequent thwacking noise of some heavy implement making impact with Mrs Holdsworth's fragile eggshell of a skull. If you've done it once, the second time becomes easier.

'We'll go to the station, and take your statement, and I'll make sure you get some lunch, all right?'

And Mrs Holdsworth nodded, her eyes searching Swilley's face, looking for some sign that she had found someone to trust, someone who would perhaps take over responsibility for the increasingly alarming tangle of her life.

SEVENTEEN
Playing Through

'Now we can move!' Porson said, rubbing his hands. 'Now we've got enough for warrants!' The machinery swung into action. Mrs Holdsworth had been put in the soft room under the care of a woman constable and given lunch while Swilley told Slider the outline of the story. She told it in professional terms, but he could not help perceiving between the lines her indignation at the way the woman had been treated; and feeling it himself.

'You did the right thing, bringing her in,' he said. 'She needs looking after – and not only because she's going to be an important witness. As soon as she's eaten, get her to an interview room and get everything down properly. We daren't risk anything being challenged later for procedural reasons.'

'But I wanted to be in on arresting Holdsworth,' Swilley complained. 'I want to see his face.'

'I understand, but you've set up a rapport with Mrs Holdsworth. She trusts you. She might not open up in the same way to a new face. That's why I want you to get her statement as soon as possible, before she has time to think about it and get nervous, or start thinking she should be loyal to dear Charles.'

'Dear Charles. Hah!' said Swilley. But she saw the necessity, and went to do her duty.

'And get as much extra information as possible,' Slider added. 'Any background could be useful.'

'It all goes to motive, I know,' said Swilley.

'"Goes to"!' Slider snorted. 'Don't give me that American slang.'

Mrs Holdsworth had said she didn't know where Charles had gone, which was a problem, because if he arrived home and found the place buzzing with police he might do something stupid like go on the run – he had already shown a stupid streak in trying to mow down Slider – and valuable resources would be wasted in catching him.

A casual telephone call to Jack Silverman's office ascertained that he had gone to lunch with a business colleague. A little further probing revealed the lunch was taking place at a certain golf club; Mrs Holdsworth affirmed that it was the name of Charles's club. 'So they're probably together,' Slider said. 'Two thirds of the villains in one place. How convenient.'

Two squad cars were despatched, with four uniformed officers, Atherton in charge and McLaren riding shotgun in case of trouble. Probably they would behave, Slider thought: Holdsworth would not want to make a scene at his club – old habits die hard. And he might still want to play wounded innocence, even though that mule had left the station days ago and was way down the trail. But if there was anything stupider than the criminal, it was the amateur criminal.

Silverman was an unknown quantity. He might have less to lose in the social acceptability stakes, and not mind starting a rumble; on the other hand, he wouldn't know how much they knew, so would probably pretend innocence. Slider thought they would both come quietly; but you never knew.

Meanwhile, SOC could go in, seal off Luxemburg Place – plenty of parking room for once, what a joy – and get to work on Holdsworth's house. If Kimmelman had been lammed inside, there might just be traces, and a murder weapon. And any paperwork concerning Davy Lane must be confiscated for supporting evidence.

Kimmelman's car must be impounded. If the body had been transported in it, again there might be traces. Even if there were not, mud under the wheel arches could be matched to mud in Jacket's Yard, and the tyres could be matched to the tyre prints taken there. And Slider wouldn't mind if a small dint were found that matched the bruise on his hip. He didn't like people trying to kill him. He'd enjoy getting Holdsworth for that.

*   *   *

Atherton was always amused to note that however fabulous the manicured rolling green acres of the golf course, the club house was usually a bit of a shack. This one was no exception: an oblong box built in the worst period of the seventies out of nasty cheap brick the colour of tinned salmon. As luck would have it, Holdsworth and Silverman were just leaving as they got out of their cars. Holdsworth gave them a blank look, and then one of dithering panic. Silverman looked at Holdsworth, scowling as though it were his fault, and snapped, 'Now, what the—?'

Atherton interrupted just in time – there was no way that sentence would end well. 'Charles Holdsworth and Jack Silverman, I arrest you for the murder of Leon Kimmelman. You do not have to say anything, but—'

Holdsworth's face was trembling, his eyes darting about. The four uniformed bods were moving into place, and at the sight of them he flung out a hand towards Silverman and shouted, 'Not me! *He* did it! Not me! *Him*!'

Silverman threw him a murderous look and, to everyone's surprise, knocked aside the hand descending on his forearm and took off, across the decorative bit of lawn that faced the clubhouse and away onto the course. Atherton whirled and was after him without thought, sensing rather than seeing two of the uniforms following him, leaving McLaren and the other two with Holdsworth. He heard a splurge of voices behind, but could not pay them attention. Everything in him was concentrated on running.

Silverman had a good start, and was sprinting with the speed of desperation, but he was older and heavier than Atherton, and a smoker. He would have no staying power. Atherton was gaining on him, and could keep this up for a long time yet. Silverman's face flashed white as he threw a glance behind, and he put on a spurt.

He ran between two clumps of trees, onto a fairway, dodged round a bunker, through some rough – that slowed him down more than Atherton – and past more trees. He bounded over a green, to the angry cries of some players. Atherton was close enough now to smell his sweat. It was the traditional moment to shout, 'Give it up! You can't get away!' but Atherton had better use for his breath. They were in the home straight now. Silverman was winded, slogging over the smooth grass by willpower alone, gasping for breath. Atherton grinned, feeling his own body's reserves, and though there was no need – the blighter would have collapsed soon anyway – he couldn't resist bringing him down with a flying rugby tackle. Beautiful!

He got him halfway down the fairway of the 7th hole – par 4, dogleg to the right, tricky bunker in the angle – having just passed a sedate party of golfers, who stared and tutted and muttered among themselves. It's all very well to play through on invitation, but such boorish behaviour brought a club a bad name.

The uniforms came pounding up in time to supply a set of handcuffs – justified now Silverman had run – and Atherton removed his knee from his back and said, 'As I was saying, I arrest you for the murder of Leon Kimmelman.'

There was a little oohing from the golfers. That'd give them something to talk about at the bar.

Meanwhile, squad cars had been despatched to Myra Silverman's office near Tower Bridge and the Silvermans' house in Chiswick to scoop up the missing third element of the conspiracy. She was not at her office. The second team found her at home, looking uncharacteristically ruffled, while assiduously burning paperwork on a barbecue in the garden.

'Of course, we don't know how far she was complicit in the murder,' Slider said to Atherton.

'The papers she was trying to burn were Davy Lane stuff,' he said, 'so she was certainly in on that. Well, we know she was – she was the one who badgered Rathkeale about it. So that's conspiracy to defraud public money.'

'I don't know,' Slider said slowly. 'She could argue she was just lobbying for a legitimate project.'

'She must be worried if she was burning the papers. And there's conspiracy to blackmail,' Atherton said.

'We don't know if she was in on that.'

'I bet she was.'

'So do I, but can we prove it? Kimmelman was Holdsworth's dog – and, by the way, we still don't know why he was killed.'

Atherton grinned. 'The way Charlie ratted Silverman out, I think we won't have any trouble finding out. They'll both be longing to talk to us. I wonder what he ran for – silly ass! You expect that from the Rudys of this world, maybe, not fully-fledged businessmen.'

'You enjoyed it,' Slider observed.

'It made a change. Still can't understand it, though. I suppose he just panicked.'

'Last chance to stretch his legs, perhaps,' said Slider.

'He'll have a stretch of another sort coming up. Are we tacking on attempted murder of a police officer?'

'We might use that as a bargaining chip,' Slider said, 'when we see how amenable they are.' He stood up and stretched. 'Meanwhile, we can now apply for all the bank accounts and telephone records, and start making out a watertight timeline. And put someone onto tracing the SUV from Luxemburg Place to Nigel Playfair Avenue. With a bit of luck, we'll get a shot of who was driving, and then it's game over.

The proper processes had been followed – fingerprints and DNA sample, medical examination and permitted phone call, and all three suspects had elected to have a lawyer sent for. Myra Silverman's was a hotshot human rights solicitor, a good-looking woman famed on TV for her almost knee-length mane of smooth black hair and her savage attacks on the government. Slider thought she was bad news, but Atherton said she was probably not well up on criminal law, and might not have been Myra's best pick, though they'd look good side by side on camera when she was released on bail, which was probably the point. Slider told him not to be cynical.

Jack Silverman's was a local man, and Holdsworth's was a woman, Angela Wilton, who exuded repressed anger as she stalked past them into the room.

'Why did she look at you like that?' Slider murmured to Atherton.

He shrugged. 'I went out with her once.' He thought a moment. 'Well, several times.'

'Oh joy. So you dumped her?'

'*Au contraire*, boss. I was the dumpee. She wanted to be the only one, and didn't like it when she found she wasn't.'

'You and your private life. We should have your trousers sewn up,' Slider said.

'Hey, I never promised her a rose garden. That's the trouble with women of her age – they've written their own script before you've even told them your name.'

'I'm going to pretend I didn't hear that,' said Slider. 'Is she going to cause us trouble?'

'Nah. She'll be professional.'

'I love your optimism.'

Holdsworth was, as predicted, eager to talk. Angela Wilton's nostrils were getting quite a work-out, but she had to take her client's instructions, which were that he wanted to talk. He was sweating, and his eyes were flitting, and before they'd even got the tape running he'd blurted out, 'It wasn't me! Jack did it!'

Wilton sighed lustily. She leaned in to him and hissed, 'Don't *say* anything until you're asked.'

When they had set up, Slider said kindly to Holdsworth, 'Let's just take things in order, from the beginning, shall we? We know what you've done, we've logged it all every step of the way. All we want from you really is to know *why*.'

'But I haven't done *anything*,' Holdsworth pleaded.

'Let's start with Davy Lane,' Slider began.

'That's just business,' Holdsworth interrupted. 'Legitimate business. There's nothing wrong with that.'

'A youth centre with some luxury flats tacked on the top. Or rather, some lucrative flats with a youth centre tacked on underneath so you could get the whole thing paid for with government money.'

'Don't answer that,' said Angela Wilton.

Holdsworth ignored her. 'That was Myra's idea. The whole thing was Myra's idea.' He seemed unable to pass up an opportunity to blame someone else. He looked sulky now. 'She's always getting me into trouble. She made me buy Lloyds shares just before the crash. She thinks she's *so* smart, the great businesswoman, but she's not so clever when you get down to it. Look at the mess she's got us into now!'

Wilton's nostrils were flaring so much she was in danger of taking off.

In her more leisurely, not to say rambling, interview with Mrs Holdsworth, Swilley had obtained a lot of background detail, which was now comfortably under Slider's belt. Since her home was still being examined and she said she had no friends or relatives, Mrs Holdsworth had now been settled in a small hotel they sometimes used, where the proprietress was well versed in keeping an eye on her visitors and making sure they didn't either run or top themselves.

To Swilley Mrs Holdsworth had confessed, 'I never liked Myra much. She was too *hard*. I don't like to see a woman like that. Women ought to be womanly. But they couldn't have children, you know, her and Jack. Charles says it's Jack's fault. I don't know. I don't think she ever wanted them. Charles says she never played with dolls when she was a child. There was just the two of them, you know. Charles is the elder, but *she* was always the one in charge. She was a tomboy – climbing trees, trespassing, breaking windows. She was always leading him into trouble, but then *he*'d be the one to be punished. "You're older than she is," his father would say, "you should take care of your sister." And he'd get beaten, and she'd just laugh. But he never had – I don't know – the *will* to refuse her. She'd say, let's do this, and he just went along with it. Always.'

'But you said he liked to dominate,' Swilley had mentioned.

'Yes,' she sighed. 'Everyone but Myra. I suppose that's why,' she added, as if it were a new insight. 'He could never win with her, so he has to beat everyone else.' And then she looked up, alarmed. 'He's not a bad man, you mustn't think that. I'm not saying he's a bad man.'

'I know what you're saying,' Swilley said soothingly.

She was getting a very nice clear picture, of the sulky, resentful little boy, bullied by his sister, who grew up to bully everyone else in compensation.

And the son who was thrashed by his father often grew up to be the father who thrashed his son. Corporal punishment was like an hereditary flaw, that got passed down the generations.

*   *   *

'Yes,' said Slider, 'Myra was so sure she could get Kevin Rathkeale to back the project, wasn't she?'

'She got that wrong as well. Still, she ought to know him, if anyone does,' Holdsworth said nastily.

'They'd worked together before, on other projects,' Slider said. 'And she had an affair with him.'

Ah, thought Slider. 'He doesn't seem a very . . . well, *attractive* person,' he said.

Holdsworth sniffed. 'Myra doesn't care about that. Power's all she's interested in. She sleeps with men to get power over them.'

Wilton murmured something to him.

'It's not speculation,' he said, sounding surprised. 'She talks about it openly. She's *proud* of it. I don't know how proud she was when she found out about his other proclivities. The rent boys and all that.' He sniggered.

'But his proclivities proved to be useful, didn't they? They allowed you to blackmail him.'

'Don't answer that,' said Wilton, and then, to Slider, 'You are not to go on fishing expeditions. As I understand it, there was no attempt made to extort money or favours from Mr Rathkeale.'

'No,' said Holdsworth. 'We never got that far. It would have worked – Myra was sure about that. Kevin couldn't afford a scandal. But bloody Leon went and—' He stopped abruptly, perhaps with a belated access of caution.

'He did a good job on your boat, setting up the camera and getting that compromising film,' Slider said.

'I'm saying nothing,' Holdsworth said, giving Wilton a smug smile. She rolled her eyes slightly.

'You don't need to,' said Slider. 'It was your boat. Leon was your employee. He picked up the boys and took them back in his company car, provided by you.'

'You have no evidence that my client knew anything about that,' Wilton said.

Slider ignored her and asked Holdsworth, 'Just out of interest, why did you say you didn't know him when my colleague first came to see you?'

Holdsworth looked flustered. 'Well, it wasn't a very good photograph.'

'He told you his name was Leon Kimmelman. You said you'd never heard of him.'

'I was . . . I didn't . . . I'm not used to the police turning up on my doorstep.'

'You were frightened,' Slider offered.

'Yes,' he took it gratefully. Then, with a glance at Wilton: 'No. I had nothing to be frightened about. I didn't like that policeman asking me questions. I didn't think it was any of his business.'

'It's police business when a man has been killed.'

'Well, I didn't know that. I thought Leon had just gone missing.'

Wilton was too professional to put her head in her hands, but Slider thought a faint moan escaped from her.

'You hadn't reported him missing to the police.'

'Why should I? He was a grown man.'

'But you told your wife you *had*.'

'Oh, she's a blundering fool. Muddle headed. You can't take anything she says as true. Anyway, I didn't want her . . .' He stopped again, his eyes shifting guiltily.

'You didn't want her looking in the garage, where Leon's car was hidden.'

'You don't have to answer that,' said Wilton.

'You don't need to,' Slider said sympathetically. 'I'm afraid it's pretty damning evidence. Leon drove to your house in that car and was never seen again. And there's the car in your garage – the same car that was used to dump his body in Jacket's Yard – and also, as it happens, the same car that was used to try to run me down.'

'That wasn't me! That was Jack!' Holdsworth cried.

'I told you not to say anything,' Wilton said desperately. 'That wasn't even a question.'

'But I'm not having that pinned on me,' Holdsworth said indignantly. 'I told Jack some policewoman had come round asking questions and he just went crazy. *He* was the one tried to kill you, not me. And he was the one who killed Leon. It's that temper of his. I told him we should pay him off, but he just lost it.'

'Why don't you tell me what happened that night?' Slider said.

'You don't have to say anything,' Wilton snapped. 'He's trying to get you to incriminate yourself.'

'But I *want* to tell him,' said Holdsworth. 'It doesn't incriminate me – it gets me off.'

'If you *insist* on ignoring my advice . . .'

'No, it'll be all right,' Holdsworth said eagerly. 'You'll see.'

'One thing about Charles,' Mrs Holdsworth said sadly, 'is that he can't bear to admit he's wrong. It's absurd, really. We used to have a cleaner – Isobel was her name. Such a nice lady – Portuguese, but spoke very good English. Well, Charles broke this cut-glass decanter – he dropped it on the glass top of the coffee table one evening, and cracked that as well. And he said Isobel must have done it. I know it was him, because I found the bits of glass hidden in the bottom of the bin in the morning, before she even arrived. But he confronted her and said she'd done it and he was going to dock it from her pay. Of course she protested, and he got very nasty with her, and she walked out. So now I do the cleaning myself,' she concluded sadly. 'It wasn't the first time he'd blamed her for things, you see. A watermark on the dining-room table. A chip out of the door frame. A person can only stand it for so long.'

'But you didn't stand up for Isobel, over the decanter?'

She gave Swilley a look, ashamed and afraid. 'I *couldn't*,' she said, and left it at that.

'He came over to supper on the Saturday,' Holdsworth said. 'It was supposed to be a sort of victory celebration. Of course, we couldn't talk about it in front of Avril. She's such a blundering fool, you can't trust her not to blurt everything out to the wrong person. But we had a few words after supper while she was out in the kitchen making the coffee. Leon said the film had come out perfectly and that he'd edit it the next day and make a copy for us. And he asked how much he was going to get paid for it. I said he'd be paid for his time, the same as he always was. And he said this was different, and he thought he ought to be cut in for a share of the profits. I was going to tell him to go to hell, but Myra jumped in and said that sounded reasonable, and we'd talk about it and let him know. And she gave me a look that meant "shut up". So I did. But after Leon had left, she said she didn't like the sound of it, that he was getting uppity, and we'd have to think what to do with him.'

'Were those her actual words? "What to do with him"?'

'Or "what to do about him". Does it matter?'

'It may do. Go on.'

'You don't have to go on.' Wilton made one last effort to check him. 'You don't need to make any voluntary statement, and you don't need to answer any question if it may tend to incriminate you.'

Holdsworth gave her a patronising smile and patted her hand. 'Don't you worry, I know what I'm doing.' He turned back to Slider, with a look that said, 'The ladies, eh? God bless 'em!' All he needed was a monocle and a moustache to preen. 'Where was I? Oh yes. Jack phoned on Sunday to say Myra was worried about Leon, that he could blow the whole thing out of the water.'

'Did he say Myra had suggested a solution?' Slider asked.

'He said we might have to pay Leon off. But as it happens, he'd had a different conversation with her, which *I* didn't know about until later.' He gave Slider, and then Wilton, a triumphant look.

'Very well. But what happened next?'

'Leon rang to say he'd finished editing the film and he was bringing a copy over. I rang Jack, and he said he'd come over too. But he arrived without Myra. Typical! She was trying to distance herself, trying to make sure someone else would get the blame, not her – just like she always did. Even though it was her idea from start to finish. Anyway, Leon turned up, and gave Jack the flash drive, and said he wanted a proper share of the money. He said he was the one who'd done all the work. Jack didn't like that. I could see he started to get angry. I asked Leon what he wanted, and he said a million pounds.' He snorted with derision. 'A million! For doing a bit of camera work! I said he was dreaming. And then he said—' the smile left his face – 'he said he had a copy of the film, and if he didn't get the money, he'd take it to the police.'

Ah, the blackmailer blackmailed, Slider thought. Very neat. 'But he was implicated himself,' he said.

'That's what Jack told him. He said Leon was just as guilty. But Leon said he hadn't made any attempt to extort, and that whoever made the approach to Kevin – which would be Jack – would be the guilty one. And that if he took the film to the police, we'd never get the money, that was the end of Davy Lane for us, and we'd all be bankrupt, so it made more sense to give him a fair whack and be done with it. I thought Jack was going to explode. I tried to calm him down. I said we ought to talk about it, and asked Leon to wait in the next room. But as Leon turned away, Jack grabbed the poker from the fireplace and hit him. Killed him.' He shook his head. 'That damned temper of his. We'd have been all right if we'd done it my way.'

'And what was your way?'

'Well, to . . .' He paused, sensing a trap. 'To sort it out later.'

'You mean, to kill him somewhere more convenient?'

'Don't answer that!' Wilton said despairingly.

Holdsworth looked sulky. 'It was Myra's idea to kill him. That's what Jack told me later. She'd said Leon would have to go, that even if we paid him, we'd never be sure he'd keep quiet. I don't suppose she meant he was to kill him in my drawing room,' he said with a kind of glee, 'but Jack always was a stupid, impulsive fool. I told her that from the start. I told her not to marry him – but she never listens to me.'

'I don't think it's been a happy marriage,' Mrs Holdsworth had said to Swilley. 'Apart from not being able to have any children, I mean. Myra's so ambitious, she *drives* Jack, and I think all he really wants is a quiet life. They both—' she looked up into Swilley's eyes – 'have affairs.'

'How do you know that?' Swilley asked.

'I don't think it's a secret. I've overheard Myra talking to Charles about it. She's quite open about hers – it's always influential people, people who can advance her – and I've heard her say, quite dismissively, that it doesn't bother Jack because his secretaries and popsies keep him occupied.' She shook her head sadly. 'What a way to run a marriage.'

'Charles has said that Jack has a temper,' Swilley said.

'Well, I suppose he does, a bit, and I don't like it when he shouts. I hate loud voices. But I don't think he means any harm, really. I can stand that more easily than Myra's ruthlessness. Jack's been a good uncle to Charlie, in many ways, but Myra never wanted anything to do with him. She was always worried about how it would affect her reputation, her career, if anything he did got out.' She sniffed. 'She's supposed to be so wonderful, such a saint, caring so deeply about all those damaged kids, but it's different when it comes to her own nephew.'

'So I told Jack he'd have to get Leon's body out of there,' said Holdsworth.

Slider guessed this was the point at which Jack had said, 'Why do I have to do all the dirty work?' He imagined the express-lift sinking of stomachs when something alerted Holdsworth to his wife's presence outside, with Leon sprawled dead on the carpet. Luckily, he had spent a lifetime training her to instant obedience and no questions.

The body must be got away, the other copy of the film discovered, and above all, no guilt must ever attach to Holdsworth. Jack could be sacrificed. Probably even Myra would agree about that. 'I can't go to prison. I have children and you don't.' But the real reason was that Charles must never be blamed for anything.

Slider felt almost sorry for Jack Silverman, who was indeed being lumbered with all the dirty work. Blackmail Rathkeale, remove the body, search the flat – and if anyone was going to get caught and jugged for it, it wasn't going to be anyone with the Holdsworth blood in their veins. Charles may hate Myra, but they evidently thought alike, or why had Jack been sent to the Sunday meeting alone?

Holdsworth ran through the rest of the story.

'Why Jacket's Yard?' Slider asked. 'Why not somewhere further away – out in the country?'

'That's what Jack said. But we didn't have too much time. The flat had to be searched and the other copy found, and Leon would have hidden it well, we knew that. And the search would have to be done during the night when there was no one around.

And I wasn't having the body left in my house while he did that. Besides, people always dump bodies in the countryside and they always get caught. I told him as long as there was nothing to link it with us, there was no problem. So we took everything out of the pockets first. And when Jack searched the flat, he took away all Leon's personal stuff, in case there was anything to connect him with me. And his laptop. But he didn't find the film,' he concluded with a brooding look.

'Where's the other copy? The one Leon brought to you?'

'Jack's got that. Or he's given it to Myra, I don't know.'

Slider imagined that they were planning to leave it a couple of weeks to make sure no questions were asked about Leon – and why should there be? A man with no friends and no family to miss him, a nobody rendered even more a nobody by his empty pockets – and then resurrect the blackmail scheme. Why not? It was a good plan. Rathkeale would really lose nothing by green-lighting it, the street kids would get a place to go, some people would get nice flats, Myra would get a good directorship and two firms would be saved from going under. An eyesore shabby terrace would be transformed into something useful, and a lot of people would have jobs along the way. Coal Sidings Road would become Davy Lane, and everybody would win. Holdsworth and the Silvermans would have performed a public good. They ought to get medals, really.

If Leon Kimmelman had not got greedy and spoiled it all – and for what? For a retirement house in the Isle of Wight. The absurdity of human ambition and human endeavour never failed to strike Slider.

Holdsworth looked at Slider hopefully. 'So you see, I really haven't done anything wrong. I'm the innocent party here. It was all Jack, and Myra. So can I go now?'

'You tried to run me down,' Slider said. 'I don't take that very kindly.'

'Not me,' he said quickly. 'I don't like driving. That's why I had Leon to drive me. My eyesight isn't so good, I don't like cars, I never drive unless I have to. I could never do that, drive deliberately at someone. It was Jack did it. Nothing to do with me.'

'But the car, you see, is in your garage. With the number plate obscured and the rear plate missing,' said Slider. 'Attempted murder is a serious thing. You are the registered owner and the car is in your keeping. You are just as guilty as he is.'

'No!' said Holdsworth. 'I haven't done anything! It was them, not me!'

Slider thought of *1984*, and Winston shouting, 'Do it to Julia! Not me!' Not to be able to accept blame was a terrible, debilitating thing. It stunted a person. There was a large chunk of Holdsworth that had never grown up beyond the boy taking a beating from his father, while his sister-ringleader smirked in the background. She had broken the window, but he had been there, he had been part of it. He couldn't see that then, and never would now. Jack had killed Leon, perhaps, but he had been there. And probably he'd been glad to have it done.

EIGHTEEN
E Pluribus Unum

Myra Silverman and her hotshot solicitor had taken the line that Myra was innocent of any involvement in the crime of murder, and as she had not been there when the deed was done, and there was no actual evidence that she knew anything about it, it was going to be tricky to include her. It depended on the wider conspiracy. She was certainly involved in Davy Lane, and had been the one to try to persuade Rathkeale to back it, but again, there was no evidence that she had been involved or even aware of the set-up and the intention to apply blackmail. It looked rather as though little Myra was going to get away with it again.

Jack had relied on the tried and traditional method of saying nothing, answering 'No comment' to every question, though with a brooding, glowering look that could have set fire to the curtains, had there been any.

Porson said, 'The evidence all points to Holdsworth, but if he keeps saying Silverman did it . . . Maybe that's the way to go. Have another go at Silverman along the lines that Holdsworth's going to get away scot-free while he's going to get jugged. See if you can prod him into giving us something. I don't like all this "no comment" business. It always looks bad when they haven't held their hand up. Get him to throw some mud at Holdsworth, which he can't do if he doesn't chirp. I don't think there's any love lost round the three of them.'

'I think you're right, there,' said Slider.

Porson eyed him. 'But not now. You're tired. You're not firing on all calendars. We've got enough time on the clock. Let him have a nice long brood overnight, and have a go at him in the morning when you're fresh and he's not.'

'Yes, sir,' Slider said. It was, however, a longish time after that before he could get away. There were reports to write and forms to sign and instructions to give. Silverman's office had to be searched; the BMW's route to Nigel Playfair researched; phone records to be collated. There was overtime available to rejoice the heart, but it all had to be organised.

Slider went home at last, late, too tired to eat, too tired to talk. Joanna wisely left him alone, to fall into bed and sleep like the dead – if the dead had huge, complicated dreams. However, he couldn't remember what they had been about when he woke, only that they had been hard work.

Over breakfast he told Joanna of the breakthrough.

'So you'll be going in?' she queried.

'I have to,' he said, and then, dragging his mind back from his case to her career, remembered, 'Oh. You're working, aren't you?'

'Seating rehearsal this afternoon, and the televised concert tonight. You were supposed to be having a day off – with George.' To his helpless look, she said, with a sigh, 'I'll sort something out. Don't worry.'

'You're a saint,' Slider said. 'What did I do to deserve you?'

'I wonder that myself, sometimes,' she said. 'But saints, like worms, can turn, so don't push your luck, Bill Slider.'

'When this is over . . .' he said.

'You always say that.'

'But this time I really mean it.'

'You always say that, too.'

'Let me have a go at him, boss,' Hart pleaded. 'Wiv my funky charm.'

'I thought Loessop was the funky one.'

'Yeah, but I got assets he can only dream about. If Silverman's got an eye for the popsies . . .'

'What, *you*?'

'I can do popsy,' Hart said, wounded. 'Go on, guv. I think I can get him to talk.'

So Jack Silverman, brooding alone in his cell after breakfast, received a visit from a tall, slim, attractive black woman in very tight trousers, a slinky top and earrings shaped like leaping dolphins, who greeted him with a cheery but not unsympathetic grin and said, 'Your wife and brother-in-law have dropped you right in it. They've jumped ship.'

'What?' said Jack.

'They've taken the only lifeboat and they're rowing hard for the shore. Which leaves you – what? Manning the bridge and going down with the ship.' She did a naval salute. 'Aye aye, captain. Glug glug. It's been nice knowing you.'

'What are you talking about?' he said, though something in his eye told her he'd twigged.

'They say it was all down to you. You alone are the guilty one. Your idea. You dunnit.' He stared at her, his face darkening. She added an extra ounce of pity to her smile. 'Loyalty is an admirable trait, but they're not reciprocating,' she said. 'In uvver words, they've hung you out to dry, old mate. Nice class of relative you've got there! They're going to swan off into the sunset, doing whatever it is they do for jollies, while you're eatin' off tin plates and lookin' at the sunset through iron bars. And if you drop the soap in the showers, for Gawd's sake don't bend down to pick it up.'

'Nice language,' he scowled at her.

'I'm just trying to make you see reality. They've done you like a kipper, and I don't like to see that. Good-looking bloke like you. They said *you* killed Kimmelman, and tried to kill our guv'nor. Blamed it on your temper. Ask me, you've been keeping a lid on it like a bleedin' hero. Good for you! There's just one more thing to do. One more step from hero to saint.'

Her smile was so perky, it would have taken enormous self-control not to say 'What?' at that point. Jack said it.

'Martyrdom,' she replied. 'You just keep saying nuffing, while they make their escape. That's what makes a hero a saint – suffering for others.'

He put a weary hand to his head. 'Don't you ever stop talking?'

'I'll stop,' she said seductively, 'if you'll start.'

So it was back in the tape room, Hart and Slider facing Silverman and his solicitor. Slider said, 'For the record, you have asked of your own volition to make another statement. Is that right?'

'Yes,' said Silverman.

'Then let's start with the Davy Lane redevelopment. That was your idea, was it?'

'*No!*' he said. 'They thought it up between them, Myra and Charles. Charles had that property to get rid of – that was typical of him, the way he got stuck with it. Trying to be too clever. He always thought he was a lot cleverer than he really was. Getting it listed to bring the price down – then he couldn't get it *de*-listed. And Myra wanted a new big project to boost her reputation. She *lives* for the press coverage. She was beside herself when they went for her over that KidZone mess-up – like, "how dare they criticise *me?*"'

'But you stood to gain yourself, didn't you?' Slider said.

'I'd have got a large contract for the building, I don't deny it, but that's my business, building things. All that would have been legitimate. But I wasn't desperate like Charles. My head was above water. My firm's ticking over all right. I mean, we all want more work, of course we do, but it wasn't life or death to me. Charles is up to his eyebrows in debt, and poor Charlie . . .' He paused. 'You know about Charlie?'

'We know,' said Hart.

'Oh.' He nodded. 'Well, Charlie costs him an arm and a leg, and he's got nothing coming in. Davy Lane went from

"wouldn't it be nice if" to "it's got to happen".' He gave a
sour look. 'And Myra was so sure Kevin would jump. She
thought she could pull his strings like a puppet.'

'She over-estimated her influence with him,' Slider said.

'Yes, and that made her mad as fire. She can't stand anyone
crossing her.'

'So she thought up the blackmail plot out of . . .?' Hart
invited.

'Temper mostly,' he supplied.

'How did she know about his . . . proclivities?' Hart asked.

'Oh, she knew him pretty well. She knew all about the boys
and the cocaine and so on, when they were working together.
I think she liked it. Gave her a hold over him.'

'Was that why he defended her in front of the House
committee?' Slider asked.

He shrugged. 'It may be. I hadn't thought about that. She
never said. But it could be.'

'So the blackmail plot was all her?'

'Her and Charles. They cooked it up between them. I thought
it was stupid – and risky. I said, just let it go. But they were
sure it would work. Myra said it wasn't as if they would be
asking for money, just pressuring Kevin to do what he ought
to do anyway. Charles had the boat, he had Leon set up the
camera and everything, and follow Kevin for a week or two
to find out where he went, and then set up the . . . what d'you
call it? The sting?'

'If you like,' said Slider.

Silverman shrugged. 'It worked like a charm. First time out
of the gate. I never thought it would. But Leon rang Charles
the next day to say he'd got it all on film, he'd edit it properly
and put it on a flash drive, then all Myra had to do was to see
Kevin, tell him about it, and if necessary show him the film.'

'D'you think it'd have worked?' Hart asked. 'Would old
Kevin have gone for it?'

'Probably,' said Silverman. 'It was pretty raunchy stuff. All
right, I know they were grown men, not boys – but it would
have blown a hole right through him being the Youth spokesman
for the GLA, wouldn't it?'

'True,' said Hart. 'But then Leon went and spoiled it all.'

Silverman shrugged. 'He wanted to be cut in. I didn't think that was unreasonable. We had a talk after he went. I was for paying him off – I mean, not what he'd asked for, obviously, but *something* – but Charles and Myra were furious. Charles acted as if one of the servants had got uppity and cheeked him. And Myra could never bear anyone trying to change her plans in any particular. Everything had to be done exactly the way *she* wanted it done. And she said, once you started paying someone off, you never stopped.' He paused reflectively. 'Which was ironic really, when you think of it.'

'Yeah,' said Hart. 'So what happened next?'

'Phone calls between Charles and Myra, all Sunday morning. I caught enough of Myra's end to know they were talking about Leon, but I didn't know what they were deciding. Finally, Myra said I had to go over to Charles's and fetch the flash drive. I said, why don't you go, and she said Charles was worried Leon might cut up rough, and wanted me there.'

'How did that strike you?' Slider asked.

'I don't know. I didn't think it was likely. But I supposed it was possible. I liked old Leon – he wasn't the brightest bulb in the box, but he was a decent old stick, very loyal to Charles. Got him out of a mess or two, with Charlie. On the other hand, Charles had always treated him like . . . well, hadn't shown him much appreciation, put it that way. And this could be the last straw. I suppose Charles might have got him mad enough to lash out. And he was a tough bloke – not big, but sort of whippy, if you know what I mean, muscular – and Charles was soft. He could have hurt him if he'd wanted. So I went over. Of course, the way it happened, it was the other way round.'

'Leon got Charles mad enough to lash out?' Hart asked.

Silverman nodded gloomily. 'Leon produced the flash drive and asked if we'd come to a decision about the money. Charles said he'd be paid for his time as always, and Leon started to go red in the face and said this was a bit different, this was above and beyond, and he deserved more. Charles said he'd get what he deserved all right. He was trying not to shout, because Avril was upstairs. I suppose Leon thought I'd be the easier touch, because he turned to argue with me about it, and Charles . . .' He hesitated.

'Go on,' Slider said quietly. 'You know he blamed it on you.'

'Right,' said Jack, his face darkening. 'The instant he saw police uniforms he ratted on me. The dirty skunk. So I'll tell you – he went behind Leon's back to the fireplace and picked up this big, heavy poker. I didn't realise what he was going to do – well, you don't, do you? But he just walloped Leon with it, across the back of the neck. Probably meant to hit him on the head. He's a lousy golfer – always missing the ball.'

Hart nodded encouragement.

'Leon went down like a sack. Not a cry. Never even twitched. I dropped down beside him to feel for a pulse, but I could tell he was dead. I said, "What the hell have you done?" But Charles was quite calm. He said, "It's the best way. We could never have trusted him again." I said, "I'm having nothing to do with this," and he said, "It was Myra's idea. And you're in it up to the hilt."'

'So what did you do?' Hart asked.

He was looking wretched now. 'I should have got out of there right there and then. I should have called the police. But I was . . . well, shocked. You don't think straight right away, after something like that. I'd never seen a man killed before. And Charles was my brother-in-law – it's not easy to shop someone close to you, not before you've had a chance to think. So when he said he'd help me get Leon out to the car and I'd have to dump the body somewhere, I . . . I went along with it.'

'Who chose Jacket's Yard?' Slider asked.

'Charles. He said there were no cameras there and it wasn't overlooked. He decided everything.'

'He took charge,' Slider suggested.

Silverman looked grateful. 'Yes, I suppose that's what it was. I was in a state of shock, and I needed someone to tell me what to do. It wasn't until afterwards – well, not until last night, really – that I thought *he* ought to have been in a state of shock as well. But he wasn't, because *he* knew all along what he was going to do. I didn't. He and Myra must have discussed it over the phone, planned it. And I got sent along as—'

'The patsy,' said Hart, with sympathy.

He looked at her with self-knowledge. 'You're right. I was the patsy. They used me like they used Leon.' He grimaced. 'What a bloody fool I've been.'

'But why,' Slider said, after a suitable pause, 'did you try to kill me?'

He returned from his inner thoughts. 'That wasn't me,' he said sharply. 'I didn't know anything about that until afterwards. Myra told me afterwards, when it hadn't worked.'

'Worked?'

He had the grace to look shamefaced. 'I would never have had anything to do with it. It was a stupid idea, but I suppose they'd just got themselves into a state by then. Charles apparently rang Myra that Wednesday in a panic because the police had been round again. He'd got your name from the police-woman and was ranting about you, and Myra said you should be put out of action, because you were heading the investigation, so it would fall apart without you. The police have so much to do anyway, they thought Leon would get shoved out of the way and forgotten about. Because he was a nobody with no relatives to argue for him. So Myra somehow found out where you were, and told Charles to use Leon's car, which was in his garage, and to make sure the number plates were obscured in case there were witnesses around.' He shrugged. 'And that's all I know about it.'

'Charles says he doesn't like driving,' Hart said. 'He said it was you driving that night.'

Silverman looked angry. 'He drives when he wants to. He just likes Leon to drive him so he can have a drink, and someone else can worry about parking. Anyway, I told you, I wouldn't have had anything to do with a stupid scheme like that. Besides, I've got an alibi for Wednesday evening. I was visiting my mother, over at Stanmore. One of my cousins, Annie, was there as well. They'll confirm it.'

'Write down their names and the address, and we'll check it,' Slider said. 'You know you should have come forward a long time ago with this whole story.'

He looked miserable. 'You wouldn't have believed me.'

'We're believing you now.'

'And they said I was implicated,' he went on. 'They said I'd be in trouble anyway, and the only hope was for us all to get away with it. One for all and—'

'They didn't give you that three musketeers *schtick*, did they?' Hart changed the word from *shit* at the last moment in deference to the running tape.

Going up the stairs afterwards, Slider said, 'They weren't entirely wrong, of course. Silverman might not have killed Kimmelman, but he got rid of the body. He's implicated in the conspiracy to commit blackmail, the conspiracy to murder, and perverting the course of justice. Once any of them got caught for any of those, they were all going down like a pack of cards.'

'Jack, queen and – what's Holdsworth?'

'Ace,' said Slider.

'Oh, is that how you pronounce it?' Hart said innocently. 'But he can cop a plea, can't he, Jack? If he turns Queen's evidence?'

'Not my problem. Let's hope the prospect keeps him on side – but as to what tariff he might get, wiser men than me will decide that.'

'*Are* there wiser men than you, boss?'

Slider winced. 'Is that what you call subtle flattery? Go and get me a cup of tea.'

Since Kimmelman's had been a bloodless killing, there was no blood in the house or car. And the poker had been wiped clean – which was in itself suspicious, because who owns a poker with no fingermarks on it? But the car with the obscured plates in Holdsworth's garage was an indisputable fact; and before the end of the day, the tyre prints had been matched to those taken from Jacket's Yard.

And now that McLaren knew where the Nigel Playfair SUV had come from and gone to, he was confident that he could find enough cameras to confirm its route, 'And with a bit o' luck,' he told Slider, 'one of 'em will give us a face as well. There are cameras on a lot of the traffic lights that face the oncoming for that very reason – to clock who's driving when someone runs the lights.' People had been known to get off a charge by claiming someone else had been driving at the time.

The other copy of the flash drive had been found in the Silvermans' house, in Myra Silverman's wardrobe. Everything to do with Davy Lane had been taken from the house, Jack Silverman's office and Holdsworth's office. Bank accounts, when they came in, ought to confirm Holdsworth's impecunity, and probably payouts to Leon to set up the sting, though there'd be no proof of what he spent the money on. Still, it all helped. And with all the phone records now in hand, it should be possible to make out a convincing timeline of Holdsworth's and Myra's calls to each other, to back up Jack's account.

'But with Holdsworth blaming Silverman and versy vicer, it's a bit of a bloody mess,' said Porson. 'We prefer Silverman's story do we?'

'It has the ring of truth. And the material evidence is all against Holdsworth.'

'All the same,' Porson said, 'it's one's word against the other. Silverman's the key witness, and without his testimony, we've hardly got a case. Let's hope he doesn't change his mind and decide to clam up.'

'I think he's pretty mad at them, sir,' said Slider. 'They dropped him right in it, and tried to get him to take all the blame. And he liked Kimmelman.'

'But she's his wife, after all. A lot of men can't do stuff like that to their wife. Still,' he reflected, 'she didn't mind doing it to him, and what's sauce for the one is goose for the other. Well, we'll see, we'll see. It's a nasty mess, and the world'll be better for having it cleaned up. Still no next of kin for Kimmelman, by the way?'

'No sir. No one's ever come forward, and Holdsworth claims not to know anything about his background. I suspect he's telling the truth about that, if nothing else. He didn't have much interest in people, except as they benefited him directly.'

'Yerss, I know the sort,' Porson said with elongated disgust.

'Throws his weight around, mollusc of all he surveys, until someone pulls the rug, then he turns into a whining heap of self-pity. They're the worst.'

Slider trudged back to his office to carry on with compiling the case, wondering whether the mollusc of all he surveyed would think the world was his oyster.

Atherton was waiting in his office. 'McLaren's got a pretty good shot of Holdsworth driving the SUV – traffic camera at Hammersmith Broadway. Good enough, anyway, to say it's him rather than Silverman. He's still looking for more, but I thought you'd like to know.'

'Yes – thanks. Good news,' Slider said. 'If we can pin that to him, it makes his killing Kimmelman look more likely. By the way,' he added, 'I was thinking where all this began, with Eli Sampson, and remembering how Mrs Sampson seemed to recognise Kimmelman from his picture.'

'Oh yes – she claimed he reminded her of Gene Hackman,' said Atherton.

'But I wonder if Kimmelman hadn't gone round there at some point, representing Target. Suppose, for instance, that Eli was behind with the rent – wouldn't it be Kimmelman they'd send to have a persuasive word with him?'

'Yes, that seems likely. So – another little mystery cleared up?'

'It's just a suggestion. But I like to leave no ends.'

Atherton cocked an eye. 'You look tired. Are we having the traditional drink tonight?'

'Yes, I suppose we should.' The team deserved to celebrate their hard work.

'Boscombe? Half an hour?'

Slider looked at the clock. 'Good God, is it that late already? You all go on, I'll join you. I'll be about half an hour behind you.'

He tried to calculate whether Joanna would be actually playing or not, and whether he could phone her, and in the end decided he had better not. He rang Dad instead and ascertained that all was well. Then, as he was going down to the car, Joanna rang him.

'Short break,' she said. 'Some technical glitch.'

'How's it going?' he asked.

'Murder. I'm knackered. My arm's hanging by a thread. Are you still at work?'

'Just leaving. I have to go for a drink with the firm.'

'Of course. Well, have fun. Does that mean you've wrapped it all up?'

'Not yet, but the rest is detail.'

'In which we know the Dark Gentleman resides. When he's not messing with the Albert Hall's acoustics.'

'Still having trouble with pitch?'

'All over the place. And the heat under the lights doesn't help – the strings stretch. The trumpets were saying they've never understood why we tune to an oboe instead of to them. Oboes are notoriously unstable. You know the old saying: what is a minor second? Two oboists playing in unison.'

'If you've got enough energy for jokes, you're surviving the experience.'

'So will you. Go and have your drink. And don't be sad. You know you always get sad after the event.'

Post coitum, omne animal triste est, Slider thought, as he drove to the pub. It was slightly foggy, a damp, mild, mournful sort of evening, fitting his mood. The moisture sparkled on street lights and traffic lights, splitting them into haloes; the roads glistened black; the first few shops had Christmas decorations in their windows. Why did that strike him as melancholy? It was the let-down after the excitement. That – and, always for him, remembering again, in the quiet at the end of frantic activity, where it had all begun.

Leon Kimmelman – a 'decent stick', and 'not the brightest' – who had broken the law and done suspect things, but on the whole had been kind to women and children. He had been loyal to his employer – too loyal – and had been poorly dealt with. Killed untimely, and his body dumped like rubbish. And there was no one to claim his body, no one to care that he had even gone, except for the wistful masseuse, Shanice, who'd said he was a lonely man. Who'd said he liked his sex plain and simple, and had been good to her and had given her presents. He had given her a watch – of all things he might have splashed out on. He had a nifty one himself. There are some men who just like watches.

Leon Kimmelman, whose ambition was to save enough for a retirement cottage. On the Isle of Wight. Did ever a villain have a more prosaic dream?

Slider was reminded of the film, *A Man For All Seasons*, and the moment when Sir Thomas More discovers Richard Rich has betrayed him in return for being made Lord Lieutenant of Wales. And More says, 'It profits a man nothing to give his soul for the whole world – but Richard, for *Wales*?'

Oh Leon, for the Isle of Wight?

He parked the car, and pushed in through the doors of the private bar, to be greeted by a gust of warmth and light and insideness. Someone shoved a pint into his hand. An amber beauty, with a head like fawn cream. The smell of it made his nostrils twitch.

There was a splurge of cheerful voices, welcoming him.

'Here he is!'

'Yay, boss!'

'The man of the moment!'

'Congrats, guv!'

'Cheers! We made it!'

People gathering round him, grinning, welcoming, praising. They liked him. As well as everything else, they liked him, and he was grateful. He smiled around at the smiling faces, and thought, this is what's important. This is my reward. He was home. Not the Isle of Wight, but wherever they gathered.

And he got to keep his soul, too.

CANBY PUBLIC LIBRARY
220 NE 2ND AVENUE
CANBY, OR 97013